THE GIRL HE WANTS

KRISTI ROSE

Vintage Housewife Books

Cover Design © 2020 Strong Image Creations

The Girl He Needs/ Kristi Rose. *-- 2nd edition*

ISBN: 978-1-944513-40-5

Previously published by Kensington Lyrical with the same title.

For DHM. None of this happens without you.

INTRODUCTION

It's tempting to ignore your heart . . .

Three reasons I'm still single by Jayne Grandberry:

1. I'm eleven feet tall and guys are intimidated by my height... okay I'm just six foot, but you get the idea.

2. My British accent makes me sound fancier than I am.

3. Running a business is hard work, and doesn't leave a lot of time for dating.

Opening a second clothing boutique is my singular focus. So I'm not even trying when my friends set me up with financial wizard, Stacey Cunningham. After my less then stellar first impression, I'm as surprised as anyone when we tumble into bed. Multiple times. For a nerdy single dad he's got a lot of skills between the sheets.

Actually, he's the complete package... but this isn't where I see my life going. I'm not wife or mommy material, and it's just a matter of time before he realizes I'm not **the girl he wants.**

CHAPTER ONE

"Why are you here on a Friday?" Amit, the gent who owns the Indian restaurant where I get my takeaway, arches his brow. "Or do I have my days mixed up and it's Thursday?"

I briefly wave my phone in the air. "What can I say? I'm a dedicated business owner like yourself." Because he's always here when I come in. I type the last sentence in the email I began composing earlier this afternoon, which feels like a lifetime ago, and press send. I check my inbox and find twelve new emails; that's over fifty I'll need to answer tonight.

I should be happy that my business is doing so well, but at this moment I only feel tired. Exhausted from the endless days, I can't determine when I did what or if I intended to do something but never got to it. It's starting to blur together.

I'm thinking the funneling of energy drinks doesn't help either.

"I had a shipment today that was wrong. According to

the packing slip, I ordered four beautifully crafted Italian knee-high boots in brushed brown leather. Also according to the slip, they were in the box that contained the slip, but according to my eyes and hands, nothing was in said box but Styrofoam peanuts. I've been on the phone making international calls all day."

Amit's bored stare tells me he'd rather not listen to me prattle on about my woes. I mean who cares that I've done takeaway from him practically every Thursday for the last few years? It's this look now that's stopped me from putting him on my Christmas mailing list. That and he's Hindu.

"I suppose you ordered the same thing?" He shrugs while reloading the toothpick dispenser.

"When something works, why change it?" I lean against the counter.

"Because you might like something new. Add a little excitement." His look is pointed.

"My parents have had no luck hiring waitstaff for their pub, three months now." I show him three fingers. "I've been working there during the dinner rush to help out. That's plenty of exciting for me." And draining. It's mindboggling how my parents do it every day, because the few short hours I go in leave me weary and desperate for a bath and foot massage.

"You need a new definition of excitement." He finishes with the toothpicks and moves to replenishing his takeaway menus.

I scroll through the emails and ignore him. That's twice today I've been told to mix things up.

This morning's fortune cookie read: *Sometimes we need to wander off the beaten path to find our true destination.*

Complete rubbish that.

For someone who finds wisdom and guidance in the prophecy of a good fortune cookie, that one was disappointing for sure. It will not be a fortune I'll tuck into my inspiration jar at home with the intention to draw it again. No thank you; I only save the really good ones. That one was immediately tossed into my cavernous handbag with a slim chance of ever surfacing again.

Being singularly focused on my goals and staying on the well-traveled path of small business entrepreneurship has brought me success. I'm certainly not going to "wander" as I'm about to launch the next stage in my Jayne-takes-over-the-fashion-world plan. First Florida, then—sooner rather than later—another state. How do you eat an elephant? One bite at a time.

And, really, how would trying something different on Amit's menu provide such a thrill it would change my life?

The bell to his door chimes as it opens and I move aside to make room for the customer that's come in. He pays and casts me a quick smile when he picks up his order.

It does smell wonderful.

"I'm excited to try the special, Amit," the guy says as he's making his way out.

"Enjoy. Come again, Joe." Amit waves and turns his attention back to me. "Joe tries something new every time he comes in."

"I like what I like and what I like is shrimp korma and naan with cheese." I *really* like the cheese.

"Why are you not going out tonight? You're too young to sit in your house probably peeking out the window and watching others. You need a date? I can introduce you to

Joe." Amit takes a bundle of takeaway orders from the waitress delivering them from the kitchen.

"What? No. I do not peek out my windows and I do not need to be set up." And not by the guy I get takeaway from either. "As if. I mean, it's Friday and Joe's getting takeaway." I cross my arms. "I worked a long day at both my own shop and my parents' restaurant. Also, I have bookkeeping that must be done or else my business will implode from the weight of all this paper and all will be for naught." I nod as if to put finality to the sentence. "What's Joe's reason?"

Amit gives me a flat look. Definitely not getting a holiday card from me. "He's a doctor. He probably just got off work."

That explains trying the special. Everyone knows doctors are thrill seekers.

Amit looks at the receipt on a bag. "Jay-nee."

"It's Jayne. No nee." We do this every time. I think it's his way of teasing me.

"But it's not spelled like Jane."

"No, it's not." I stare into the chaos of my overstuffed handbag, preparing for the dive in to retrieve my money. A scarf and several bits of paper in various sizes, mostly receipts and notes, obscure the view into the depths. Funny—or is it ironic—the bloody fortune from this morning is right on top as if chanting its false wisdom. With vigor (likely due to equal parts hunger and frustration), I plunge my hand into the bag and dig for my purse. When I find it, I pull it free with a feeling of victory. As it would happen, I also pull free a newspaper clipping, which flies out and lands on the counter, facing Amit.

The headline reads: *Young entrepreneur invents menstrual undies and makes first million by thirty.* On a Post-it note, Mum has scrolled *This could be you, time is ticking!*

Embarrassed, I snatch it up, crumble it in one hand before tucking it back into my handbag.

Amit stares at me, his lips pressed into a thin line, a puzzled look on his face. I don't have the energy to explain that my mum frequently leaves inspirational messages such as this one in my handbag, on my car windshield, or clipped on her schedule board at the pub.

I count out the dollars needed to make my escape while silently cursing mum and her obsession with the business side of my life. Most mums plead for grandbabies. Not mine, she wants me to have a set amount in the bank before I bring anyone else in the picture. The second year after I opened my shop, she went as far as making a motivator for me, drawing out a thermometer on the large chalkboard she kept in her office—the top being my target net worth—and tsking when I fell short at the monthly check-ins she required. I've refused to participate each year and, even though I've yet to reach the goals she's set, I've come really close. Though in Mum's eyes really close and success are not equal.

Amit hands me my change.

I snatch my takeaway bag from the counter and exit as fast as I can.

The drive to my flat—or as my friend Paisley likes to correct, townhouse—is quick and loaded with yawn suppressions. When I pull into the lot facing my place, too lazy to park in my garage, the obnoxious growl of my stomach has replaced my yawning as the tangy yet sweet aroma of my shrimp korma keeps my salivary glands working overtime. I'm hungry enough I could eat in the car. But I'll likely fall into a sleep coma afterward and perhaps my car isn't the best place. What does it say about me that I'm ready for bed at half past nine?

Spinster? Workaholic? Loner?

I wouldn't hear that from Mum. She'd applaud any of one of those, surely.

Before I go inside, from the seat I grab the wrapped in wax paper extra fish I nicked from Mum's pub. Behind the shrub next to my front door, I've placed a small bowl where I dump the fish.

"Kitty, kitty," I say, calling the feral tabby arsehole that's been coming around.

I say he's an arsehole because he, like all men, deigns me with his presence when it suits him. Not that I asked him to come around. When he first popped up, I tried to shoo him away and for my efforts was awarded several eight-inch claw marks down my arm. Not before I felt his jutting ribs and the lack of meat between his skin and bones. I'm not keen to be a crazy cat lady, though. Which is why I tried to make him scamper off in the first place. Pushing thirty, the last thing I need is a horde of cats. Are you married? Have children? Pushy folks always want to know your status. I don't want mine to be that I have more cats than fingers and toes. That's a meme if there ever was one.

Still, he's terribly scrawny and I can't bear to see him looking the way he does, those big green eyes blinking at me. Hence the fish from Mum's. I wait a few beats but there's no sign of him.

See Jayne be an absolute sucker.

Once inside, I toss my ledgers on the table. I swear I'll get to them at some point this evening but first...food. Without bothering to change from my dress, I devour the bread while standing in my kitchen. My phone chimes an alert, reminding me I have a new client appointment first thing in the morning. I inspect my chipped nail polish, ruined from helping bus tables and working the dishwasher at the pub. To show up like this tomorrow will not do!

Right, first things first. Nails and food then books. By then I hope to catch my second wind and be able to power through the paperwork. Who doesn't like to do typing and paperwork with pretty nails? Masochists, that's who.

Bonus, I fancy the gel polish that doesn't require a special lamp to process. I love that it cuts down on the nail painting upkeep, as it lasts longer. Though it does need several coats. Excited, I change into yoga pants and a t-shirt, because I'm an expert at getting a food stain out of my clothes, but not nail polish.

I set up the polish next to the remainder of my food and click on the telly. Starting with my toes, I apply my favorite color. Mum calls it dirty slag red.

"Should I stop wearing it?" I once asked, humoring her.

"Is this the color a smart, successful business woman selects? Just be mindful that you're drawing in the wrong sort. Sending the wrong message," was her response. Tonight, I shall ignore her warning.

I aim to see eleven o'clock. But to do so means none of the standard telly for me. Good as my favorite shows, Graham Norton or *Downton Abbey* reruns are, they'll knock me out. I've a free trial to one of those premium channels and after nine p.m. things get a wee bit racy. Does an accelerated heart rate from soft porn count as cardio? I hope so. That'll be the catalyst for my second wind and give me the energy to do my ledgers.

If my clients could see me now they'd never believe it. Posh Jayne Grandberry with the immaculate clothes and style, painting her toes while eating a large portion of shrimp korma from the box it came in. Thankfully, my first impression is usually cracking good. It's in the privacy of my own home where I cast off that mantle. Here I wear manky yoga pants and mismatched fuzzy socks. I show this side only to my family and closest friends, who happen to be a small group of women that came together nearly two years ago.

I complete the coats of polish on my toenails and start my fingernails. I'm placing the first coat on one hand when the melodic ringing of my phone forces me to pause. I click the sound of the telly down, lest the vixen who's currently getting a massage starts moaning, as people in these types of shows tend to do.

Paisley's name shows on my screen and I hesitate. She's supposed to be on a blind date, and our mutual friends Josie and Brinn are with her. What could she want with me? A rescue? Paisley already has two guys on the hook. When I saw her earlier today at my shop, she didn't seem keen on a third. Rescue seems the likeliest.

If I answer, there's a good chance I'll have a hard time saying no.

If I ignore it, I will keep to my plan and my workday will have surpassed the twelve-hour mark.

See Jayne rescue her friend and be a hero.

I stifle a yawn before I answer. "Hallo." I stare longingly at my food, knowing the odds of not finishing it just increased. Quickly, I shove a food-laden fork in my mouth. My gaze settles on the half-empty—or should I be an optimist and say almost full?— glass of wine. Had I finished it I wouldn't be able to drive, so I'll give her props for timing. It's a shame to waste it. Can it be funneled back into the bottle to save for later?

"Jayne, what are you doing? Right. Now," Paisley calls into the phone. I can tell she's overly excited because her southern drawl gets thicker and her voice goes up a few octaves.

I make her wait while I chew then swallow. *"Right now, right now?"* I ask, a trace of sarcasm in my voice. She sounds too happy for me to be alarmed.

"Yes, right now," she answers, a bit impatiently.

I glance from the telly, my nails, the food, and my bag with the ledgers. Truth is, I'm terribly behind on the administration bit of my business, which in turn means I've neglected the private clients I do personal shopping for. All this combined affects the color of my bottom dollar. I prefer black, but if I continue with my current habits then red it will likely be. Which is why I've also decided to paint my manky nails the motivating yet forewarning shade of *Russian Roulette* (AKA sultry slag red) instead of my typically encouraging *Midnight Fog*. I've still only one hand emblazoned with the bold red color, though it's streaky and needs the second coat.

"Well, let's see. Right now I've Colin Firth on the other line begging me to fly in and see him. Graham Norton keeps texting me to leave this small hick town to do wardrobe on his show, where he promises I shall meet more eligible men than I can handle, and Ryan Reynolds is naked in my bed as we speak. So make this quick."

"So you've got nothing going on. That's great!" Now she's fairly singing with excitement.

"What's so great about my pathetically boring existence and that I'm home on a Friday night?" I sigh wearily, seeing now how I must have appeared in Amit's eyes. A young woman who can't even be bothered to meet a young, and in hindsight somewhat handsome, doctor. I really am a sorry sod.

"Nothing except now you *do* have plans. Get your bum off the couch and put on something pretty, but casual. Meet us at Maggie May's. Oh and brush your teeth. I bet you've had Indian food."

I huff. "I always brush my teeth." But I'm saying it to the air because she's already rung off.

CHAPTER TWO

I hop up and get moving, because Paisley's
punctual and will be ringing me incessantly if I'm not there
in the time she thinks appropriate. I'm curious as to why
she's invited me on her blind date. Likely it's to be a buffer,
and I'm interested to see how awful this guy is that he
requires an intermediary. There's no use counting on Josie
and Brinn. They're only good for the beginning portion of an
evening, typically, as the night progresses they lose focus in
everything and everyone but each other.

Truthfully, I'm excited to be getting out. My books can
wait until tomorrow. Besides, I'll be refreshed and more on
top of it all then. If I'm honest, today, I'm too knackered for
anything more than mindless conversation and laughter.

I don a pair of light pink skinny jeans, a gauzy tunic with
a pastel floral print, and belt it using a silver pressed metal
chain. I eye my shoes; my toenails look fabulous, so open toe
it is! I've two pairs that will work with this outfit. One flats
and the other modest heels. If I wear the heels, small as they
are, I'm more than likely going to be taller than any guy I

may come across tonight. My accent does a good job of attracting men. Once I stand, however, even being British can't overcome my height. I settle for flats.

A quick fluff to the hair, a light dusting of blush followed by an even lighter coat of powder, and a swipe of gloss to plump up my lips and I'm ready.

The streaky nails glare at me in the mirror.

Shite. The smart thing to do is take the time to soak and remove the polish, let my nails go naked. But that'd be ten minutes at least, and any other method of removal would destroy my nails and make my hands look bloody awful. Besides, I'd like them done for tomorrow's meeting. I weigh my options. Why'd I have to use the bloody gel polish?

I decide to paint on the drive to Maggie May's—I can get the second coat done on the way over. Put the topcoat on in the car park. Drying time isn't exceptionally long. The whole routine will take less time than doing a removal and tomorrow my morning won't be frantic, which has the tendency to set the day off poorly.

I drive and paint, changing gears only when the whine of the engine is unbearable. The bottle, resting in a cup holder, bumps the sides as I take corners. It's a skill, driving, shifting, and painting. The yawning's started up again; the wine I imbibed hasn't helped. I have two nails left when I pull into the lot, so I park, turn off my car, and complete the job. I place my hands on the dash to dry and tilt my head back against the headrest while I wait. My eyelids drift closed.

The subtle beep from a car on the street jolts them open again. I do several deep blinks in hopes of improving my state of arousal.

Blimey, this isn't going to work. I'll be asleep before I get the topcoat on. I consider canceling, texting Paisley to tell her I'm too knackered, and once again I hear Amit's remarks. From between the slats of my blinds, I *have* watched others come home from a late night out. Plus, I'm certain my phone is buried in the bowels of my handbag. There's no point going through all this nail work only to have it ruined by digging into the bag. I do a quick brush of the topcoat and return my hands to the dash, rest my head on the steering wheel and blow gently on my nails.

I yawn and slip into blissful darkness once more.

Startled by a sudden rapping sound, I jerk up, only to discover my left hand is affixed to my cheek.

"Bollocks," I say, coming alert and blinking rapidly as I try to clear the sleep from my eyes.

Where in the hell am I? I squint at the neon sign.

Maggie May's?

Ah, yes. I remember. Paisley's phone call. The drive over. The nail polish.

The *wet* nail polish! Of course. That explains why my hand is stuck to my face. Apparently, while I was dozing I slid my hand under my cheek to cushion it. Hence, the bonding.

I tug slightly and my pinkie gives way, leaving a burning sensation in its place.

Fabulous.

Only three more to go.

"You okay in there?"

I scream and, with a tearing of flesh, press both my hands to my racing heart. A pale, ghost of a face swarms toward the window. "Do you need help?" he says and jiggles my door handle.

"Don't kill me," I scream at the same time and click my locked door button. Did I fall asleep only to wake and find the zombie apocalypse has begun? I really shouldn't watch such disturbing shows alone.

I can see my death unfold. Ironic how I was safely comfortable in my home, bemoaning my lack of life, and now I'm facing certain death. He'll drag me from the car. Tell others I've had too much to drink and that's the end of Jayne.

See Jayne dead. At least her outfit was cute even though her nails were a manky mess.

I brave a glance toward him.

He's in possession of a longish face, a square chin, and spectacles are tucked into the pocket of his faded and slightly fraying oxford. He's wearing a t-shirt underneath, and either it is in desperate need of some bleaching or my window needs to be cleaned. Could go either way.

He's unremarkable, aside from the piercing blue eyes and strong simple facial features; he's the perfect serial killer. No one would remember what he looked like.

I take a second glance, attempting to commit something to memory should I manage to escape, while feeling for my handbag and hopefully finding my keys.

He's pressed one large hand against the top of my car door; the other is leaving his palm imprint on my window. He removes it to rake a hand down his face.

I make a mental note to try to preserve the print in case he truly is an ax murderer and these my last few breaths on earth.

Silver lining? Mum and dad will be quite comfy with the life insurance policy I took out against myself.

"Jesus, you scared the hell outta me." He shakes his head.

"I scared you?" I cry. "I nearly wet my knickers. What's wrong with you? Sneaking up on a sleeping person?" I rub my stinging cheek. The rough patch of skin— likely residual polish—is tender to my touch.

"What are you doing sleeping in your car at a bar? I thought maybe you passed out. Or worse, were someone who had more than their limit and had intentions to drive." He levels me with a pointed stare. "Considering the establishment, the time of night, and your...um...position, the odds are in my favor."

"Oh sure, paint yourself to be the Good Samaritan and me a menace to society. But what if *you're* a nutter? What if you've already measured out my boot to make sure my body fits?" I say through the window, the only barrier between us, while motioning to the backend of my car.

"Listen, lady. I came out here to look for someone—"

"To murder?" I finish and use my own well-honed stare to make my point. Fumbling with one hand, I dig in my handbag and find my phone and quickly bring it up for a snapshot. Bless the designers who made that possibly with two strokes.

The flash blinds us both.

"Jesus, you're crazy," he says.

When the halos from the flash fade, he's rubbing his eyes. He shakes his head, does a long blink, then stands, hands on his hips. Mercy, he's tall. I stare at what I'm sure beneath his shirt will be his belly button. For a possible serial killer, he's well built. Slender yes, but solid. His arms corded with sinewy muscle. Not a tattoo or distinguishing mark to be found.

The better to lure you with, my dear. This generation's Ted Bundy perhaps?

Seriously, who sneaks up on a person sleeping in their car?

"I'm over here," he calls. Likely to his accomplice.

I fumble in my purse for my keys before I realize they're still in the ignition.

Paisley's face comes into view outside the window. Her wild red hair is pinned back in the cute mother of pearl barrettes I gave Josie for her birthday last year.

"Hey, you found her," she says to the tall killer. "We were getting worried. Why are you still in your car?" She leans closer to the window. "What's happened to your face?" The tip of her finger touches the glass, smudging his palm print.

Damn her.

"Nothing, I—" I glance into the rear view mirror and gasp. Four large red-welted dots run up from the corner of my mouth to right below my eye, inflamed. "Bloody Judas Priest." I gently press on a dot and it blanches. Allergic reaction to the nail polish. Why not? This evening has been special thus far. An allergic reaction is a perfect scarf to complete the ensemble.

"I need to get some hydrocortisone," I say to Paisley. "Sorry, I can't stay."

"I understand. You gonna be okay?"

"Yes, of course." My eyes dart to the man's belly. He's become a rock, not moving, simply standing there radiating his irritation.

"Oh, gosh, I sure thought this would go differently but...." She tugs the guy's arm, forcing him to look back in the window. "Jayne, this is Stacy. He's Brinn's president of finance. He's moving to the area. Stacy, this is our friend Jayne."

We stare at each other through the glass. Even the way he blinks his blue eyes expresses his lack of interest or, perhaps, his distaste for crazy women who sleep in their cars and accuse strangers of being psychopaths.

"We've met," I say, focusing my attention on him. Levity would be welcome. "I suppose your murdering of women will have to cease while you're here. Now that I'm onto you and all." Unfortunately, I suck at imparting the joke. I try to smile but moving the right side of my face is difficult.

"It's bound to happen. Cops were on my trail anyway. A hiatus is called for. Guess you lucked out," he deadpans before turning and walking off.

Gawd, there's something adorable about a man who has a sense of humor.

"Lucky me," I say and fire up my car. I look toward Paisley. "You fancy him?" Maybe Josie's wrong about Paisley's feelings for Hank. It would prove my point about love being fickle.

Paisley shakes her head. "Do you?" she whispers.

"No," I say, though without conviction. There was something very appealing about him. Perhaps his eyes? "I should go."

"Yeah, okay." She looks to the retreating Stacy and back at me, puzzled. "Do you think he's cute, at least?"

"He has killer eyes," I say and shift into reverse.

Wouldn't Mum be proud? I met a man.

And I scared him off in under thirty seconds.

CHAPTER THREE

Knowing I had a long day ahead of me and being short on sleep, I used my *feel better* fortune cookie jar and its slips of wisdom to set the tone for the day. Secretly, I wished it would encourage me to shop. Those are my favorite. Usually pulling from the jar gives me a bit a fun. Sometimes, the tiny slips of paper are spot on with their message.

Even if they are a tad disappointing.

Like this mornings: *The road to riches is paved with paperwork.*

Don't I know it. Today, I did not let paperwork cast its dark, nasty shadow over me but rallied my strength and dug into it with vigor my Viking ancestors would be proud of. I completed and submitted my loan application, seeking preapproval, and because I'm calling today a win for Jayne, I printed up and arranged nicely in a binder all my recent budgets and number thingies.

I also made a note to stop letting Josie see my books and hire an accountant. Every time she sighs when she sees how delinquent I am with inputting all the important figures, it stresses me out.

You must do this weekly, Jayne. Not monthly.

This is something I am acutely aware of. I just loathe it with a fiery passion.

But the day is coming to a close. Well, the business end that is.

Now for the best part, the evening and hanging with my friends. I predict large amounts of chocolate and wine in my future. I need no fortune cookie for that!

Josie's hosting an impromptu get-together, which can't be counted a girls' night out as Brinn and some other guys will be there, according to Josie. Which means instead of letting my hair down as I hoped, I check my French twist and replace a few bobby pins to keep it in place. The inflamed skin from my nail polish fiasco had reduced to resembling dry patches of skin easily concealed with foundation.

I smell slightly like fish, as I rushed from my shop to my parents' pub to help with the dinner rush. Another article about a self-made bazillionaire woman who managed this great feat before she was thirty was waiting for me. Mum tucked it in my pocket so I wouldn't misplace it.

Several cars out front tell me I'm late when I arrive at Josie's and let myself in the front door. Cutting through her large open living room, I see my friends gathered outside around a fire pit, laughing. Brinn is alone by the grill. There's an assortment of food laid out on a long table and I beeline for it. Brinn comes up next to me and places a tray of sausages with steam rising from them, a vapor invitation.

"Burgers up next, Jayne." He hands me the tongs and disappears.

I load my plate, famished as I am I don't hold back as I would if I weren't among friends.

After adding a sausage, I reach for the slotted potato salad spoon, excited about all that glorious mayonnaise, when my hand collides with another.

"I beg your—ack!" My apology is lost when my gaze meets that of the car park murderer. I should definitely stop thinking of him like that. It's clear the only thing he's culpable of is killing it with numbers, according to Paisley and Josie, who natter on about him often. Which makes no sense as Paisley says she not interested and Josie says she's doing it to help Paisley figure out exactly what she is interested in. The topic of love has reduced my friends to ninnies.

"It's you," he says, jumping away. The spoon's handle clatters on the table before coming to rest half in the bowl and half out.

"This is awkward." Covertly, I attempt to check him out. It's his lovely blue eyes I remember the most. They make quite an impression. Gawd, he's tall. It's a pleasure looking up at him, a treat really. If I focus on his bewitching eyes and charming chin dimple, I can block out the atrocities he calls clothes. The Albert Einstein t-shirt and faded jeans say college bum, not numbers genius. "We could pretend this is our first introduction and ignore that one the other night."

"Steel trap." He taps his temple with a long index finger.

"In my defense, I was disoriented from being startled awake. Up close and in the light you don't look like a murderer. Apart from the—" I start to point to his ratty clothes but clue in quickly that I should shut up. I turn my point into a whole hand sweeping motion. "Well, you don't look like one at all."

"I've never been accused of being a serial killer before.

Nerd. Dork, even. In college someone once accused me of cheating. But never a killer." He rubs his chin in thought.

Fearing I've offended him greater than I initially thought, I screw up the courage and scan his expression. The slight upward crinkle of his eyes tells me he's teasing.

Instant relief.

"Nor have I been accused of being such a lush I pass out in a car park. Though perhaps when you weigh the two side by side, your assumption is more likely."

"Shall we begin a *reductio ad absurdum*? Perhaps yours has a basis of merit."

"Er...."

His chuckle is deep. "Sorry, math talk."

"Ah." I shift, causing my hip to bump the table.

Unexpectedly, he lunges toward the table and catches the potato salad spoon, stopping its flight from the table to the floor.

I'm caught completely off guard by the litheness of his movements. There's something graceful yet sexy and predatory about it. Not car park killer-like. More the sort to take a woman up against the wall.

I do a long blink to try to get the image of this man and me up against a wall out of my mind. I must stop watching that naughty channel. Just last night this sort of thing played out between a package deliveryman and a romance writer.

Unsuccessful at erasing the vision, I stare openly at him and try to fixate on his clothes instead of how full his lips are.

"Why are you staring at me?" Balancing his plate on his palm, he takes a step back.

"Er, was I?" I look over his shoulder to where my friends sit. Paisley's giving me the thumbs up.

"Yeah, you were."

"I think I'm overly tired. Been working loads. There's a good chance, probability you might say, that I'll suddenly fall face first into the dessert—it's lemon meringue, a favorite of mine—and catch a good snoozer. So I, er, am not so much staring as I'm trying to stay awake."

He's quickly loading his plate.

"Not that you're boring or anything. This is titillating conversation. Oh, er...perhaps interesting is a better word." I picture his large hand ripping off my shirt.

"Okay. Sure." He does a quick shuffle backward. "Good seeing you again, Jayne—right?" He splits faster than too-tight britches.

I nod. Of course I'm still watching him when he looks back, having mentally redressed him as the deliveryman.

Crikey. It's Paisley's fault, all this staring. She made him out to be such a saint. 'Stacy is a single dad, isn't that amazing? He's really funny and was looking forward to meeting you, not killing you! He'd only gone outside to look for your car. Duh, Jayne.' And 'Stacy is such a revered mathematician.' (How easy it would be for him to make calculations regarding body weight to boot-size ratio.) 'He did an internship at Cambridge, and Stacy...blah blah blah.'

I quickly finish loading my plate and make my way to my friends. Sliding into one of the two remaining chairs, I face the gathering of women who are as important to me as my family.

"So?" Paisley asks.

"So nothing. Stop with the matchmaking." I shake my head. "Not going to happen. And remind me to cancel my cable." I look around the table. "Where's Heather?"

"She's on her way." Paisley dips a chip into her favorite comfort food, spinach and artichoke dip.

"Did you work the pub today, too?" Josie asks me.

I nod. "Still no good candidates and with Dad's broken leg—"

"Wait." Kenley stops me. "When did your Dad break his leg?"

"Last week? Didn't I tell you?" Has it been that long since I've seen any of them?

I've seen Paisley the most.

"You told me." Josie nudges me with her elbow.

"And me," Paisley adds.

"That's good, because I thought I'd lost it for a moment. I knew I told someone." I focus my attention on Kenley. "It's only rush hour where they need me the most. Thankfully, I have Shara. She's amazing and runs my shop perfectly, which has been a relief as it lets me focus my worrying on Mum and Dad." And worry I do. This accident of Dad's not only highlighted how thinly spread they are at the pub but how long their hours are and, the most disturbing of all, that they're getting older.

After Dad's accident it was clear that contingency plans were not something they'd discussed nor was short or long-term disability. Something that I purchased right away as my shop is my sole income and an accident to me is lost money. I ponder the article in my pocket. If I made a small fortune, I would be able to offer them an early retirement.

"If they need anything, let me know. I'll cover a few shifts too." Josie puts a comforting hand over my forearm. If I were gifted a sister I'd pick her. She's getting married in a little over two weeks, is scheduled to take the bar exam, and is helping her fiancé, Brinn with his new start-up company. The second one for them in as many years.

"You're a love," I say as we slide into a side-arm hug.

"Anything at any time."

"I don't know much about waitressing, but I'm off work until school starts up in August. I'll help any way I can," Paisley says before munching on a chip.

"Hey all." Heather slides into the chair next to me. "Guess what? I have a job interview. Finally. Maybe I can get out of the hellish cycle of temporary work." Heather, mum to sweet-faced Tyler, a preschooler with special needs, has recently become a single woman. Though her divorce isn't final, she's decided she can't afford to be one hundred percent dependent on her soon-to-be ex. Hence the job seeking.

"Where is it?" Kenley, Heather's sister-in-law, asks.

"Oh, um...it's a receptionist position at the hospital. The hours align with Tyler's school so it's perfect."

"Being a teacher is perfect too, and you only need one more year of college for that." Kenley takes a chip from Paisley's basket.

Heather rolls her eyes and Josie, Paisley, and I sit back, away from the row that is about to take place.

"I've told you. I'll go back to school as soon as I can. Right now I want to make sure I can afford to feed Tyler and myself if Justin doesn't pay his support money."

"You could live with us," Kenley says.

"I'm going to the restroom." Paisley jumps up from her seat. Confrontation in any capacity is hard for her.

"Yes, because living with my brother and his wife is a step up from my current situation of a soon-to-be divorced loser who can't even support her own child."

"Hey." Paisley stops her flight. "I'm divorced and I don't think I'm a loser."

Heather drops her head on her palms, sighs, and then

looks up at us. "I desperately want to do this on my own. Can you understand that?" Her gaze swings from Kenley to Paisley. "I'm sorry. You aren't a loser. I didn't mean it like that."

Paisley drops back onto her chair. "I know. If it's any consolation I sorta know what you're going through. I mean, I don't have a kid but it's an adjustment period, and I think you're doing an amazing job."

"You are too," Heather says, reaching for Paisley. They clutch each other's hands.

"Josie?" Brinn stands over her, having come up behind us while we were all watching Heather fall apart.

"What?" She tilts her head back and looks up at him. A secret exchange of looks passes between them.

"Oh, right. Okay." She pushes back from the table. "Excuse me, everyone," she calls out.

I look around. Having only paid attention to the food and my friends, I now see Erik, Brinn's business partner, and Brinn's younger brother, Vann, are standing next to the grill talking to Stacy. Erik, who I've known the last few years, is a minor nuisance who comes and goes sporadically. Our interactions are limited; I can count them on one hand for this year alone. My guess is that Stacy will be the same. Limited.

Which, if I were interested in playing delivery man and romance writer with him, I'd find limited chance of future paths crossing a bonus. That's the first checkmark on my chat-someone-up-checklist checklist. I prefer not to mix intimacy with my sex.

Josie says, "I would like to take this moment to formally introduce our friend and chief financial officer, Stacy Cunningham. Stacy worked with us on that start up with Erik a few years ago when we partnered up. Wow. That seems forever ago." She takes Brinn's hand and leans into him.

"And look at the two of you now. About to play house officially," Erik says. He has this bloody awful habit of hiking up his pants while his hands are in the pockets, which he does now. It poofs out his groin region and draws one's eyes in that direction.

It's very awkward.

I find comfort in the fact that they aren't pleated.

"And we wanted to thank everyone for all their help then and now." Brinn raises his beer. "You all are awesome."

"Don't anyone show Stacy they're crazy until after he's situated." Josie winks at him.

"Too late. Why introduce him to us before he's all moved in?" Paisley waves at Stacy and he waves back.

Everyone laughs. We are a motley crew, for sure.

"Hi Stacy, I'm Heather." She waves and flips a golden lock over her shoulder.

My car park murderer waves back. He scans the group and when his gaze meets mine he gives a small shake of his head.

I lean toward Paisley. "You can hang up your hopes of anything between me and your swoon-worthy nerd. I think he might be afraid of me."

"You think he's swoon worthy?" Excitement is written all over her face.

Josie sits down between us and effectively cuts off any reply. "All right. Let's get to gossiping."

"He seems nice," Kenley whispers, her gaze on Stacy.

"He's very nice. I like him a lot and so does Brinn. You all know Brinn doesn't have many friends. It's hard to keep them when you're a workaholic. But he and Stacy fit well together and even though they're working long hours they still do fun things together. Brinn needs that. I need that for Brinn. And, we couldn't do this new start up without him."

"We're very excited for you all," Kenley says.

I switch the focus to Heather. "Let me know what you're wearing to the interview. I can help you pull something smart together. You'll wow them," I say quietly.

"Thanks," she whispers. "Will do.

"Okay, here's the lineup for the wedding," Josie says. "Vann is the best man, and he'll walk with you, Jayne. Will is walking with Daanya, who will also create a fabulous mandala on my back. Like the one she did when I went to that charity event with Brinn a few years ago. Remember that, Jayne?"

I nod. I most certainly do. The picture I'd taken of Josie in the silver gown with the delicate filigree design her brother's wife, Daanya, had created on her back, had inspired a stroke of genius. Since then, I keep a henna artist on call to do such creations for my customers. It's very profitable.

She unfolds a sheet of vellum and produces a picture of such beauty we all gasp then sigh. "Amazing, right? Daanya is incredible. If she ever gets tired of being a surgeon she can totally do this." Josie gently caresses the picture. "Anyway," she continues. "Paisley, you're walking with Stacy."

"Oh, speaking of beautiful. Lucky you, Paisley," Heather says. "That Stacy fellow is F.I.N.E."

Surprised, we all stare at Heather. She's never been so overt before.

She giggles and covers her mouth before saying, "I mean, you know, he's cute."

"For the tall, nerdy type," Kenley says.

"Like Clark Kent," Heather replies. She directs our attention behind us and we turn.

The guys have abandoned the grill to start a game of beach volleyball. Whether intentional or not, they've taken off their shirts, and surprisingly enough even Erik is sporting a form that could make some girl warm.

I swing my gaze to Stacy. Sweet mother of Oscar de la Renta, the man has a body like Superman.

"I think he's perfect for Jayne," Paisley says, her machinations obvious. Bless her.

"I think Hank is perfect for you." Josie's quick with the barbs that cut close.

Paisley pops up again. "It's my turn to get the drinks. I can mix something up with Josie's blender. Or get some more snacks. Anyone want any food?" She doesn't wait for any response.

"What are we going to do with her?" Josie shakes her head.

"Give her more time. She'll figure it out." I nudge Josie with my knee. "You did."

"How did you ever bear to watch?"

I respond with an eye roll. Not everyone gets a natural disaster to help them figure out their lives. Only Josie required an act of God, as he's the only one with enough patience and strength to face off with her. Well, God and Brinn.

"Hey all," I say. "I would like to discuss something that is really exciting." I pull my list out of the satchel that I use as my briefcase.

"Remember how I've talked about expanding? How keen I am to tap into different markets. Many of my personal clients come from all over and I've talked, well dreamt really, about reaching more of them." I unfold the paper. "Here is my plan to expand. It's really happening."

"You'll have to hire a bookkeeper," Josie cautions. "You're up for that, right?"

I jab my elbow in her side. "I've decided that it's time to do it. I've narrowed down my list to three. These are the top choices for where I'm going to open my next shop. Which do you like best? Miami, Buckhead, or Dallas?"

"Are you going to relocate?" Heather asks.

I've run this by Josie and Paisley a few times, so they're already up to date on my expansion plan.

"Temporarily. Until I get it off the ground and running smoothly. Likely, I'll commute home a few weekends a month. Shara can run the shop here and this new shop and my personal shopping clients will be my primary focus. Today the United States. Tomorrow the world." I hold up my paper in Dr. Evil fashion and try to emulate a wicked laugh.

Indeed, this new business plan to expand is scary, but I'm ready, and if there was ever a doubt, the recent situation with Dad's accident and Mum working ragged has swiftly ceased it. One day, Mum will be too old to make scones, her hands gnarled with arthritis, and Dad isn't so much as a cook. It may not happen by my thirtieth birthday, but I might make my (and Mum's) financial goal two years after said milestone birthday.

"Which do you prefer?" Kenley asks. "And which is your least preference?"

"Honestly, Miami is my first and only pick. It's the priciest option and my greatest obstacle will be finding a location. But I might also use this venture to get into some real estate, as I'll need to buy a building there instead of lease space. I selected the others because I need a contingency plan, but I'm hoping to not have to go there."

"Let us know if we can help," says Paisley.

Josie raises her glass and the others follow suit. "Dream big or go home, I say. Here's to Jayne. May she have great success in this new adventure."

CHAPTER FOUR

As is now my normal, I start my day at my shop and end it at my parents' pub. It's only Tuesday, though it feels like it's later in the week.

Though working both jobs is exhausting, at least the pub is home away from home. The lovely smells—the fish, the spicy meat of shepherd's pie, and hops—help the stress and anxieties roll right off me.

Serving, though hard on the feet and legs, is a mindless state for me. Table ten gets this. Twelve gets that. All right, easy enough. As opposed to adding figures in my ledger. I'd rather bang my head repeatedly on a concrete wall than do my ledgers.

The sight of Mum standing by the fryer, humming, also relaxes me. This was my everyday as a child.

In between serving food orders I nick some of my mum's fish and chips. The Chinese food I ate earlier did little to curb my hunger, but—*huzzah!*—the fortune was brilliant.

A new pair of shoes will do you a world of good, it read.

Too right! I'd been eyeing these smashing "sultry slag

red" heels I bought for a client on my last trip to Italy. She broke her ankle and was off heels, and, not having the heart to sell them to anyone else, I decided to say thank you, Mr. Fortune Cookie, and buy them for myself. No matter that I'll be equivalent in height to a baby giraffe when I wear them. Today, I don't give a rat's arse. I've been wearing them all day.

As I do with all my good fortunes, I'll save this one, put it in the jar to pull out again when I need a pick me up. Which, with my luck, could be as soon as tomorrow.

"How's it going, love?" Mum sings to me as she loads chips into a wrapper, laying the fish on top. She places the bundle in a basket and moves the basket to a tray.

"It might be slowing a tad." I place the tray on the counter, take in another breath then I lean to kiss her cheek. "Smells heavenly."

"When was the last time you ate?"

"You mean a proper meal? Not the bits of fish I've helped myself to?" Mum waits for me to answer as she dips and batters more filets.

"Lunch."

"No dinner?" She hands me a breaded filet. I generously sprinkle malt vinegar over it and eat it while leaning over the sink.

"I've got plans." It's a bend of the truth. After I eat and help out a bit more, I plan to head home to watch naughty telly while working more on my books. I'm nearly done and I can't wait to get it over with so I can have two weeks off before I start the painful ritual again.

See, plans.

I hide a yawn by tucking my face in my shoulder then

wash my hands before I take the ticket next in line and load the tray.

"Jaynie-girl, go home already." Dad balances a mixing bowl against his extended belly and turns the dough, precisely as Mum has harped at him for the past twenty years. He winces, pauses to shift his weight, his awkward, cast-encased leg extended in front of him. Likely his source of discomfort. He stepped into a hole while taking out the pub's rubbish and broke his ankle in four places, his leg bones in two, and required more pins and rods than a seamstress constructing a bodice from boning.

"I will soon." I drop a kiss on his bald spot. For the last year, staffing has been an issue. Most people want to work in pubs along the beach. While ours is popular with locals, its inland location makes it difficult for tourist to stumble across, and therefore not ideal when the bulk of income comes from one's tips.

"Why bother, Thomas?" Mum asks. "She doesn't listen. I keep telling her this is energy she could spend on making her fortune. Yet, she's here instead."

"Mum, please. I want to help." I knead my hand over the knots at the base of my head, stretching the tension from my neck at the same time. I don't point out that they'd have one server if I weren't here and where one is too little and three too much, I balance it all just right.

"Go home, darling. You worked hard enough today. I'm sure this new shop you want to open takes lots of time and mental energy. Did I tell you how proud I am of you for your shops? There's nothing better than owning your own business. Sometimes I kiss these bricks." She leans in closer. "Doing this will ensure you aren't dependent on a man,

Jayne. You alone can make your dreams come true." I've heard this saying my entire life.

Mum shoos me away from the tray then moves to the fryer to remove the cooked fish. The sight of her hands always takes my breath away. Red, chaffed, and spotty with small scars. Lately it's the knobbiness of her knuckles, the telltale sign of arthritis, giving me pause. How much longer will she and Dad be able to keep up this pace and run their business?Dad's dream of a restaurant/pub English style was the impetus for them moving to America in the first place. I believe Mum would have been content to stay and work in her family's pub, to split the lion's share of work.

"You've listened well, Jaynie-girl," Mum says, using the nickname Dad gave me twenty years ago when my adolescent and needy self thought Mum, who was working day and night herself and newly married to Dad (he's not my biological father), would have more time for me if I were more like Lisa Marie. Desperate for her attention and smart enough to use her frenzied love for Elvis, I teased my hair out, walked around with squinty eyes (which caused many a stumble) and requested that everyone call me JayneMarie. My middle name is Elizabeth.

Dad, a southern-born, dark-haired American, quickly changed it to Jaynie-girl and called me an original. I loved him from that moment forward.

"Not marrying too soon before you know what you want. Look at me. I could be working in my family teashop. But no, I'm here working my hands to the bone, standing on my feet all day." She cast a narrowed gaze at Dad, who harrumphs with admirable pseudo-disdain.

"Take me to America, you said. I can't pour another cup of tea, you said. You just used me to get to Graceland." Dad winks and slides the bowl of dough down the counter toward Mum then takes a second, different bowl from the counter and begins his stirring, this time with increased vigor.

"Stir it like I taught you, daft man." Mum lovingly shakes a wooden spoon in the direction of his head.

This is their thing, their shtick.

"Jayne," Mum calls as she swivels back to me. "I made you a new visual motivator. It's in the office. Go get it." Her prolonged stare makes me trudge down the hallway to the office. Sure enough, once I step inside, a giant, tri-fold poster with a newer, grander profit thermometer waits for me. Its side panels open as if waiting for a hug. Silver lining? It's not on her chalkboard for the world to see.

This time the goal isn't a somewhat reasonable cool million. Mum's added a quarter million to the total.

Motivation or pressure, they've become synonymous.

To make matters worse, the thermometer, likely drawn by Mum's hand, looks remarkably like an outline of a penis with one giant uni-ball.

I stifle a laugh and lean against the desk. If I had my phone I'd send a pic to my friends.

"What do you think?" Mum calls.

"Well done, Mum," I call. I catch sight of a stack of folded papers on the desk, OVERDUE stamped in a bold red on the top one. I shuffle through each of them without hesitation.

Bills every one of them, and there's eight. Utilities, food delivery, and advertising.

I scan the desk for others and find a different stack of unopened envelopes. Though my fingers itch to slide a letter opener through them, I let them be.

I weigh my options. Do I go out to Mum and Dad and

ask about them? Do I write the checks now to cover them and then discuss it later? I know they work hard. I'm also aware that they're slowing down, Dad even more so after his accident.

I twist my earring and ask the universe for a sign, some sort of direction to tell me what to do.

I place the stack where I found it and stand. Timing will be everything.

When I reenter the kitchen, I watch my parents for a moment. Should I pause my expansion and sink my money in their business?

Dad catches my gaze and winks. I nick another piece of fish. "It's nice, Mum. I'll let you know if I get off track." I stuff the filet in my mouth.

"Well, you have it in you, Jayne. You can take this to levels I will never go. You're talented and clever and I'm so very proud of you." She pats my cheek, her hand warm from being close to the fryer.

No other staff is in the kitchen. I take the opportunity. "Er, Mum. Dad. In the office I noticed some...er...unpaid bills." Please let a bolt of lightning strike me right now. This is a moment I never envisioned. Who pictures the scene where they ask their parents if they're paying their bills? Gads. "Is everything all right?"

Mum looks to Dad and I strain to interpret the silent message that passes between then.

"Everything's well, Jaynie-girl. I've just been a bit tired. Especially after the accident. But everything's caught up. You saw old statements." Dad nods as if to reassure me further. I curse myself for not looking at the statements' dates, having been mesmerized by the large red OVERDUE.

I glance at Mum. She's nodding too.

"If I can help with anything?" I don't want to say the word money and trample on their pride.

"You can make that thermometer I made you all red. That would help." Mum smiles but loses it to a yawn.

I press my hand to hers. "Have you thought more about my offer to gift you an entire weekend on Amelia Island? If you're tired, a break might do you well." I figure since they plan to attend Josie's wedding they could turn it into a mini-vacation and go up a day before and spend two glorious nights and three days to relax there.

"Oh, I don't know." She looks at Dad. "There's so much to do here." Says the woman who never goes on a spontaneous holiday. She and Dad spend seven days a week in their pub and never less than eight hours a day. Dad, who should be home resting, comes in every day because hiring kitchen staff is not in their budget.

"Jeff can cover," I say. Our former dishwasher, who's worked his way up to cook, has worked here since the place opened. He's never been more than part time, but that's because Mum can't let go of control.

"We'll think about it."

"I'm just going to do it. Book the room and then guilt you into taking it because I can't get a refund. It's okay to take a break now and again, Mum." They barely leave as it is. Closing one week in the spring to fly back to England so Mum can visit her sisters, another long weekend in Memphis to group-mourn the week Elvis died—known as dead week— and only one week for Christmas. It takes the state health department to keep either of them in bed when they're sick. It tears me up to see this. Life should be getting easier for them. Not harder.

She glances at Dad again. His stirring has slowed and his

mouth is a thin line, likely from the pain. "All right. We'll do it," she whispers.

"Wonderful." I clasp my hands together in joy.

"Love you," she says.

"Love you more." I kiss her cheek.

She moves away to batter the fish. "If you take this to table ten, I'll get some going for you. I'll make it extra crispy like you like."

"Deal." I slip on a fresh Union Jack apron. Silk does not respond well to grease. I ease the tray up on my right hand and head out to the floor.

The dinner rush is finally waning. A few of the regulars are at the bar and only a couple of tables are occupied. I head to table ten.

"Two fish and chips," I call as I balance the tray and put the baskets and vinegar on their table. I turn to smile and look into the face of Mr. Car Park Murderer, also known as Stacy. Gracious, he has stunning blue eyes.

CHAPTER FIVE

One basket for him, the other for the small girl he's sitting with.

"Looks as if we're destined to keep running into each other." I look at the girl, who can't be a day over...oh, I don't know. She feeds herself and doesn't wear nappies; it's anyone's guess as to how old she is. "Hallo," I say to her.

Stacy stands and places a hand on the child's shoulder. "This is my daughter, Cordelia. Cordie, this is Jayne. She's a good friend to Josie and Brinn. Go figure." He cuts his eyes to me and shrugs, but the small tilt to his lips tells me he's teasing.

Nice memory. Though I suppose being called a serial killer is not something people easily forget, or perhaps it was the uncomfortable staring I did at Josie's. Either way, not the best first or second impression.

"Obviously we got off on the wrong foot. Perhaps we should start again, considering our mutual friends and the likelihood we'll come across each other...often."

He pauses, his gaze bouncing between me and Cordie,

then tucks one hand in his front pocket (Gads, I can see the liner of said pocket poking through a hole in the jeans) and says, "I think I can manage starting over." He's got a wry, endearing smile.

"So you're here. I mean, you've moved down, then." I gesture for him to sit.

"We got here yesterday and furniture came today." He looks at my apron. "I thought you owned a store or something like that."

"My parents own this place. I'm helping out. Where did you settle?"

"I took a townhouse in the Ormond Beach area. Timber Lakes. Paisley turned me onto it."

I live in Timber Lakes and there was a flat across from me for let. I wonder if he took it? I do a mental rewind of my neighborhood car park from this morning. I don't remember seeing a moving truck. Perhaps he didn't take the flat by mine after all. Of course, I did leave before nine and haven't been home all day, not even for lunch.

"So then you're all moved in?" If Paisley had a hand in it, then it is the flat across from me and the chances of running into each other increases exponentially. Oh, wouldn't he be impressed with me using math terms?

"Well, we've got all the boxes in the house. We took the townhouse across from you. So I'm told." He meets my gaze; his blue eyes are soft and gentle. Not overly dilated like the other night. Not that the flash on my phone had anything to do with that. Or as hypnotizing as they were at Josie's "I was worried about that—our safety and all—but Josie and Brinn assured me you're harmless." He winks, a smile dancing upon his lips.

I return it, not the wink but the smile. Our gazes lock

and a surprising hum of pleasure runs through me. I look down at his cherub-faced daughter and reason with myself. I don't do, date, or even entertain the idea of doing or dating men with children. No matter how keen my girly parts are on getting to know his boy parts. At this stage, I'm confident they'd be interested in just about any age-appropriate boy parts that come their way. It's been a bit of a dry spell.

"You'll love the neighborhood," I say to Cordie, girl of poor unfortunate name. "Plenty of kids your age and a park." I assume they're her age. They look about the same height.

"We really like the place and the neighborhood. Don't we, Cordie?" She's hoovering food into her mouth. She nods and keeps plowing through. As if she's been without for days.

Perhaps they have been. Maybe they're into fasting. Or only eat meat on certain days. If that's the case, I feel terribly sorry for this girl. No wonder she's inhaling the fish.

Stacy glances down at his basket, and I'm prompted into action.

"Eat," I say. "Before it gets cold."

He's still standing, only now looking down at me, hand resting on the chair he's pulled out. "Would you care to join us?"

"Oh, that's okay. I'm not hungry." Why draw out all this awkwardness?

"Here you are, love." I turn to find Mum behind me holding out a basket of fish and chips. "You said you were starving so I thought I'd rush this out to you." I ignore Stacy's quiet chuckle.

"Mum, this is Stacy and his daughter, Cordie." I turn to the tall man. "I'm sorry. I don't know your last name." I'm sure Paisley or Josie mentioned it one point five million times.

"It's Cunningham."

Oh, well that's a lovely name. "This is my mum, Millie Grandberry." We all say our pleasantries except Cordie. She continues shoving food into her mouth as fast as she can.

My mother looks at Stacy's daughter and bends to talk to her. It's moments like this I wonder why she never pushes me for a grandchild. "Cordie, eh? I'm guessing that's short for Cordelia. It's a lovely name."

Cordie licks her fingers. "I hate it. It's ugly," she tells Mum.

"Mm, I imagine you would think so. My name is Millicent and I hated if for a long time too."

"You like it now?" Cordie asks.

Mum nods. "It's grown on me. How'd you like those fish and chips?" We all take in Cordie's empty basket.

"They were good. Thank you," she replies.

Nice manners and she's quite cute. She has Stacy's eyes and sweet smile.

"I'm guessing you're what? Ten?"

"I just turned nine."

"Oh, my. Well, you do seem so much older." Mum feigns surprise then replaces it with a puzzled look on her face. As if she doesn't buy it.

Cordie puffs out her chest and smiles. "It's because I'm an only child."

"You and my Jaynie-girl are much alike." Mum winks. "I'm not sure if you're still hungry or not, but I've got an assortment of ice cream in the back. Not for all the customers, only the ones I like." She looks at Stacy. "Is it all right?"

"Please don't feel you—" he starts. "I mean, we don't want to be any trouble." "Nonsense."

"What do you say, poppet, care for dessert?" Mum holds out her hand and waits while Cordie gives her dad a silent look, asking for permission, perhaps. He nods.

Mum takes Cordie's hand and off they walk toward the back, chatting.

I stand there with the tray and my basket feeling awkward, at best. Because if he extends the invitation again I'll have to use utensils or at least make an attempt.

"Please join me." He slides out the chair for me and waits until I sit. "I promise to not commit a crime against your person."

"I'm not going to live it down, am I?" I hesitate for a breath then ease into the seat.

"Probably not. Are you sure that's okay?" he asks, nodding to Mum and Cordie.

"Oh yes, It's a nice break for Mum. She'll scoop her some ice cream and bring her right back. Glad the move went well."

"It could've been worse I suppose. It's going to be an adjustment." He sprinkles vinegar on his food and takes a bite of fish. "Mm, this tastes like it's right out of Oxford."

"I'm glad you like it. 'The Fox and Hound, a lovely and quaint establishment that is a small slice of our hometown, Oxfordshire, England.'" I say, quoting the first ever ad my parents made and have framed and immortalized by hanging it in the bar.

He nods. "I think we might be eating here a lot. The moving company lost some of our items. Like kitchenware."

"Seriously? What are the odds of that happening?"

"Well, when you want to figure how to get the odds, you first have to—"

I put my hand up to stop him. "It was rhetorical." I smile because I'm sure he probably does know the odds of the moving company losing a portion of his household goods.

"Sorry, habit," he tells me, shoving some of the extra crispy, crunchy chips to the side of his basket. I assume he's relegating them to the don't-eat zone.

"Do you mind? These are my favorite."

After he shakes his head I nick a chip from the pile. He pushes his basket closer to me.

"They not only lost my kitchen stuff but a good portion of my clothes. And Brinn and I have a big meeting on Friday."

I laugh and can't help but say, "So, they did you a favor."

"Hey!" Feigning shock, he sits back against the chair and rubs his hands down a T-shirt that should have been banished to the rubbish bin years ago. Though I'll give him credit; his jeans fit in all the right ways. "I like my clothes. They're well loved."

"Mm, you do know I'm in fashion? I personal shop for people." Here's my chance to make a better impression. Not that it should matter or anything but funny enough, it does. I've wondered, since we met, what he must think of me. If Paisley has chatted about me as much as she's done about him, he must struggle to reconcile his encounters with me to the picture she paints. I once read that first impressions can't be undone and knowing he may think I'm a loon is difficult to accept.

"Yes, but how is that going to help me? The last thing I want or have time to do is try on clothes. I'm confident nothing in your boutique will work for me." He takes a drink of his beer and winks.

"Did you understand me when I said I do some personal shopping?" I rise from my chair, quickly skirt around the bar, lift out two more beers, pop off the tops, all before going back to my seat. I hand him one.

"Why don't you clear it up for me?" He leans his chair back, tilting it up on the back legs a wee bit, and picks up the new beer, raises it up in a silent toast to me, and takes a swig.

"*I* could get some clothes for you. You can unpack and get Cordie situated all while I'm restoring your wardrobe." I smile, push my basket away, and then lean back much like he is (with the exception of tilting my chair as the likelihood I'd tip over is guaranteed).

"You would do that for me?" He rocks forward, leans toward me.

"Yes, because I love shopping for men. It's one of my favorite things. Doing it for you would give me great plea-sure. But you'll have to trust me. Can you do that?" I silently pray for this opportunity to make a better impression.

"Sure, but don't go all pink and crazy patterns. I'm not that type of guy." He runs a hand down the front of his black T-shirt

"When you say they lost your clothes, does that include your pants and socks too?"

"Yeah. Shirts, pants…oh wait you mean…" He pulls out the waist of his jeans and glances to what's underneath. Which is not just tighty-whiteys but rock-hard abs. I'd like to bounce a quarter off them as I've seen done in videos.

"Yes, those too."

"How do I pay for this?"

Still thinking of the abs, I struggle to get back on target.

"Er, um... We can set a budget you're comfortable with. You are a thirty-four, thirty-six, yes?"

Surprised, he asks, "How did you know? Oh, right, fashion. Guess you're something of an expert. I really only have what was in my suitcase, so I could use a good amount." He seems to be pondering.

I talk more for myself as I make a mental checklist but aloud in case I'm assuming too much. "You'll need a few things for your meeting and some everyday clothes. But I'm also guessing you'll need shoes and ties as well." I don't want to push him. I know nothing of his finances.

He nods. "We have some really big meetings coming up. In person. I'm used to doing this through video streaming."

"You need a power suit. I know just the thing." And it won't be Hugo Boss or any of the like. That's not the vibe I get from him and sending him into a meeting feeling awkward in clothing would be a fail on my part. Even if he'd look divine in a three-piece, double-breasted navy suit. "You mentioned paying. Typically, first-time clients give me a retainer on a card or something."

"I don't do credit cards. All the compounding interest adds up. Can't seem to get past it." He smiles.

"Let's do a budget and I can just bill you."

"Are you sure?"

"I happen to know where you live. I think you're good for it. I'll cover everything. You'll pick from the selection and pay from that. I'm aces with staying on budget." Not so much aces with balancing the books afterward, but he need not know that. I've moved into shop mode, my exhaustion long forgotten. The opportunity to shop has me fairly excited. Can I help that my addiction is my job?

I pull the pen from his pocket and refold the napkin then

sketch out a plan of what I think he needs with some input from him. I guess his size bang-on for all things except shoes. For those I'm only a tad off. We come to an agreement about the budget and I'm pleased with the challenge that's before me.

"Well, I think I'll start tonight. How about I pop round later this evening with what I have? Is nine too late?"

"No, sounds great." He leans forward and rests his elbows on the table. I swear to heaven his blue eyes twinkle. "I'm real appreciative, Jayne."

I wave off his gratitude. "Come on, I'll show you where Mum has whisked Cordie off too." We both rise and I realize that even with my new red shoes, he's taller. At this height, our mouths come close to lining up.

Bloody hell. I've got to stop inserting this man into my fantasies. The only way I'm going to know what his lips feel like is if something awful happens to me and I need mouth to mouth. Give me those odds. Even then I'll likely be unconscious so, to put it in Stacy speak, odds are *never*.

It's not often that I'm smaller than a man. It leaves me feeling womanly. Something I've only been able to achieve through clothes. I don't have it easy like my friends. Josie is a petite, yet stacked, knockout. Paisley is a leggy, rail-thin country girl who embodies a sincerity that makes any stranger her instant friend. Heather is the quintessential girl next door, and Kenley, though tall, is still three inches shorter than I am. She's got the perfect height and the exotic skin tone that comes from having racially different parents. Me, I've got the pale Welsh genes and lackluster blond hair that, when coupled with my height, make people think albino before Amazon. Even my cousin, Pippa, whose coloring is much the same as mine, has a lack of height to her benefit.

She's a pixie and I her oversized, non-pixie-like relation. So it's understandable that I would be wooed by the uniqueness of this new experience I'm having with Stacy. It only makes sense that I would fantasize about something I've never gone through before. Who doesn't do that? Perhaps the naughty free channel I've been watching isn't doing me any favors as well.

"Any chance of scoring more fish wherever it is we're going?" He follows behind me as I lead him toward the kitchen.

"You chat up Mum long enough and she'll make you anything." I laugh.

"Hmm, we may never go home."

We share another laugh and it's nice. Friendly. Easy. Well, once we got past all the awkwardness, but talking clothes always makes me feel comfortable. I deposit him into the welcoming company of Mum but not before I purposefully ignore her questioning look. Last thing I need is for her to call me after Stacy and Cordie leave and remind me of my goals. Her single-minded, tyrannical fixation on them is exhausting. She'd make an awesome coach on one of those weight loss shows.

CHAPTER SIX

I show up at Stacy's half past nine with bags in tow. Finagling some blinding deals has left me on a shopping high. Stacy is getting a good number of clothes for his quid. I might have done better had I not been kicked out due to closing time.

I rap lightly on the door, in case Cordie is asleep. He swings it open seconds later and smiles.

"Jeez, are you sure you didn't go over budget?" he asks, eyes sweeping over the bags.

"Better, I came in under budget. You're a joy to shop for." I hand over several heavy bags of my finds.

"Come in, come in." He gestures with his head, arms already full.

His place is a mountain of boxes in various states of unpacking. He's managed to set up the den with two sofas and telly. It appears to be the only habitable room.

"Did you say the movers lost some of your boxes?" It's hard to image there being room for more.

"Yes, about ten all together. Can you believe that?"

"Unbelievable." I take it all in. "Though seriously, how does that happen? Don't they load the boxes onto the same lorry? On the same day?"

He rubs his face and shakes his head. "I've given this a lot of thought. Best I can figure is the truck left point A at ten a.m., but half the truck veered into a parallel universe, a worm hole if you will, and my matching end tables were unable to stay together." He nods to a lone end table.

I raise my brows. "Math joke?"

He nods.

"And they lost the other end table too?"

"Yes, or it absconded with my clothes and kitchen stuff to set up its own house. Either way, it's all gone. The mathematics of it is astounding."

"Crikey! But you're adorable. I bet you've been thinking about it loads." I laugh partly because he's so earnest but mostly because I can't believe I said he was adorable aloud. It just popped out.

His cheeks turn a faint pink and a new awkward moment hangs there, leaving us staring at each other. Following a glance to his lips, I jerk my attention back to his broader features only to watch his eyes do the same thing. Down toward my lips and back up.

He licks his lips and afterward the small muscle in his cheek pops. Something wonderfully unfamiliar hits me. Anticipation.

I'm attracted to him. Something about being near him has me struggling for a steady breath. Like the moment before a much desired first kiss when hope's at its highest.

See Jayne get wobbly-kneed.

I sigh with delight. It's a heady feeling I haven't felt since my time at University when I was a naive girl learning about the highs and lows of love. Sure, I've been attracted to men since but I've come at it pragmatically, engaging with men who wanted what I did, a casual affair.

I can't speak for what Stacy wants long term. I haven't asked. And I'd wager a year's worth of cracking good fortune cookies it's not what I want. But in this moment, if I were to guess by the way he's licked his lips, he wouldn't push me away if I made a pass.

I don't romanticize this powerful physical attraction, simply sink into it and let it wash warmly over me.

We take a step toward each other and the bags in my arms push up against those in his; the loud crinkle sound of them colliding, the way they cling to my damp skin, jolts me out of my reverie.

Clothes. Business. Focus!

"I, er... Let me show you what I've managed." I take a step back, waiting for the moment to dissipate.

After dumping everything out on his couch, I sort out jeans, khakis, some dress trousers, and shorts in various colors. Then a variety of shirts. My attention stays on the clothing, my internal dialogue reminding me I seek to make a better impression and to be professional.

"Right, see you can put this shirt"—I hold up a short-sleeved shirt in a plaid of various shades of blue—"with either these trousers, these shorts, or these jeans." I group everything into sets.

He looks between the shirt and the trousers, his expression...befuddled. He may even have gone a bit pale.

Gently, I ask, "You're overwhelmed, aren't you?"

"Truth? Yeah. I was just doing the math in my head about the number of combinations and well.... Actually, I'm not real good at matching clothes. I'm ah, colorblind or something." He stuffs his hands in his pockets.

"Right, well then. I suppose I could take pictures of sets and you can use that as a reference." I shrug. I've done it before for other people. Lots of people.

"Could you? That would be fantastic."

"I'll do a bit for you now to get started. Here, try on these shoes." I hand him a box of leather Tod's I picked up for such an incredible deal it feels like stealing.

He slips them on. "Wow, these are nice." He tests them by walking around a few boxes. "I could wear these without socks."

I gasp. "Promise me you will never do that. You will also never wear them with white athletic socks." I hold up a bundle of trouser socks. "Only these. If I find you breaking the rules, I will take them back." I shake the sock bundle once more before dropping in on the couch.

He tosses back his head and laughs before he says, "You will pry these shoes from my cold dead feet."

"That good, right?" I smile. "Perhaps Jayne knows her stuff?" I smirk as I use my smartphone to snap pictures of outfits.

"Perhaps she does." He smiles back. "Hey, can I get you something to drink?"

I step away from the clothes I've arranged and look over at Stacy. He's wearing the same manky t-shirt from today with those low-slung, threadbare jeans and the new shoes that, when not on sale, cost as much as his now lone end table.

And he's lovely. I see why Josie and Paisley speak so highly of him. He seems easy going and I find I'm feeling more like Jayne, at home, than Jayne, the shop girl. "I would love a glass of wine. But"—I gesture to the boxes—"I'll take some water, please."

"Red or white?"

I'm pleasantly surprised. "You've got wine?" I know when I moved in I had a case of wine but I'm sure that's the last thing he's had time to think of.

"And beer. You don't think I could tackle all this without it, do ya?" He laughs.

"White then, please." I smile at him as he leaves the room. I'm snapping shots of clothes when he comes back and hands me a cup of white wine. By cup I mean plastic blue Solo cup.

"Sorry about the stemware."

"It's no problem. If I were a stemware snob I'd run over to my flat and get a glass, but this will do just fine."

"Well then, here's to making good friends, good luck, and a smooth transition." He holds his cup up for a toast.

"Cheers," I say before we each take a sip.

"Listen, I was wondering if you wanted to carpool up to the wedding? My folks are coming to town—"

I shake my head. "Sorry, I'll be flying up from Miami. I leave Wednesday for business there and go straight to the rehearsal."

"If your plans change, let me know." He tucks his hands into his front pockets, his smile so boyishly charming it makes me want to change my plans or at the very least cup his face and suck on his top lip. I'm instantly thankful I really do have to be in Miami or else a two-hour ride with him—alone—could lead to trouble.

"Now, I'm going to text you each picture with a caption of which shoes go with the outfit. This outfit here should do nicely for your meeting Friday." I point to the navy blue dress trousers and light gray pinstriped shirt. "But this is the *pièce de résistance*." I pull out a dark gray necktie and present it to him.

"Are those quadratic equations on that tie?" He stares in disbelief.

I shrug. "Dunno, looks math-ish to me. So I bought it."

"This is incredible. Jayne, you're great. Thanks for bailing me out here." His face lights with pleasure and once again I'm a superhero of the clothing world. I'm capable of eating dinner with the queen, hanging with the Beckhams, and sitting front row during any and all fashion weeks. Paris, Milan, New York—I am dresser of people, hear me roar!

I snap back to reality. "Oh, it really was my pleasure. I had such a good time shopping for you. Truly. I'm glad you gave me the opportunity."

He steps closer and takes the tie; our hands brush each other's and the flare of heat that travels up my arm causes me to suck in my breath. It's as if this man has an energy field around him that reels me in.

Resistance is futile.

Still smiling as I look up at him and he down at me, I'm instantly pulled into a second, better fantasy that involves being thoroughly kissed and possibly thrown onto the couch for insane passionate lovemaking. Oh, or better yet, across a large box. Doesn't that sound pleasantly dirty? How wonderful would it be to stretch up when being kissed?

I sigh and refocus.

He's holding the one shirt I questioned of all the purchases. I wondered if it would fit across his broad shoulders.

"You should try that one on," I murmur. Because he should but also maybe I'll get to see his bare chest up close.

Dear Lord, I've turned into a lech. A desperate, window-peeping slapper whose salivary glands are on full water works.

"Okay." He reaches over his head to pull his t-shirt off. Right in front of me.

See Jayne expire from delight.

I'm holding my phone and the Solo cup of wine but they fade away as all I can process is the broad, beautifully sculpted, picture-perfect male form before me.

"Gracious," I murmur and lick my lips.

"Hey, watch it," he calls, snapping me out of my fantasy of having my needs topped off.

"Oh, I'm so sorry." My Solo cup lies on the floor, my phone balancing precariously from my fingertips. Apparently, I need to calm myself down as he befuddles me more than I thought. So much for being the cool Jayne I know and love.

He tosses his old t-shirt on top of my spilled wine, pressing his toes over the cloth to absorb the liquid, while flinging the new shirt over his shoulder. I can't draw my eyes away from his broad shoulders and delicious chest. All those bulky muscles begging to be caressed.

"You're staring. It's the scar, right? I know it's unsightly but it used to be a whole lot worse." He looks down at his chest.

"Pardon?" Not one single ounce of him is unsightly.

"The scar. I was in a bad car accident. Impaled."

At the word "impaled" my girly bits surrender and get tingly with want.

I stare at the quarter-shaped scar over his right pec muscle and swallow. "I hadn't noticed."

"You're being kind." He rubs the scar and I want to lick him. Like brownie batter off a spoon.

"My arse," I whisper and blink several times trying to break the stare. "You're dishy."

Briefly, he ducks his head. "I like to swim."

When he meets my gaze the message is clear. It's the same raw look of desirability I saw a few moments ago, the one that sent me into a daydream and at this moment continues to keep my body ringing.

We step closer and a nervous laugh created from the anticipated excitement of what is about to happen, combined with my eagerness to touch him and see if he feels like I imagine, threatens to erupt. Without further thought or words, we're pressed together, his warmth permeating my silk blouse, and I praise the fashion gods for the sheer fabric. I thank the Florida heat for making lightweight fabric a necessity because the only thing better would be skin.

He wraps an arm around my waist and pulls me in closer and I lose the capacity for common sense. One moment we're talking outfits and the next his tongue's in my mouth and I've expired and gone to heaven.

He backs me up against a wall between two boxes and deepens the kiss. I grip his shoulders, trying to crawl on him, in him, or whatever it is that will feed this insatiable craving for more.

"Jesus, Jayne. I didn't see that coming," he says, his temple pressed to mine, our chests rising and falling together in a steady rhythm.

"Er...." Not that I hadn't thought about it, but who needs to say that?

"I just ended a relationship..." He nuzzles my neck and I'm unsure if he's telling me this for full disclosure or working it out for himself, only aloud. I slide my leg up the side of him and wrap it around his waist.

"I can't offer anything more than a night here and there." I give him my standard line. Lay out the rules right away.

"And I've got Cordie...she really"—he kisses the space under my chin—"doesn't need"—kisses and moves lower—"any more"—kiss, kiss—"to handle." He stops at the space where my neck meets my shoulder, gives a long sucking kiss before moving across my collarbone. I confess, I may have heard what he said but I'm not listening.

My eyelids flutter as my body relaxes into his and I moan low and deep.

This tall, broad-shouldered fantasy of mine who, with my luck, is likely a closet knuckle-dragging caveman who wants a *little woman* has swiftly rendered me a strumpet after a few mere kisses. I'm keen to put on an apron and pretend I can cook. I also want to wear nothing else underneath that apron.

My mind's eye conjures up domesticated visions I've never had before.

That's a dose of cold, harsh, no fun water.

Alert! Screams my heart. *Warning!* Scolds my brain (in Mum's voice). Mind the gap between reality and fantasy.

I shift slightly to the side, trying to put space between us. It's difficult, especially when one wants no space whatsoever. "Right, well this can go from innocent to naughty in a flash."

His head comes up slowly, his blue eyes cloudy with want and I debate telling my conscience to stuff it. Caution be damned.

"You want me to stop?" He whispers roughly as if it's going to be an exceedingly difficult task.

My body trembles with delight. It's unfair how keen I am for him, how flawless he is.

"Dad," his daughter calls from above us. I suppose from the top of the stairs. We come apart in a flash.

Flaw discovered.

No matter how I might yearn for his form, there is no way I'm going to let our bits co-mingle when there's a child in the picture.

"Yeah, kiddo? What's the matter?" He jerks the new t-shirt off his shoulder, flips it open, and pulls it quickly over his head. His movements are smooth and masculine and once again, I say a silent prayer for the naughty free channel as I think I'm going to call upon it tonight.

I turn my back to him and try to do at least one deep calming yoga breath; I know I need to do about ten but one's a start. I pick up my Solo cup then put it on the end table.

"Can you bring me some water?" Cordie calls.

"I'll bring it up in a minute. Get back in bed," Stacy answers before returning his attention to me.

"I'm sorry about the wine," I tell him, avoiding his gaze.

"Jayne, I—"

"No, don't say anything. Let's just leave it." I grab my purse and shove in my phone.

"But we should—"

I turn to him and put my hand up. "Please, Stacy." I back out of the room. Would I be leaving if he were the new single (childless) stranger across the street? Probably not.

"I owe you money."

"I'll bring a bill over. Don't worry about it. Have a good night." I'm out of the flat before I can convince myself to stay.

CHAPTER SEVEN

It's the last girls' night out before Josie gets married. We hadn't planned on getting together, having carried off a smashing good bachelorette party this past weekend for her. The week is heavy with extensive to-do lists and last-minute errands, but this is the quiet we'll need before the chaos.

We meet at the Fox and Hound. A quiet table in the corner.

Josie's nursing a whisky sour; she spent the afternoon collecting her family from the airport and getting them settled at Amelia Island. "The two-hour buffer isn't enough," she says.

Having met her mother, I would agree.

Paisley slides into a seat across from us. Her face is red and blotchy and at first I wonder if she's had too much sun and am about to remark on it when she bursts into tears.

Covering her face with her hands, she says between her fingers, "I'm sorry. I should go. I'm not going to be much fun."

"What's happened?" Both Josie and I change seats, moving into the ones next to her.

She shakes her head and cries harder.

"Is it Hank?" Josie rubs her back.

Paisley nods and we simply wait, rubbing her back and cooing encouraging words, until she's gained some control.

"We had a terrible fight. Awful. And everything I knew would happen, did. I told him friends with benefits didn't exist. It was a stupid idea. Stupid!" She grabs Josie's drink and downs it. She fills us in on the specifics and I try not to meet Josie's eye over Paisley's head.

"So you're no longer sleeping together and you're no longer friends?" Josie signals the waitress for a refill.

"Yup. That sums it up." Paisley wipes her face with a bundle of napkins, little hiccups the remaining clue to her sobs.

"And how do you feel about all that?" I lock eyes again with Josie, who's likely thinking all would not be lost if Paisley would simply admit that she's in love with Hank. But Josie has little problem speaking her mind, unlike the rest of us.

Paisley's not just in love. She's desperately, madly in love. Probably has been since the day she met Hank, which was when she was in nappies. Her excuse that he's her best friend's brother is a poor one for sure, but I get where she's coming from. There's more at stake than their feelings, so many of their family is involved.

Paisley shakes her head. "I don't know what to think. I've never seen him so angry. So disappointed." Fresh tears course down her face. "What will I tell Gigi? She just accepted that we've been fooling around and now I have to tell her he doesn't want to be my friend anymore." She ends her words on a wail.

We wait in silence.

Paisley continues, "I'm sorry, Jo. You're getting married in a few days and I'm nothing but a downer." She's caught her second wind and is back to searching for composure.

"Do you think I care about that? I care about you. I care that you're happy." Josie hands her a new wad of napkins.

"I don't even know what happiness looks like anymore." She looks at me. "Let's change the subject. If I keep on about this, I'm going to go to a dark place."

"Because you love him." Josie smacks her hand on the table. "You see that right?"

"Jo," I warn.

Paisley shakes her head and hones in on me. "Any chance something is going on between you and Stacy yet? I saw you on the phone last week and you were blushing. It was him, right? He mentioned you two might ride up together—"

"Stop." I hold my hand up and look between my friends. Funny thing is I'm talking to both of them. Josie's primed, itching to make Paisley see that she's gutted over Hank because she's downright head over heels for him, but Paisley's in no space to hear it. Paisley is too scared to look at what's before her so she's deflecting to the rest of us. Courage, she'll find it when she's ready.

"I was not on the phone with Stacy that day. I was on the phone with Josie and we were talking about you."

Paisley gasps.

"We were saying that we hoped you'd bring Hank to the wedding and I was embarrassed that I was caught. I'm sorry. As for riding with Stacy, he did suggest it but I'm going straight from a meeting with a loan officer in Miami to the rehearsal. There is no Stacy and me. And there won't be." If her crisis is any sort of presage, I'll keep to that resolve.

"I'm sorry I keep trying to force him on you. It's just that he's very nice." She pressed her palms to her eyes.

I pat her shoulder. "I'm sorry about Hank. In a round-about way I was doing the same thing." While Paisley's eye are covered, I shove Josie in the shoulder to get her to settle down.

Paisley uncovers her eyes and faces Josie. "I'm sorry, Jo. I know you thought he was for me, Hank that is, but...I just...I dunno."

Josie side hugs Paisley and rests her chin on her shoulder. "All that is irrelevant. I only want you to be happy. If I can help, I hope you'll let me." Paisley hugs her back. Not one to be left out, I fling my arms over the both of them. We're still like that, laughing, when Heather and Kenley come in moments later.

"Did we miss everything already?" Kenley asks and sits across from us.

"Nah," Paisley says. "Just a small breakdown. I'm good now."

"So what's new, everyone?" Heather asks and takes a lone chip from the basket. I may have eaten the bulk waiting for them to come.

"Besides me getting married?" Josie smiles. "And my mother already threatening to disinherit me if I bail on this one like I did the other two?"

We all laugh because the thought is ridiculous. Josie's other two engagements were farces. Brinn is the real deal.

"I hope there are single men at your wedding, Josie. I'm looking to meet someone." Heather scoops up the crumbs from the bottom of the paper-lined basket.

We all look to Kenley for a hint of how we should react.

"Um, I'm not judging, but are you sure you're ready for dating? I mean, you and Justin are still working out the particulars of the divorce...." She clasps her hands before her, touching them briefly to her lips before continuing. "Ah, you know...this is all so new. Maybe you should take some time?"

Heather cuts her eyes to Kenley. "Time for what? I know what I want, or more specifically, what I don't want. I'm not very good at this single thing. I don't like being alone. Dating is the natural solution." She turns to Josie. "So, single guys?"

Josie's gaze cycles around the table. "Yeah, well I think there will be a few. Like Vann and Erik, and Stacy."

"That Stacy is something to look at," Heather says.

I duck my head in case it's turning the telltale shade of *busted*. One look and they'll know, likely Josie before anyone, that I've given Stacy an overly friendly welcome. They'll want to know how much of my body was pressed against his while I explored molars.

I look for a distraction. Damn that empty chip basket. I lean across the table to take it back to the kitchen and get more when Paisley asks, "How's the new shop plans coming along, Jayne?"

Bless her.

"Well, I should know more after Wednesday as that's when I meet with the banker. I'm very excited. Little worried and stressed, of course. But I'm going to try to focus on the excited."

"I'm excited for you," Paisley says.

"Holy shit. Is that who I think it is?" Josie rises from her seat.

I follow the direction of her gaze and groan loudly and for good measure.

"No," I say, shaking my head. But there's nothing to stop my smile. "I will this vision to go away. This is not happening. Simply not happening."

"Hallo, my lovelies. Surprise!" Pippa says. Her voice is soft and lulling and gives the impression that she's a flighty, dimwitted hippie. If I didn't know her as well as I did, it would be an easy assumption to make.

My cousin, with her thin, wispy blond hair that she's streaked—apparently haphazardly—with orange, clasps her hands before her and bows slightly.

From between my fingers I ask, "Pip, what are you doing here?" It's not like it's a quick drive from where she was staying. I'm guessing multiple flight connections were involved. "Weren't you living at some yoga commune in India?"

"Namaste, Jaynie-girl. I wouldn't miss Josie's wedding for anything in the world."

"Yay!" Josie moves from around the table and hugs Pippa. She can be over the top and there have been times I'd rather tackle Mt. Everest without oxygen than suffer through spending extended time with her. She's always trying to get me to eat healthy and exercise. It's too much, really, how thoroughly she loves me. Particularly when I've been a shite cousin half the time.

Though I do love her so. Most of the time. And not three minutes here and we've slipped into our familiar roles: me the annoyed pseudo-older sister, and Pip the one who pushes all my buttons.

With full glare affect, I say to Josie, "Did you not think I was serious when I made that monetary offer for you to lose her invite?"

"Oh, Jayne. You missed me." Pippa wipes what I presume is a tear from her eye.

"Just a wee bit, Pips," I say to my cousin, who throughout most of our childhood was but mere steps away from me, as her mother put the nut in nutter.

She comes around the table and hugs me from behind.

"I assume you'll be staying with me?" Part of me is glad my always quiet home will have some noise.

"Already dropped my bags off. I saw Uncle Thomas and Auntie Millie and I'm on the schedule to help."

Josie pulls a chair up for Pippa, who surprisingly plops into it. This is uncharacteristic for my cousin, who normally strikes a yoga pose everywhere, and I make a mental note to approach her about it in private.

"What were you all talking about?" Pippa asks after going through a series of warm hellos and welcome backs from the girls. She is well liked, my freaky cousin.

Paisley pushes the pitcher of water toward Pippa. She rarely drinks alcohol.

"Jayne is going to expand her business," Paisley says.

"For realz?" Pippa faces me. "Finally! This has been her plan since she was accepted into her design program at University." She reaches out and takes my hand, squeezing it.

"We were also talking about this hot guy that's in Josie's wedding. His name is Stacy." Heather wags her brows.

I stifle a groan.

"Oh, tell me more about him." This from Pippa.

"He works with Brinn. He's the numbers guy that they brought in on that start up Brinn did two years ago. Now they're venturing out into building an airline. He's a genius with numbers," Josie says.

"He's really tall. At least six-five," Heather says. "I'm willing to bet he's a swimmer or something."

She'd win on that bet. But I keep my mouth shut.

"Tall, smart, hot. He sounds like all the things," Pippa says, looking at me. "What do you think?"

Pippa believes in love, the magic that surrounds it, and that a heart will shrivel to resemble a raisin without it. "He has sole custody of his nine-year-old daughter," I say. Putting an immediate stop to any crazy notion she may get. She faces the crowd.

"That answers that question. Who else wants him? Heather, you divorced and ready to date yet? Maybe I can have him?" Josie laughs and Paisley groans.

"I don't understand this thing about a child," Kenley says. It's not a new discussion.

"She says she's not maternal," Paisley adds and follows it with an eye roll so exaggerated it's a wonder she doesn't get a cramp in those little eye muscles.

"Oh, she isn't. I can attest to that." Pippa raises her hand as if she's about to take an oath and solemnly swear to tell embarrassing, yet true stories about me. I lean back in my chair, wine in hand, and wait for the stories to unfold.

"Once when she was supposed to be watching me, she let me play with scissors. I cut all my hair off. I had these beautiful ringlets. Hacked them like errant shrubbery limbs. As you can well see, nothing but limp, straight hair since." She caresses her silky, honey-colored strands.

"Poor you." I sigh.

"That not so bad," Kenley says, making eye contact with me.

"Cut it to the scalp." Filling in the missing information makes Paisley and Heather's mouth form little O's.

"Also, the time you let me drink six bottles of fizzy drink and eat that spicy sausage. I was sick all night long," Pippa continues. She's got a treasure trove of them. Let us not forget the time I forgot her at school, or when I tried to pierce her ears without numbing them first, or when I fed her uncooked hot dogs for three days straight.

In my defense, I offered her cereal. She said no and requested the hot dogs.

"Do you remember that, Jayne?" Pippa asks.

"I remember. Mum made me hold your hair while you vomited. Disgusting."

Apparently, the wail of a baby does nothing to my uterus or my lactation system, as I can easily tune it out much like I do a fire alarm or an alarm clock. Which is why I have so many *gone wrong* stories.

"Okay, so whatever. Jayne's not maternal. But passing up on a great guy like Stacy—I don't get it." Paisley crosses her arms over her chest.

I want to tell her to take a good look in the mirror. That she's held Hank off for far less serious reasons. I shrug. "What's going to come from having a fling with him? Tell me that."

"He could be *The One*," says Kenley.

I want to laugh but she believes her husband, Doug, is the only man for her on this earth. I think she could find a dozen more.

"I've never subscribed to the romantic notion of 'the one' or soul mates." I shrug. "I just haven't. I'm not a romantic. I've said this before. I don't believe everyone gets a magical and passionate love and rides away on a unicorn. Two of you at this table can attest that love can go horribly wrong." I look to Heather and Paisley.

"It comes down to risk for Jayne." Josie supplies.

"But we're talking about just having some fun with him," Paisley says.

I fix my stare on her. "Are you? And how do you define fun? I imagine for you it's not just one night." I give her a meaningful look; isn't that how she started her fling with Hank? Wasn't she bawling her eyes out earlier over losing him?

I continue, "What if I do 'just' have your version of fun with him and it wanes like most initial attractions do? What then? Do we all continue to hang out and act as if nothing ever happened?"

Josie shakes her head. "I call bullshit because if you split amicably then I don't see a problem with us all hanging out. So it's awkward for a bit. Who cares?"

"What if we 'fall in love'?" I use the quotes to emphasis how ridiculous I think this sentiment is for someone like me. "What happens if we go through all that and then it falls apart? He has a child, right? We have to consider her."

I look at each of them before continuing. "It's like that Adele song. The one where she says love either works or it hurts instead. If you need proof of how tragic the effects of an unsuccessful love can be then by all means please read about Pyramus and Thisbe, Romeo and Juliet, or better yet—"

"Bonnie and Clyde," Josie says waspishly.

"—I was going to say Sir Lancelot and Queen Guinevere. The annals of history are loaded with stories of love gone wrong, and I'm sorry but I'm keen to avoid drama such as that. It's not for me."

I face Pippa and dare her to use my reference to draw attention to my own mother's tragic love story. My real father, biologically that is, is not the man I call Dad and love with all my heart. No, my bio-dad is a black-hearted wanker who discarded Mum eight years after I was born. It seems he had a second family and couldn't decide between the two for a while so he kept us both. Then, after what Mum describes as a terrible but common row, he came clean about his other family and left us for them. That experience helped form what I want from love and a life partner. Or specifically, don't want.

"You never have to marry, Jaynie-girl. There's comfort in making your own security," she would tell me. Late at night, I'd hear her sob in her bed.

Marriage? Thanks, but no. Never mind my own experiences have been shite. How about that one guy I dated in college? Come to find out he was using me to get closer to my roommate. Or the Aussie in design school whose ulterior motive was for me to do his work? I was so eager for their attention and touch only to be humiliated when their true intentions were revealed. How many of my friends at this table have had a man look up at them like a hunter to a wild animal and say, "I'm game?" That's happened to me more than once and it doesn't do a whole lot toward romantic notions for the opposite sex. For me, it's about lining up the pieces that fit, wanting common goals. Making the most of what each other has and brings to the partnership. It's about a solid companionship.

"No," I repeat. "It's not for me."

CHAPTER EIGHT

Though I've lived in America for eight years now, I simply can't do coffee in the morning. The aroma of ground beans does not bring forth a sense of calm. It does not ease away my tension, and the lack of a teabag to bob in the steamy water removes that essential moment where time feels as if it's standing still, waiting for me to map out my day, before it begins its forward charge at breakneck speed.

I scan the paper as I fry an egg. The timing of the bagel popping up in the toaster and the egg cooking to a perfect crispness around the edges is a skill I've perfected since college, when this meal became my morning standard. Along with my tea, of course. I compile my breakfast and move it along with my cup to the table.

The knock at my door is so unexpected I question my hearing. Through the peephole, I see Stacy, his hand resting on what I assume is the top of his daughter's head. Not that I can see her since their heights are so drastically at odds. But it's a safe guess.

I smooth the front of my natty pink robe, wishing briefly

for something sexier. But when I slipped it on over my silk bed gown, I wasn't expecting anyone to come round and certainly not as I was steeping my elixir of life.

He knocks again.

I crack open the door and peer out.

"Hallo." Bollocks, it's a terrible time to realize one's teeth haven't been brushed. Who gets up and brushes their teeth first thing? Perhaps I should consider doing that to avoid these occasional and awkward moments.

"I'm so sorry, Jayne. We've had a—" Stacy begins.

"Fire. Dad burned the bacon." Cordie looks at me with the same beautiful blue eyes she inherited from her father. "Can't you smell it on us?"

I tuck my robe in tightly, which only makes the threadbare spots more obvious, before pushing open the door. "That's not the smell of bacon. Bacon has a delightful smell—"

"Until you burn the fat," Stacy says.

"That smells like...rubbish." Involuntarily, I curl my lip.

"You should smell our house," Cordie says.

"No, thank you," I say and smile. "How can I help you?" I gesture for them to come in and step back to allow them, him, room to pass.

"Part of the reason I burned the bacon was because I was distracted with an issue Cordie is having." Stacy looks at his daughter.

"Another reason he burned the bacon was because he set the microwave for five minutes and not thirty seconds."

"Which I would have been aware of had we not been trying to braid your hair and looking for your belt.' I glance at the waistline of her cute dress; the belt loops hang limp and empty.

"Listen, Jayne. I know this is early and we've clearly caught you at a bad time."

He nods to my robe. "But any chance you know how to do a, uh, what did you call it?" He looks at his daughter. "A fishtail braid? I tried watching the videos. I can't do it." His tone is frustration mixed with a bit of sadness, or is it self-recrimination? "I really tried." He has such sad, pleading eyes when he looks at his daughter that I'm compelled to make it all better.

Because I can. It's so easy to fix this.

"It's okay, Dad. I know you tried. I can wear my hair loose."

"Nonsense, I'm an expert braider, I'll have you know, and I'm sure you have a lovely belt for that dress, but I have an amazing scarf that would go perfectly with that outfit. Are you interested?"

"Sure, because we can't find the belt in any of the boxes. We can't find anything because of all the boxes."

"Thanks, Jayne." Stacy wraps his large hand around my upper arm and squeezes gently. Tiny gooseflesh dances down my body and I inadvertently sway toward him, wanting more gooseflesh and tingly skin.

"Right," I say and clasp my hands together over my chest to hide the evidence of how pleased my body is to see him. "I'll just pop into my room and grab that scarf and elastic for your hair. Have a seat." I pull out a chair at my kitchen table.

Stacy steps toward me; I step back. My hands holding the lapels of my robe together.

"I'm gonna run home and air out the house. It smells pretty bad in there. Is that okay?" He whispers the last bit.

"We're fine," I say.

"It smells worse that bad. It smells horrid. Repugnant,

vile—"

"I got it, Cordelia. Thanks," her father says before slipping out my front door.

"That's quite a vocabulary you have." Is it common for a child her age to have such an extensive one? "How old are you? Nine, right?" I may have not heard correctly once he said he had a child, as I was likely caught up in the disappointment that he quickly became off limits.

"Yes. I'm in the gifted program. Dad says I don't talk like I'm in the gifted program."

"How do gifted children talk?" She's quite cute with her cheeky, matter-of-fact attitude. She sounds like she's in the gifted program to me.

"I dunno. I guess I'm supposed to use bigger words. He says I say dumb too much." She shrugs. "Whatever."

I hold up one finger before popping into my room for a quick change into some yoga pants, a bra, and t-shirt. I swish some toothpaste then find the scarf I was thinking of and an elastic, and head back to my front room. Cordie is sitting in a chair reading the paper. The comics.

"Do you like this?" I hold up the scarf.

Her eyes go wide. "It's too pretty for me to wear."

Her dress, a cute navy and pink combination, is accented with tiny white stitching.

My scarf, white with strands of navy, matches perfectly.

"It's a scarf and you must admit, it's perfect."

"It really is."

"Here, stand up and I'll tie it around." When we're done, I lean back and smile.

Heavens, I love putting clothes together.

"You're the one that helped my Dad get his clothes, right?"

"That's me."

"You did a great job. He looks kinda cute for a dad."

"If you think so."

"Don't you think so? Most of the moms at my old school thought so. Jill thought so."

Jill?

"I think everyone looks good in nice, well-fitting clothes. Sit." I pat the chair. "Let's do your braid." I brush out her long strands, and I'm taken back to when Pippa was this age and I'd mess with her hair all the time. After the scissor incident, I spent serious quid trying to buy her forgiveness by acquiring headbands and clips for her in effort to do up her nearly shorn head. She always had cute hair thanks to me. "Is that your breakfast?" She points to my plate.

"It is."

"What is it? I don't mean that to sound rude." Her gaze is fixed on my plate.

I laugh. "It's a toasted bagel topped with a fried egg and baked beans. Not your American-type baked beans made with honey and bacon. These are Heinz goodness that I have to find in specialty stores. Looks gross to you?"

Her stomach growls. "Nothing looks gross next to Dad's chocolate chip waffles. You should have seen them. I didn't think it was possible to do that to a waffle. And the bacon. After he tossed it in the trash can, smoke continued to come out and he just stood there staring at it."

I suppress a laugh. "At least he tried."

"Yeah. My Mimi always made me chocolate chip waffles on important days like the first day of school."

"That's not today?" How can that be? I try to mentally conjure up an image of the calendar but all I get are accessories and skirts.

"It's the first day of nerd camp," she says quietly. "Dad thinks I can meet friends here before school starts."

"Are you nervous?"

"Yeah."

I finish her braid and sit next to her. "I would be too. I hate first anything. Dates, client interactions, business meetings. They all suck immensely."

She smiles, the edges wavering ever so slightly. Her stomach growls again and her gaze darts to my breakfast.

"Can I try that?" She slides the plate closer.

"Are you sure? Most people don't like beans."

"I'm sure." She nods emphatically.

"Let me warm it a bit." Fifteen seconds in the microwave does the trick. Then I cut it in half, sliding one portion onto a plate for her. Sitting into the chair across from her, I push one plate her way and pull the other toward me.

"Are you sure you want to eat beans on the first day of meeting others? They might make you windy."

Cordie looks between me and her plate, her fork poised, ready for action. "What does that mean?"

"Windy is flatulence." After slicing off a bite, I slide it through the gravy of the beans, scooping as many as will load onto my fork before devouring it all in a manner Mum would deem horrifyingly unladylike.

For me, food is decadence and reward. With the same passion I seek and take pleasure in eating, I loathe exercise. And therein lies the issue. My solution, shapewear.

"Wow, this is really good. I mean, I thought it could really suck but after seeing what Dad made I figured I might be okay with this."

"So hunger, plain and simple, brought you to try it."

"Yeah." Her smile is filled with pixie mischief that shines

from her eyes. She shovels the food in at such an alarming rate I fear she'll choke. When she's done she takes the plate to the sink, rinses it, then comes back to sit across from me.

Sodding hell, she's a better roomie than Pippa, who whole-heartedly believes kitchen gnomes will suddenly appear and magically clean the kitchen.

"Don't tell my dad I ate that. It'll hurt his feelings." She quirks her lips to the side. "Please," she adds, possibly an afterthought.

"Want a spot of tea to wash it down?" I tilt my cup her way.

"Does it have caffeine? I'm not allowed to have caffeine. Dad says it will stunt my growth."

"Is that so? I hadn't heard." Or paid much attention.

"I thought all adults knew that. It's your job to make sure us kids don't do stupid stuff, right? That's what Dad says."

I rise, nearly six feet in my stocking feet, the living contrast to her statement. Unless it did stunt my growth? Imagine that. "I've drunk tea since I was maybe a tad older than you." I don't mean to sound defensive. Honest.

"You're tall. I'll probably be ginormous like you because Dad is so tall." Her gaze travels my length several times.

"Thanks. But what about your mum? Maybe she's not so tall." I refill my cup with hot water and add a second bag to steep. I don't know how long it's going to take Stacy to air out his house, but I'm going to need strength from the gods, as I usually don't enjoy talking to people early in the morning. Hence, the earliest my shop opens is ten.

"I don't know my mom. She ditched me after I was born. Dad said she played volleyball for the college. Not that I've seen many volleyball players but she looks tall in her pictures."

What does one say to that? Poor child.

"My condolences then. Trousers will be a bloody nightmare, but you'll always look good in a skirt."

It's an interesting tidbit about Stacy. Is he the sort to prefer athletic women? I file the information away, to use later with the girls should they harangue me about how I should be jumping his bones. I am most decidedly not athletic. Two very good reasons to stop thinking about my hunky neighbor. One stands in front of me and is likely armed with a bazillion more reasons.

"Who's Jill?" I ask, despite my resignation that I wouldn't.

"Oh, Dad was going to marry her and then we moved here." Marry? So he wants a wife? Or did at one time.

"You don't say?" Because I was never in the gifted program, it's all I can come up with.

"Yeah, then she dumped him," Cordie states matter-of-fact.

A knock at the door is followed by Stacy pushing it open from the outside and poking his head in.

"Hi, may I?" His gaze darts between his daughter and me. One brow lifted. Was he expecting a brawl or something?

"Sure." In one gesture I indicate he should come in and stop being ridiculous.

Easing the door closed, he says, "I'm afraid there's no hope in getting that smell out of the house. We'll have to burn everything and start over."

Cordie pumps her fist. "Good. Then we can move back to Mimi's."

Stacy's smile is wan. "She's not happy being here," he tells me.

"I'm in the room."

"I'm not talking *about* you; I'm explaining to Jayne why —" He shakes his head and grunts. His daughter has since crossed her arms over her chest and looks ready to deliver a lippy comeback. I've seen the same stubborn look on Pippa's face many times.

Time to offer some assistance. "I know of someone who might be able to get the smell out. A cleaning lady of sorts. She can work on it while you both are gone." I have no intention of refereeing a fight this morning or any morning for that matter.

"Can she unpack the boxes too? Because it's no fun living in a cardboard city." Cordie directs an irritated look toward her father, who's turned a lovely shade of pink.

"Now, Cordie—"

"She'd certainly help with the boxes."

His gaze swivels to me. "Seriously? Because that would be amazing. Amazing. With the business trying to start up and getting Cordie settled...there's little time to unpack." His look is one of pleading hope.

"And he hates it," Cordie says.

"That too."

Laughing, I say, "I'll ask but I'm certain she can use the money. Not that you'll have to pay a tremendous amount or anything. Leave me a key and I'll pass it along." Stacy begins to pat his pockets, presumably searching for his keys.

Cordie sighs heavily. "He does this a lot."

"Those jeans look nice on you by the way. You have good taste in clothes," I say, tongue in cheek.

"Sending me pictures of how to put everything together was a life saver. You should do that for every man."

"Are you looking for this?" I touch his hip where a single

key hangs from a D-ring. When my finger makes contact with the fabric a tingle of pleasure, likely because I've made him forbidden fruit, travels up my arm where it bursts free and heats my body.

Stacy touches the key and laughs. "Yeah. Thanks." He removes the ring and places it on my outstretched hand. The tips of his fingers graze my palm and I'm forced to fight the impulse to close my fingers around his.

"I'll leave it under my flower pot for you when you get home. I'll be at my shop late. Josie and I are finishing up her gown." I pull in a slow, steady breath, hoping to focus on everything but my primal need to touch him again.

"Thanks for your help." He tucks a hand in his front pocket; the movement forces his shirt to stretch over his chest and my attention is drawn to the spot where I know a scar lies underneath his shirt.

Suddenly, I feel a wee bit breathless.

From the back of my place, upstairs, a bellowing guttural yawn breaks the moment of silence. An even louder burp follows it.

"Oh dear," I say, making my eyes go wide, feigning surprise though I'm clearly not. Soft, sweet Pippa can be quite crude.

"Man, I'm sorry, Jayne. I assumed you were alone. We didn't mean to interrupt," Stacy says, fumbling his words, hands reaching for his daughter.

"Oh, it's no bother."

The sound of someone breaking wind, a loud release, echoes through the rooms. Cordie snickers. I close my eyes, biting back a chuckle.

"Really, Jayne. We didn't mean to interrupt. I...it was stupid to assume you were alone. We'll leave before your friend comes out. Thanks for—wow, Cordie's hair looks great. Did you get that from a video, because I couldn't figure it out." He grips his daughter's shoulder and pivots her toward the door.

Above us, Pippa shuffles heavily in the direction of my loo, lets another one rip, and a door closes. I fail at holding back my laugh. She'd be mortified if she knew.

"Flatulence." Cordie joins me in laughing.

Stacy pushes her forward. "Again, I'm so sorry."

I wave off his apology and sink down into a chair, laughing. The poor man is obviously embarrassed. Perhaps he doesn't want his daughter exposed to my den of sin. Clearly he thinks I was entertaining a man.

They're out the door before I can compose myself. When I do finally gather my wits, I stand at the foot of the stairs, and when I hear Pippa come out of the loo, yell, "Are you all right there, Pips?"

"Airplane food. It destroys my gut," she says then moans. "I know better but I get so bloody hungry."

"Feel too tepid to earn some cash cleaning up an apartment and unpacking some boxes?" I ask when she come to the top of the landing. Clean up behind herself? No. Clean for cash? She's a champ.

"Aye-ya. Once I get some quality food in me, I'll be spot on." She has her runners in hand.

"Headed to the grocer are you?" It's a standing joke between us that the food I stock does not meet Pippa's standard of quality. If it comes from a box, she turns her nose up. Whereas, I forgo a salad for a cupcake.

"You're lucky you're so tall. If you were my height and ate like you do, you'd be round like a circle."

We've had this conversation so many times I can recite it

in my sleep. Fortunately for me she's easily distracted.

"Here's the key." I place it on the table. "It's flat twelve, across the street. He burned some bacon and apparently it stinks. Also, they just moved in so maybe, if there's time, unpack some boxes. You'll need cleaning supplies." I move to my purse, remove some cash before placing it on the table next to the key.

"Who lives there?" She's lacing up her runners.

I groan inwardly and go for vague. "It's Brinn's coworker. He just moved here."

It takes two beats for her to put the pieces together. "Oh, it's the Stacy guy. If I see anything that indicates he's a weirdo, I'll let you know. Can't have you pining for someone who's mad."

"You know how I am. I'm not going to get involved with him," I say. She does know me best.

"Aye-ya but that won't stop you from pining. Fantasizing about him. You may think romance movie are mere fantasy but—"

"Go away, Pip," I say and move to warm up my tea. Stacy is cute, sweet, and underneath that nerdy dad cloak he wears is a hot, hot man who's taller than me. Sex with someone where our parts line up is a luxury I've rarely had. But that won't happen here. This is not a clean, get-in-and-get-out situation. He lives across the street, he works for my best friend's soon-to-be husband, and he has a child.

What I need is casual. I'm planning to expand my shop, develop more personal shopping clients, and tuck away more money for Mum and Dad's retirement. There's no space in my life for anything other than simple and easy.

Stacy and Cordie are beyond that.

They're messy.

CHAPTER NINE

It feels as if I've packed a solid week in these few short days, and I'm still going non-stop. My pre-meeting with the bank went well and I successfully found a building in Miami to buy that might actually increase my income faster than I expected. I'd crunched the numbers on my phone's calculator several times, running different scenarios. I'm feeling on top of the world.

Invincible.

Exhausted.

Having flown from Miami last night in time for the rehearsal, I fell, face down, onto the beautiful and downy coverlet of my well-appointed, I-could-get-used-to-this room in the hotel as soon as all the pre-wedding events were over. Only to be up early and going for the wedding.

I watch Josie's reflection in the mirror as I help her slip from her wedding gown. She's uncharacteristically quiet and looks sadder than a newly married woman should. Expertly, I place the dress on a padded hanger and tuck it into the garment bag that her parents will assume responsibility for while she and Brinn honeymoon in Europe.

Everything, last night and today's wedding, has gone off without bump or bluster (I don't count the tears shed by both bride and groom), and with the lively and surprisingly fun reception winding to a close, I admit I'm a wee bit sad to have it over. Things will be different now between Josie and me. Sure, she and Brinn have been together these last two years, but now married they'll eventually have the should-we-or shouldn't-we-have-kids conversation. If they decide to add to the McRae clan, it will make two things we no longer have in common. Husband and child.

I hand her a beautifully crafted navy slip dress that matches our bridesmaid gowns. The back drops low and exposes the amazing silver henna design Daanya crafted on Josie's back.

"The wedding was so incredibly beautiful, Josie. It couldn't have been more perfect." I help slip the sheath over her head.

She nods slightly, and then sucks in a sob while bringing her fingertips to her eyes in an effort to hold back the tears.

"Are you all right?" I ask. "What could possibly be wrong?"

Josie shakes her head. "Nothing is wrong. Everything is better than I ever thought it could be. Will and I are as close as we used to be as children. I have you and the other girls; I have a home and place where I belong." She takes the tissue I offer and dabs at her eyes. With a watery smile, she says, "And I have Brinn. I have the love and adoration of a man who I love and adore just as much. How did I get so lucky?"

"Oh love. You're supposed to have this. You worked hard—"

"You should have this too. I want this for you." She grips my arms with a seriousness that's surprising enough I laugh.

"It's not meant for everyone." If it were there would be no such thing as divorce or lawyers that benefit handsomely from them.

Her eager expression gives way to worry. "I don't believe that," she says. "It can't be true."

She is my best friend. This is her day. She's come a long way. So I say what she needs to hear. "I'll have it. When the time is right."

"But I'm afraid you'll miss it. You're like Brinn. So focused on business and your goals that life is passing you by." She tugs me closer. "Promise me you won't get too focused on your professional goals that you'll forget about what Jayne needs personally."

Pippa comes into the room and gathers up the basket of birdseed to hand out to guests.

"Of course, I always take care of my personal needs when the issues arise. I've yet to meet anyone that...you know...." Was interesting or worthy of more than the few weeks I gave them.

"That's because you purposefully pick men that can't go the distance. Most girls have an ideal guy they want to end up with. But not you—"

I drop my voice to a whisper. "Josie," I caution. I know where she's going. She's brought this up before.

Instantly Josie's melancholy turns into irritation.

"That stupid list. Had I made a list and stuck to it, Brinn and I would never have gotten together. Your list is so blah and unimaginative, well frankly, it's like you settle every time."

"Shush." I look over my shoulder for my cousin. I don't

want to have this conversation with her and especially with Pippa in the room.

One bleeding night of too much booze and I tell her about my list. And she faults me for it? This is not the time to point out that she did make a list...of sorts. Only hers was mental. Because what girl doesn't have a wish list? Who says, "Oh any man will do?" No one, that's who. And though I've never pictured myself marrying for mad passionate love (which burns out quickly to be sure), I do have some idea of whom I'd like to spend time with, or rather not spent time with. I'm not completely addle-brained. Eventually, I'd like to have a partner to travel with and share life's events with and I don't expect it to be any of my friends or my cousin. If I do bring a man in the fold, I have my list to ensure I make a good decision.

"Oh please." Josie rolls her eyes. She calls across the room. "Hey, Pip. Know anything about Jayne's man list?"

"Josie!" I punch her in the shoulder with the heel of my palm. The last thing I want is Pippa knowing about my list and telling Mum...and anyone else who'll listen.

"Oh yeah. The Watch-out-for-Wickhams List, I think she called it. Though it was more a Do-it-like-Darcy list. Read it in her journal years ago. That's where she logs all those creative man fantasies she has." Pippa comes around the corner; her arms laden with baskets of cutely decorated bags of birdseed. "It's amazing really how you took one of the greatest love stories and reduce it to a cautionary tale." She shakes her head.

"Because it is." I sigh with annoyance. My list is a measure to ensure I not get conned by the Wickhams of the world. Made sense then when I crafted it and makes sense now, ten years later. Besides, Elizabeth took one look at

Pemberley and suddenly she was in love. Not blooming likely. She saw security and a man who took care of what he was responsible for. She was reminded that she could have easily been snared by Wickham had she been a less cautious person.

"Yet, I don't think you're hopeless," Josie says.

I ignore the bride and focus on the intruder. "This journal-reading intrusion. Does it happen often?" I cross my arms and try to level Pip with a stare but she's clueless. I should know better than to waste my energy.

She shrugs. "All the time. When you leave it out like you do, how is one supposed to know it's not a novel or something? Reads well, by the way. So insightful."

If I had something to throw, I'd aim for her head. "Pippa, I am going to murder you. How dare you—"

"Save it for after. And, if you're so protective of it then don't leave it on your dresser or night table."

She rolls her eyes with such exaggeration I hope they get stuck and she's forced to be cross eyed the rest of her life. Imagine how complicated tree pose would be when one's eyes are looking inward. It would serve her right.

Clearly, she thinks she's done nothing wrong. Going into my bedroom and helping herself to more than my clothes and shoes. I make a mental note to lock my bedroom door or, better yet, lock her out of my home.

"Jayne." Josie takes my elbow, turning me toward her. "I love you. You're my best friend. Please don't wait to be happy."

"I am happy." It's the honest truth. Lonely, perhaps. But happy, yes.

"Happier," she says, a wry twist of her lips. Her lip

piercing winks in the light. "I think you catching the bouquet is a sign."

"I think you aimed for me." I hand her the heels we paired with the dress a few weeks ago in my shop. Feels like ages ago.

"Not true. I was aiming for Paisley. I was hoping to hit her in the head and knock some sense into her." Her smile alights with mischief. "Perhaps I knocked some into you instead?" Her expression is hopeful, her brows raised.

"Sorry. No. Because I don't need it."

"Says you." She grabs my shoulders and gives me a slight shake. "Don't be like me. Where you have to lose everything just to figure it all out. It's way easier if you just go willingly. now."

I laugh, wrapping her in a hug. "Eat a crepe for me in Switzerland and bowls of pasta in Italy."

"You and food," she says with such dryness.

"All right, dear. It's time," Josie's mother says, coming into the room and clapping her hands together twice briskly. "Chop, chop."

Josie whispers, "Yeah, chop, chop, Jayne. You better get out of here before she puts you to work. Think about it, okay?"

"Okay," I whisper and hold onto her for a second longer than her mother probably wanted to spare. "I'll see you in two weeks when you get back."

We separate and are both wiping away the moisture that's collected on our lower lids when she says, "You have to text me and tell me what happens with Paisley and Hank. Don't hold back anything." She wags a knowing finger at me.

If Paisley's about to get her heart broken, that's the last thing Josie needs to be thinking about on her honeymoon.

"If you're sure." I hold my hands up in deference to her wishes.

"I'm sure about loads of things now," she says mimicking my accent.

"You've come a long way, baby," I say, mimicking hers and doing the finger-gun point.

OUTSIDE OF THE BRIDAL ROOM, I wait with my friends. Paisley hands me a bag of seed and proceeds to chew her thumbnail.

"She's almost ready," I tell her.

"I'm a terrible friend. Wanting to leave is so selfish," she says, taking her nail from between her teeth for only as long as it takes to make her statement.

"Josie understands. Besides, it's over when they're gone." I pull her into a side hug. "It'll work out."

She may think I mean between her and Hank but I mean in general. Everything always works out. Even if, at the moment, it's not what we want.

"What if it doesn't? What if I had the chance to have it all and I let it go because I was too afraid...and stupid. Mostly too stupid."

"Oh, Paisley." Before I can continue, the double doors from the reception hall open and out step Josie and Brinn to a loud, excited cheer from the crowd. When they step onto the oversized patio, birdseed fills the air.

They hustle through the crowd, Josie stopping long enough to hug her brother before they get into the waiting limo. She looks at us, Paisley and I, and I assume makes eye contact with Paisley as she motions to the car park and mouths "go" before slamming the door.

Paisley's off at a run and the cheering from our small group continues.

"Go get him, Paisley," someone yells. Paisley's friend Gigi maybe? Who, ironically, is Hank's sister.

I erupt with laughter and watch the cars fade into the evening. One friend firmly wrapped in the arms of love experiencing (I hope) the sort of bliss that inspires love songs, bestsellers, and poetry that spans centuries. The other friend running toward that same happiness and the man she believes holds the key.

CHAPTER TEN

Love.

Like chasing a high, people do the unimaginable for a taste of love. For the chance to hold it forever. Online dating sites, personal ads, and singles mixers abound. Is there any greater product we crave?

I'm struck wondering, not for the first time but certainly more often recently, what my life would look like if I were made more like my friends. If I believed the love they have, or seek to have, can be had by anyone and will be reciprocated and pain free.

Unfortunately, I know better.

Mum's experience of blissful love and subsequent devastation, her parting gift, me, is all the education and fair warning I needed. When an eight-year-old watches her mother fall apart and only the firm hand of her own mother, my nana, was able to put her back together, it sticks. Forever.

Even if my stepdad is a peach of a man who has loved me and cared for me as his own. Who caters to and greatly loves Mum. But what's the point if love's end result is losing a wee bit of oneself like Mum did? I'd rather skip all that, if that's all right.

But wouldn't a taste, if such a safe sample existed, be a lovely, wondrous thing?

After the cars have long faded from sight, I scan the crowd for Pippa. Maybe she'll be up for a drink at the hotel bar.

"Care to join some of us for drinks?" a man says close to my ear. A large hand cups my elbow, gently turning me toward him.

I face Stacy, who motions over his shoulder toward the hotel's outdoor bar that wraps around the side of the building and faces the beach. "The others will meet us there."

I nod, not ready to end the night. Mum and Dad are around here somewhere enjoying their much-deserved downtime and I intend to do the same. I'm not going to worry whether shifts were covered or about this loan. I'm going to enjoy the moments I have right now. We walk in silence the short distance and when we come around the corner, a tray of shots is being delivered to a table of my friends, including Brinn and Josie's siblings.

"To my brother and his wife." Vann holds up a tricolored shot known as a jellybean.

I suppose the colorful concoction is more celebratory than biting a lemon and licking one's hand.

We each take a glass and raise them in the air.

"It was the luckiest day of his life when we picked her up on the side of the road," Vann continues.

We all laugh and I'm reminded of the Josie who blew into town searching for her brother and found love, too. I glance at Will, who's holding a carbonated drink, his eyes glassy with moisture, and I'm willing to wager he's thinking back the couple years when Josie, stranded by a broken-down car, hitchhiked to Florida in search of him.

"To Josie and Brinn. May they love each other for eternity. Cheers," I finish and everyone echoes me.

Except Heather who says, "Pfft," before tossing her shot back. After a wince and a shudder, she meets my gaze. "What? I'm jaded? Are you really surprised by that?"

I shake my head. "Would you prefer to make the next toast?" I ask when a second tray is delivered. One glance at Vann's sheepish grin tells me he's the culprit of this round.

"Absolutely." She snatches a glass off the tray, spilling a wee bit on her thumb. She licks it off before continuing. "To Brinn and Josie. Let's hope they can beat the odds." She raises her glass in the air.

There's a long pause. Someone, Pippa maybe, clears their throat.

"To my sister and her husband. May they learn to hold tight to each other when the road gets rocky and may they always find their way back to each other if they lose their way." Will clinks his Coke to Heather's shot glass.

"Yeah, that's what I said." She tosses back her drink.

The piped-in music is cut off as a band steps onto the stage at the far end of a dance floor. "Let's celebrate," the lead singer yells into the microphone and not a second later they launch into a loud cover of a popular eighties dance song.

"Oh, I love this song," Pippa says.

"Me, too." Heather grabs her and says, "Let's dance," before pulling her to the dance floor.

Others peel away and I'm left with Will, Daanya, and Stacy.

Stacy and I order a red wine, and though the band is loud, we manage a conversation.

Wasn't Josie lovely? Do you think they'll go sightseeing in Europe or stay in the room? The standard pleasantries made following a wedding.

Everyone is feeling lighter and free.

The ambience is dreamy. It's cliché, I know, but that's the best word to describe the ocean stretching out to the horizon before me. The dunes and gently swaying sea grass between the water and us. Besides the band and dance floor, which is a squared-off area devoid of tables, a large fire pit sits off to the side and is surrounded by cushioned stone bench seating.

There's a slight autumn crispness to the air and I pull my shawl in tighter, covering the goose bumps that texturize my skin.

"Hey," Will says leaning toward us, closing in our group. "Want to join us by the fire? Daanya's chilled."

"Sure," Stacy answers for me and places his hand on my lower back, guiding me to the fire pit. Every nerve ending in my body comes alive.

I scan the crowd of my friends and realize nearly everyone is paired off, aside from Heather and Pippa. Well, and Stacy and myself. Though the ambience and all this talk about true love makes me wish—somewhat—that I had someone to share this night with, I make no move on anyone. I scan the crowd and don't see anyone even remotely interesting to chat up.

Not that I've been able to see past Stacy. I've noticed Heather watching him, too. If the atmosphere is working me over, has already done a number on Paisley, then it's likely

Heather's feeling the effects,too. To what end? Hard to say at this point.

I sink in the spot next to Daanya, which removes any chance Stacy could sit by me, and forces him to sit in the awkward corner of the sectional style bench or move further away. He picks the further seat. Unfortunately, with his long legs and my lengthy sticks, our knees brush each other every time one of us moves.

I glance at his profile as he talks to Will. His nose is straight, his chin strong. He doesn't look like a father tonight. He looks dapper in the tux I fit him with, the bow tie hanging loose around his neck. When he catches me staring (again, gads), a rush of heat warms my face.

"Did you do all the tuxes?" He leans back against the bench and rests his arm along the top of the empty seat next to him.

"I did."

"You're really good at what you do. This custom dressing of people."

"Thank you."

The band switches to a slow song and from the corner of my eye I see someone approach.

"Want to dance, Stacy?" It's Heather, who happens to already be swaying, and I'm not so sure it's because of the music.

"Actually, ah...these shoes are killing me. Why don't you join us? I can get you a drink. Some coffee, maybe?"

Her shoulders slump and she swings watery eyes in my direction.

Bless her and her broken heart that she's currently wearing on the outside for everyone to see.

"I was thinking about getting some more dessert. Want

some?" She's a sucker for sweets like me and I'm hoping I can ease her pain through food.

She shakes her head and looks back toward the dance floor. "Nah, I'll just go join Pippa."

We watch her shuffle away. Will pulls Daanya up and leads her to the floor and I wait until they're out of hearing range before I face Stacy.

"You might have danced with her." It's hard keeping the irritation out of my voice.

He levels me with a stare. "Come on, Jayne. What kinda guy would I be if I danced with her knowing she's looking for something else from me and I have no intention of providing it? A shit bag, that's the kind."

"I should try to get her back to her room," I say.

"As long as we keep an eye on her she'll be okay. She probably needs to be around people anyway."

We both turn to watch the dancers and when he shifts his leg brushes mine, which creates a soft buzzing in my head. Must be all those horniness chemicals exploding in my brain, having been overcharged from his mere touch. They were already humming from being so close. I blink slowly and try to gather my wits.

"Your cousin's really bendy," Stacy says.

I scan across the crowd until I find Pippa doing her mating dance. Looking for someone who's willing to practice downward dog with her. She's transitioning between standing split pose and tree with some awkwardly placed hand gestures in between. Much like a gymnast does before the run across the mat to tumble. Only all it would take Pippa to yoga her way across the floor is one well-placed and purposeful look from any interested guy. Pippa embraces free love.

Heather on the other hand. Yikes, I've never seen such angry and lonely slow dancing with oneself. Her movements are jagged but quick as if she's punching ghosts surrounding her. She stops to toss back another shot then goes back to her boxing.

"Er, Doug, is there something I can do for Heather?" I ask her brother, who only moments ago came off the dance floor.

"Jesus," he says after spotting her. "Ready to call it a night, babe?" he asks Kenley.

"I'm ready to take this elsewhere." She backs up her words with a salacious wink.

That we all witness.

Doug tugs her into a brief but powerful kiss. "Get the key ready, babe. I'll get my hot mess of a sister." He swivels on his heel and stalks across the room. Kenley plops down next to me and squeezes my knee. Heather, oblivious to his arrival, continues with her angry dance until, in one swift move, he tosses her over his shoulder, fireman style, and holds her legs tightly so she can't kick.

He ambles back toward us, I presume, to collect his wife. "You all have a nice night." He offers Kenley a hand up.

"I hate you, Doug. You're the worst brother in the world," Heather says and pummels his back.

"You can thank me tomorrow. I haven't seen you like this since college when you and Dax broke up. And look where that got you."

At the mention of this Dax person, Heather gasps and pinches his side but he reciprocates by pinching her calf.

I lean forward, curious about Heather's reaction. Has love trampled on my friend more than once? Poor Heather.

She gets so few nights away from her son and the stress of her life and this is how she spends it.

"I told you to never say his name." Heather pinches her brother again.

"You do that one more time and I'm gonna drop you on your head." Doug turns to the side and says to us, "Night, Stacy, it was nice to meet you. Jayne, stay cool."

"Stacy?" Heather arches her back so she can lift up. She sees us and smiles widely. Her eyes are glassy, a clear sign she's past the limit. Not that the dancing wasn't clear enough.

"I hope you had a nice time, Stacy," she says. "It's too bad we didn't get a chance to dance."

I watch Stacy form his mouth to make words but nothing comes out. Doug walks away, Heather still looking at Stacy.

"Maybe next time." She does a finger wave as they move away. "Night, Stacy."

"Night," I call but she ignores me. I fall back against the cushions and cover my mouth with my hand. I can't wait to tell Josie this. This behavior is opposite from the Heather we know; I can't help but laugh.

One day when Heather's come out the other side of this divorce, she'll laugh too. Maybe then I'll ask her about this Dax.

Stacy leans back and our shoulders brush. He looks between me and the dance floor. "What was that out on the dance floor?"

"I'm not sure. Maybe she's exorcising a demon?" It's my best guess and all I'm going to share about Heather and her rocky road of late.

"I feel for that Dax guy. That got a rise out of her. Is that her ex?" He faces me and I turn to him as well. We're closer than I expected. So close I can see the ring of silver around his blue eyes.

His fingers brush my shoulder. "No. Justin is her ex. I've no idea who Dax is and honestly I'm afraid to ask."

He travels his fingers up the column of my neck, lightly stroking skin along the way. His hand slides around to cup the base of my head. "Please don't. I need a neighbor who can come to my rescue." He smiles.

I stare into his eyes and smile back, shifting closer to him. A warm fuzziness comes over me and dulls out everything but him.

The next moment his lips are pressed to mine. When I close my eyes all I see are flashes of light and sparks and then he's gone as quickly as he came.

"I'm sorry. I couldn't resist," he says after he pulls away. But no sooner are the words spoken are his lips on mine again, his tongue gently probing, waiting for an invitation from me.

I know I should push him away.

I can't.

Because I don't want to.

One more taste and then I'll do the right thing.

With his arms around me, I experience the sensation of weightlessness. As if I'm floating on a cloud and there's nothing more significant than this moment. I grip both of his shoulders, hold on tight, and go for broke.

Funny thing, intentions. I absolutely, one hundred percent mean to thank him for the kiss and make my escape. I'll comfort myself with another bottle of wine and a hot bath in the garden tub in my room.

I stay because I want this moment, this memory. One day in the future, I want to hear the song the band is playing on the radio and remember this. I'll recall how our chemistry was exceedingly strong and how unquenchable our desire was for one another.

When we part, his stare is intense and loaded with one question, waiting for an answer.

I scan the room. Pippa is talking to one of the musicians. The others have all slipped away to places unknown. No one is watching.

"I can only give you tonight," I whisper. "No strings. Tomorrow we go back to being neighbors and new friends."

"Like we're in Vegas." His lips twitch. "We leave it here."

"Precisely." I run my hands down his lapels. "I need you to understand that this can't happen again once we leave."

"And that reason is?"

"It's several reasons. Mainly, I'm insanely busy trying to expand my business, what little time I have I give to my friends. Also, I don't have affairs with men who have children, ever, and anything after tonight would only make everything else more complicated. You see that, right?"

"You have something against children?" His thumb caresses my cheek, his hand on the back of my neck. Can he feel my racing pulse?

I shake my head. "No, but the last things they need is a person to come into their life who already has an exit plan."

He searches my face, and I keep my gaze level and sure. He nods, pulls me in for another kiss, and I know we've sealed the deal.

"My room is right around the corner. Yours?" he asks, between traveling his lips to my ear.

"Upstairs." I turn my head to give him greater access. My face is cradled in his palm and I nibble on the fleshy area of his thumb.

"C'mon. Mine's closer." He stands and pulls me up against him and runs his hand down my arm before circling my waist and pulling me close.

We walk out of the bar that way, me tucked into Stacy's side, his thumb caressing my hipbone and my girly parts tingling with need and anticipation.

I want him to love me the night long. I need to explore every bit of him and let this moment be what it is, two people desperate for each other's company. We'll burn through this attraction and be able to peacefully coexist.

When he pushes his room door open, I rush in ahead of him. Stacy no sooner locks the door then I'm in his arms. We fit together even better than I imagined. My dress is sliding off my body, his tux is a black heap on the ground. We touch, eager to take our fill. We caress, grip one another, and taste. I let myself go, hold nothing back. We come together, calling out each other's name. And this has only begun or desire for me. Tomorrow and everything that awaits me is forgotten. I only have space for him.

CHAPTER ELEVEN

FIVE LONG DAYS HAVE PASSED SINCE MY TRYST WITH Stacy. Not that I'm avoiding him or anything like that. Which is hard to do when someone lives directly across the street. Circumstances just made it so. First, because I promised Mum not to limit my options, I went to Atlanta, where I half-heartedly looked at property that came up lacking. Nothing there captured my love like the building in Miami. Though I have a high percentage of clientele that come from the Atlanta, it's not my first pick.

Following a brief stop at home to change out clothes and repack my travel bag, I was then off to Miami with hopes to cement the deal I'd been dreaming about since I first imagined it with the real estate agent those few weeks back. First the loan and then the building. Then everything went sideways.

I try to harness this crazy panicky emotion that's churning inside me. A mix of desire and desperation. I desperately want to increase my presence in the fashion world and I have an insatiable desire to reach that monetary goal Mum set for me. I'd love to see the expression on her face when I show her I've achieved it.

Now, sitting in my car in my garage I can't muster the energy to leave. But staying is not an option. At least for much longer. I can't avoid the insurmountable paperwork waiting for me.

That, and I need to pee.

I trace the stitching that binds the leather cushioning on my steering wheel. My nail polish is chipped and in desperate need of attention, as is everything else in my life. The red I painted a few weeks ago long gone, replaced with the *Midnight Fog* I favor. The color as black and murky as my mood.

"According to these documents, it's unlikely you're a candidate for a loan of this size," the impeccably dressed woman with Botox lips told me today. Bursting my dreams of expanding into the Miami area with a swift poke of her professionally polished talon.

I rest my head against the top of the steering wheel.

Location. Location. Location. Unfortunately for me the location that would be best for my shop has nothing for lease, only buildings to own, and my hopes of being an owner hang by the thinnest thread.

I should be happy that I still have Atlanta. Or even Dallas. I can lease there. But a new state will be more expensive for me to start up the new shop. New state laws and forms and taxes. Miami would have been so easy.

In the meantime, I'm to get my books together for an audit if I want to continue pursuing Miami. Silly me, thinking my business plan, taxes, and statements would have sufficed. It's a last ditch effort but I'm not ready to let the dream go.

When I step from the car, I hear the softest mewing. So soft that for a second I think I've imagine it.

I tiptoe as quietly as my two-inch heels will allow and peek around the side of the garage. There, sitting against my house, is the tabby, licking his front paw. I've tried an assortment of names—Chester, Felix, Linus—all to no avail. Then I tried more butch names such as Bruce and Jack.

"Hallo, kitty, kitty." I do a mental perusal of my fridge and cupboard looking for people food, as that's his preference. "I've nothing to eat but just the little bag of cat food I picked up at the grocer."

I squat slowly down and remove the bowl (yes, I keep one in the front and back) from under the shrub. I step quickly back into the garage, fill it, and then go back to where he waits, still fastidiously grooming.

"Looky." I slowly lower the bowl back to its spot under the shrub. I don't dare reach out to pet him.

The tabby stops licking, paw still up, and looks across his body to the bowl before looking back at me. He meows a great loud sound of what I interpret to be disgust. He puts down his paw and meows again.

"That's all I've got." I nudge the bowl in his direction.

The arsehole swipes at me and would have landed another blow had I not been anticipating it.

"Hey!"

But he just turns, tail high, sphincter puckered tight like the arse he is, and saunters off.

Giving him the two-finger up-yours makes me feel better.

Once inside I call for Pippa but she's nowhere to be found.

Before the back door closes behind me, Paisley sticks in her head.

"Knock, knock," she says.

"Come in. I just got here myself." I'd forgotten she texted and asked if she could come by for clothing help this evening. Naturally that was before my bank appointment when I lost the will to move forward in this day and hoped to come home, eat a box of Hostess cupcakes, and fall into bed, ready for a do over.

"Is it a bad time?" She closes the door behind her, a garment bag of clothes flipped over her arm.

"Truthfully, I might not be at my best so there's my disclaimer. Want one?" I hold up a cupcake.

She shakes her head. "No, thanks. After Hank, you know, left, I finished off two gallons of ice cream. If I slow down enough to eat I might fall apart again. So, I'm keeping busy."

After Paisley had sprinted from Josie's wedding to Hank's house with the single goal to declare her love, she came back even more broken then when she left.

"You ready to talk about it?" It's not the first time I've offered. A few nights back we stayed up late, chatting on the phone and talking about everything but men, specifically Hank.

She turns watery eyes to me and I have my answer.

"I'm here when you are." I squeeze her shoulder.

She crosses my kitchen where she hangs the garment bag from my cupboard door. "Sarah Grace and Dan are celebrating their anniversary. I need a cocktail dress and I can't seem to decide." She leans against my counter and starts gnawing on her thumbnail.

"Paisley." It aches to see her hurting so.

"Can we talk about something else please? I just need to focus on other stuff."

"Okay."

"So what went wrong today?" She nods to the nearly finished-off cupcake.

I toss the remains of the treat in the sink. "I was told—not outright, mind you, just hinted—that there is no way I'll qualify for the loan I need if I want to purchase the shop in Miami."

"What about leasing a place?" She pours herself a small glass of wine and takes it into my living room where she sinks into my couch.

"I've looked. Nothing in the area I want. I could wait, I suppose. But it's still a gamble whether anything will come up. I found this building. It's ideal for my shop and I could make extra money on renting out the other two spaces." I poke my head into the fridge to try to figure out dinner. A quick sweep tells me what I already know. Nothing in there but leafy greens and wine. And an old orange that is composting in the lower bin.

"I'm ordering take out. You want any?" By heart, I dial the number for the nearby Thai restaurant and, because I need a pick me up, I reach into the cupboard and pull out a fortune cookie from my secret stash.

"No." She shakes her head and, following an exasperated sigh, continues. "Wait, get me a spring roll. No, better not. Jeez. Nothing for me. I'll just watch you eat and drool."

"You need to eat." I open the cellophane wrapper and break open the cookie, shoving the smallest piece in my mouth. As usual I'm put on hold without waiting for a response regarding whether I'll wait or not. I point to the phone and mimic food.

"I already ate. I can't afford two dinners." Following an eye roll, she chugs her wine.

When the guy comes back on the line, I mention who I am and that I'd like my standard order of Pad Thai. We exchange brief pleasantries before I end the call then toss my phone on the table. After collecting the wine bottle from the fridge, I take it into the living room, refill her glass, and raise mine in a toast.

"Here's to tomorrow. It's a new day with new opportunity. May it go our way, and if it looks like it might not, may we take control and make it our day anyway!"

"Hear! Hear!" She clinks her glass to mine and we laugh before taking a drink.

"Do you think men get depressed because someone tells them no?" I ask.

"Yes," she says. "Duh.".

"I mean aside from sex. I mean in business. They just plan around it, right? But I'm all weepy because someone told me to get my books together for an audit and they *might* change their mind. So, I'm going to spend time I don't have because I'm a hopeful person and believe all opportunities are open to me." I wave my fortune in the air. "Unless my answer can be found here."

I unfold the tiny paper and read it aloud, "It could be better, but it's good enough."

Deflated, I droop onto the couch next to her.

"Can I help?" She kicks her heels up on the ottoman.

"How are you with adding columns and entering info?" I do the same with my heels. It's an amazing feeling to relax back into the couch, knowing food is going to be delivered, and having someone to talk with.

"Not very good. But I know someone who is." She cocks her head toward my front door.

"What are you talking about?" I murmur, sniffing my wine, the tension in my shoulders melting away.

"I'm talking about the dude across the street. The one who is handy with numbers." Her stare is pointed.

"Oh, right. Duh. I dunno—"

"Why would you *not* ask him?"

"Well, it's awkward—" I cut myself off. I hadn't told anyone about my one night with Stacy.

Her brows raise. "Why would it be awkward?"

"Er, to show him my finances." I do lightning quick thinking. "Lay myself out there, so to speak."

"Oh. I thought you hesitated because of the S.E.X. Because you *want* to sleep with him."

"I do not—" Before I die I want to master the art of masking a blush. A skill that would come in handy right now.

She cocks her head to the side. "You do too, and that's okay. Any of us would hesitate if we needed help from a guy we want to bang." She narrows her eyes.

"Paisley—"

"You slept with him, didn't you?" She sits up and faces me. "Didn't you?" I blow out a slow steady breath and meet her gaze.

"Oh, boy," she says then slaps her knees. "I knew the two of you would work together."

I sit up. "Wait. Don't go there. It was one night and we agreed to never do it again. We got caught up in the moment. The wedding, the shots—we did some of those after you left. Don't make it into anything because it's not. It can't be."

She searches my face. "You sure about that?"

"Positive." If I knew an oath, a magical unbreakable vow, I'd give it.

"So why won't you ask for his help? Are you afraid you'll repeat that night?" She relaxes back into the couch.

"Er, well. I haven't seen him and it feels awkward." I settle next to her.

"Which would you rather? An awkward moment with no one around or when Josie and Brinn return from their honeymoon?"

"Good point."

"Listen," she says, sitting forward again and setting her glass on a tray I've placed on the ottoman. "I don't know much. My life is a hot mess. It's taken me a long time to figure stuff out and because of that I missed out on time with Hank. It may be over for us." Her voice catches and after a deep breath she continues. "One thing I do know is our group is a tight circle and Stacy is now a part of that."

"What are you saying?" My shoulders clench, folding inward.

"If you don't want the others to know you slept with him then you need to get that first encounter over with. If you think you might want to fool around with him some more just be aware of the consequences." She gestures to herself. "If Hank doesn't talk to me, if we can't resolve this somehow, then it changes my relationship with Gigi and his parents. They're just as important to me as my own family and I stand to lose them too, in a roundabout way." A single tear rolls down her cheek.

"It might still work out." I swallow but I don't have the conviction people of faith have.

She palms away her tear. "I've emailed him every day, sometimes several times a day. I've heard nothing but I know he's able to email because Gigi says he's been emailing their mom."

From what I know, from the little bits she's fed me and I pieced together, Paisley confessed her feelings to Hank right after Josie's wedding but they did not have a lover's reunion. Instead, he told her it was too late and to complicate it further had to leave for work. As a Naval Intelligence Officer his location and duration of time away are unknown.

"I hurt him a lot. That's a hard thing to live with." She takes the tissue I hand her.

"What are you going to do?" Is she worried about the worst-case scenario? A broken heart that never mends or does she already have that? My naive heart can't begin to fathom what she must be feeling.

"I plan to celebrate my sister's wedding anniversary and get ready to start back to work. I love the beginning of school." She smiles but it's wobbly and looks forced.

"And Hank?"

"I survived my divorce. I can survive this too." She pushes up from the couch, going to her garment bag. "My sister loves pictures so there will be a photographer. For once I'd like to not look like a train wreck. Which one of these do you think works best?"

Subject change noted. I get up and stand next to her. "So it's cocktail, not formal."

"Right."

"Let's take a look at what you've picked out."

She slides down the zipper. "Okay, I can take any of these back. I was in your store the other day and your employee told me to stick to earth tones because of my hair. Or else I would have bought something there."

I spin toward her in surprise. I've taught my staff that

certain tones definitely do look best on some people versus others, but hues are the trick for any color. And sticking Paisley in earth tones is so nineteen ninety-nine. "She said what? Please tell me it wasn't Shara."

"No, the other one. She knew we were friends. Told me to talk to you." Paisley grimaces.

"Brilliant. This feels like an omen. Like I'll need to be looking to replace her soon. I'm sorry. She's a...well, never mind. Let's get you sorted." I add the worry to my list and push it aside, instead pulling out the three gowns she's tucked in the bag.

"Is this event inside or out?" I spread the dresses beside each other. The navy gown she wore in Josie's wedding, next to a simple black dress more suited for a funeral, and the last a peach gown with a sweetheart neckline and a beaded bodice.

"It's both."

"All right. Take this back on your way home. It's bloody awful and will wash you out." I tuck the peach dress back into the bag.

"It's an earth tone," she says fingering the material. "But the fabric is kinda scratchy so back it goes."

"This black one should be your back up. Wear it with the silver heels from Josie's wedding. Hang on."

I find what I'm looking for in the back of my closet and join her in the kitchen a few moments later. "Use this shawl and bag." I snap a picture on my phone and text her because I know she'll get freaked out in the moment and will need the prompt.

"Okay, so go with the bridesmaid gown?"

"No, I've got a lovely bright green gown in the shop that's perfect for what you want. It's fresh and will look amazing in pictures. Come tomorrow and try it on." I tuck all the dresses back into the bag and zip it up. "You okay with that?"

"Yeah, for sure." She grabs my hands. "You're the best, Jayne. Whatever would I do without you?" And I know she's talking about more than the dresses.

I roll my eyes and keep it light. "The horror. You in an ill-fitting or poorly colored dress will never happen on my watch."

We laugh and are interrupted by the chiming of the door.

"Goody, food," I say. "Want to stay? I can share." I find cash in my purse then open the door to the delivery guy. I'm on a first name basis with him.

"Thanks." I hand him the money and he hands me my lifeline.

"Anytime, Jayne. Have a good night," he says.

I stare across the car park toward Stacy's house. Paisley's right, not only is he in possession of a mathematical brain, I also need to make sure it's all good before we're surrounded by our friends.

"What are you thinking?" she asks.

I turn to face her and kick the door closed. "That you're right. I'm going to ask for his help. I'm not going to take no from these banks, not until I've exhausted every avenue."

"Good for you." She takes down her garment bag, only to freeze in motion at the halfway point. She stands there blinking.

"Paisley?" I place the food on my table before taking a step toward her.

"You know what?" she says, turning to face me. "I'm not done yet either."

I wait for more.

"I'm going to take this gown back and get home so I can email Hank some more. Just because he's not responding doesn't mean he's not reading them, right?" She bumps her shoulder to mine and there's a new sparkle in her eyes that wasn't there earlier. "See ya tomorrow."

I bump back. "You got this."

When she's gone I lean against the door and silently wish it to work out for her. My skeptical self fights to have the last word but I reason that Paisley already paid some sort of price by being married to a cheating bastard. Isn't she due a lucky break?

Desperate to eat but knowing I need to shed the day from me, I quickly change into yoga pants and a loose t-shirt, to deliberately hide the pooch of my tummy that's being pushed up ever more by the tight band of my pants.

But I'll be buggered if I'm going to spend a second thought over it. I am, after all, in fashion and therefore able to select clothes for any shape. Including ones with pooches.

While enjoying my Pad Thai, I pull ledgers from my messenger bag and straighten out papers, droplets of sauce falling to the pages. I need to sort them before I can ask for help. They're in such a state it's the least I can do.

While logging the numbers on the computer program Josie installed for me, I let myself fantasize about being rescued from this task. Better yet, of receiving a suitcase of money, left to me by an old distant relative so there's no issues about thievery. Then I can buy the building outright and step up my game.

Weary, I sigh.

See Jayne stall and her dream fail due to her own inaction.

It's no use. If I were able to put these books into a decent order, then I wouldn't need help. Tossing the fork on my table, I stand and stride purposefully out my door and across the car park, stopping at Stacy's door. I knock, wipe my mouth on my shoulder, and search for the words I want to use.

CHAPTER TWELVE

My mind races at the million and one ways this can be awkward. Will he misread it as a ruse to get his attention? My desire for success wins out over personal pride in this instance. One look at my ledgers and he'll know I'm not making anything up.

Cordie swings the door open. "Dad, it's Jayne," she calls over her shoulder.

"How's camp?" I'm not so ignorant with children that I can't make pleasant conversation or be aware of what's going on in their world.

"I hate it. It sucks."

"I'm sorry," I say.

Stacy comes from the kitchen, folding pizza boxes in half. Dinner is in the air.

I read his expression as surprised.

"Yum, pizza." I smile widely at Cordie. What kid doesn't like pizza?

"For the third time this week." There's a measure of disgust in her voice.

"Wow, that's a lot." Even I can't do pizza three times a week. Thai or Indian takeaway perhaps but not pizza.

"Hey, Jayne. What's up?" He tosses the boxes in a bin before tucking his hands in his front pockets. He's wearing low-slung jeans (that I picked out), which emphasize the exceedingly long length of his legs. Lord, how I fancy him. I mentally slap myself in the head.

His t-shirt spans the width of his shoulders, showing off his swimmer's physique. It's a cute graphic tee with some unknown-to-me math equation on it. Probably his favorite, he's such a nerd for math.

I have a mini-fantasy of us back in the hotel bed, his large hands running the length of me.

Stop! I scream in my head then mentally bang it on the wall.

"Er, I need your help."

"Need something manly done. Should I get a hammer?" He looks excited.

"Do you own a hammer?"

"Yeah, and a laser level." Definitely excited.

"Actually, I need math help. Er, um...book-keeping guidance."

"Okay," he says then shrugs. "Let's see it."

I point behind me. "I left it at my house. I suppose I could have brought it with me. That would have been help-ful." I'm ill prepared and I hate how it looks.

"Okay, well. Let's go take a look. Cordie? You wanna go or stay here? I should only be a few minutes."

"I'll stay. Can I watch TV?" She's already moving to their living room.

"Yes, lock the door behind me. I'll take my keys. If you get scared, call my cell and I'll come home. I'll be right at Jayne's." He motions in the direction of my house.

"I'll be fine, Dad. Just go already," she says with the telly remote in hand.

He follows me out. An awkward silence fills the space between us. I consider bringing up the amazing shag just to get it over with but the car park seems like the wrong place.

"I appreciate you taking a look." I glance over my shoulder and try to see where he's looking.

"No sweat." He's looking straight ahead. I wait until he's next to me.

"I'm trying to land a loan and er...well, I need to provide more information. But I'm having issues pulling it together." Understatement, show thyself.

Once in my house I head straight for the table and the pile of papers. "Here you go." I want to shove the disaster into a bag and send it home with him.

He slides into the dining chair and looks up at me. "You're kidding me, right? You still do this old school?"

"Well, no." I push my laptop toward him. "Josie set me up with a program that tracks purchases and deposits, but I need to manually log other expenditures. Which I haven't yet. Sorry."

He rubs his chin as he surfs through my computer and accesses the program. "I'm guessing they want to audit you, so you'll need a few years of figures."

"Right." I slip into the chair across from him. I'm so glad I did this now. I can't imagine getting this moment out of the way in a different venue where we're making forced pleasantries over chicken wings and veggie sticks.

"Okay." His attention returns to the screen.

My phone chimes to indicate a message. It's from Shara,

my star employee. I would not be able to do any of this without knowing she was at the helm of the shop.

Her text reads: *Check your email.*

So I do and what awaits me is the final straw.

Shara has up and quit.

Apparently, having been inspired by working for me these last two years, she's applied to New York School of Design. She'd been wait-listed but that's no longer the case as she's just received a call accepting her to the dream school. Classes begin next week.

She's leaving with no notice whatsoever and though it's in an email, I can hear her bubbly, "I know you're just as excited as I am" and "of course you understand" as clearly as if she's standing next to me and saying it.

"Bloody hell," I say.

Chiefly, I understand, but her good fortune leaves me with Amber, now my sole employee. A sunny and willowy college girl who doesn't know how to count money back and tried to use her babysitting certificate as college credit for gym. She's brilliant with the high-paying customers but shite with everything else. Paisley's earth tone comment is case in point.

"You okay?" His voice breaks me from my toxic thoughts.

"My best employee just gave notice. By notice I mean up and quit." I stare at my phone and blink away the tears. I'll have to look at my timetable and rethink my plan. My time, which I planned to use to pull the paperwork together, will now be spent in the shop. I'll have to reschedule personal shopping as well. Though, thankfully I managed to get some in while in Miami. I suppose one good thing came from that trip. Then there's the pub. Covering the extra shift. Had Pippa not shown up I'm not sure this last week would have been manageable for my parents.

I pull in a shaky breath.

"I'm sorry, Jayne. How can I help?"

When I look at him, his focus is on me.

"Help me with these books?" I ask, slightly pleading.

"Done." His lips lift in a slight smile.

I could get lost in the memory of how gently he uses those lips, a distraction I could well afford on this crummy day, but it wouldn't be wise with him sitting a few feet from me. I can't be held accountable for my actions. Instead, I push from the table and with the intention to toss the now-cold food in the bin and straighten up, I reach for the containers of Thai food.

He grabs my arm. "What are you doing with that?"

"I was going to chuck it."

"Leave it. It smells good." He picks up the fork I'd tossed down earlier and takes the Styrofoam container from my hands. "You put any soy sauce on this?" He raises his gaze to meet mine.

"No, but I have soy—"

"No, this is perfect."

"Shall I warm it?" I reach for the container again.

"No, I'm good. How about some of that wine?" He nods with his chin toward the bottle on my ottoman before looking through some papers.

"Sure." I get him a glass and collect mine, pouring us both a healthy amount. My hand trembles and I think of the awkwardness that Paisley mentioned.

"Did you not eat pizza?" I ask, avoiding what I really need to say.

"Ah...see, here's the thing," he says, stopping what he's

doing. "I've run out of meals to make and we're reduced to take out. Cordie can be picky so I've been getting pizza."

I picture his daughter eating my beans and bagel and the word that comes to mind is not picky.

I roll my eyes, which gets a chuckle from him. "You mean you're unimaginative."

"That too. My mom used to do all the cooking. Something I took for granted." He shakes his head. "We're so sick of pizza; Cordie barely touched it tonight. But I can't keep feeding her mac and cheese and salami. This used to be a lot easier when my mother did it."

I do like a man who can poke fun at himself.

"You could hire someone." Another fantasy I have. A full-time chef.

He shakes his head. "This is the first time we've lived without my parents and I had these great ideas of Cordie and I really bonding. Part of that being cooking together. I thought all kids liked to be chefs."

"Do they?" I hadn't.

"Apparently not. Or mine is broken." He stabs at the food in the little bucket. "Not that I'm much of one myself."

While he works on my computer and my food, I go into the kitchen and set about preparing my favorite meal of eggs, beans, and a bagel. "Call your daughter and tell her I'm making beans and bagels if she wants some." If he's this hungry, surely Cordie is as well.

His look is puzzled but he does as I request and, after ending his call, says, "She'll be here in a minute. I'm not sure she'll eat it."

"She will."

I move to the table. Now is the perfect time to say what I

need to say. Yes, I recognize that I'm being a coward using Cordie as a buffer.

"Stacy," I say and wait for him to look at me.

"Yeah?" He's focused on the papers.

"About our night at Josie's wedding." That gets his attention. Both the fork and paper are suspended in air.

"Yeah?" He sounds a little strangled.

"Oh Lord, I'm not pregnant or anything," I say, knowing I accidentally set it up like that. Not that I would know something like that in five days but still.

"Okay," he says and gets back to business.

"About that night," I say again.

He raises a brow, apparently his way of asking me to continue.

"I don't want there to be awkwardness between us—"

"So long as we are both under the same impression of the terms, I imagine there isn't really a margin of error for awkwardness." He holds the fork midair.

Why am I surprised this is going easier than I anticipated?

"That being said, these things are managed better when the parties involved don't see each other on a regular basis." I avoid using the word couple.

"True."

"And with us being neighbors and with having the same friends, I don't want anything to be forced."

"Okay."

A few other words from him would be nice. "I'm open to having a genuine friendship. Please don't feel that you owe me anything or I have certain expectations. It was one night. A very good one at that." That gets a smile from him. I gesture to my ledgers. "You don't have to do this because we—"

"I know I don't, Jayne. I'm a big boy. I can take care of myself." He starts eating again.

I think of Paisley's words earlier that night. "We're going to be around each other a lot and if there's something unspoken between us...."

"Jayne," he says. "I hadn't given it a second though. You made everything clear that night. I'm recently out of a serious relationship and it was refreshing to know exactly what was expected. I'm good. Are you good?"

Meaning just let it go, already! He hasn't given it a second thought. Such flattery.

I nod my head. Stupid Paisley and her dumb words.

"I'm not a dope. I know the score. You're not looking for anything serious and ultimately, I am. You don't want children and I'd take a few more. It was one night. We're good. Can I?" He indicates to the papers.

The familiar push of heat creeps up my neck. "Yes, please," I say and turn to open the door and wait for Cordie.

That was easy.

I sigh.

CHAPTER THIRTEEN

Another long day on the books, as they say. While at the pub I noticed their standard imported beer was out of stock, something that's never happened before. When I asked Mum about it she dismissed it with a hand wave and blamed it on the distributor. My own business plans appear to have stalled, or perhaps are sputtering. I should go home and get my advert ready for Shara's replacement but I'm exhausted and in need of some laughter, human contact, and my friends.

Josie and Brinn are back from their honeymoon and profess jet lag; hence the late evening get-together. It's precisely what I need. When I pull up to their single story home, the sun is slowly sliding lower in the sky and the hickory aroma of a barbecue tugs me forward. I'm planning on eating my way to a carb-induced slumber.

Josie swings open the door before I'm upon her landing. "Jayne. Finally. You look like shit. Tired."

"Wow. Thanks. And here I put this look together for you." I slip out of my heels; leave them to dangle from my fingers, before we do a hug. It's good to see her again. "How was the trip abroad?"

"Wonderful. It was good to get away and have nothing to think about but sightseeing and sex." She wags her brows while ushering me in. "But, we're home and Brinn s back to being hyper focused. He and Stacy have been holed up all afternoon."

"Back to the grind." I drop both my shoes and purse on the bench inside her foyer and subtly try to check my image in the mirror hanging above it. Josie's right. Dark circles are blooming under my eyes. My hair's come out of its French twist and hangs at awkward angles due to being pinned while still damp and I'm pale. I make quick work of pulling out the pins.

"Yeah, I think Brinn was getting twitchy the last few days. I brought you a ton— seriously, it weighs a ton—of chocolate."

"Bless you," I say, my mouth watering in anticipation.

Outside the double sliding doors, the ocean beckons. A large deck extends the house toward the water and a fire pit, much like the one from the hotel used for Josie's wedding, crackles. Immediately my gaze goes to Stacy, who's reclined in a chair, his long legs stretched in front of him. Our eyes meet and the heat from the inevitable blush creeps up my neck.

I'm so glad we've seen each other before this moment. Now I won't wonder if he thinks about how urgently we stripped each other and didn't make it to the bed. Or recall when he took me in the shower. Who am I kidding? One glance at me and he more likely wonders if I have extra take-away than thinks about our one night. But I'm such a pathetic sod, my mouth goes dry and my knees wobble, so I collapse onto a chair and break eye contact, pretending to scan the group; only the images from that night are all I see.

"Orgasmic," I say when someone says my name.

"Pardon?" Paisley says. "I asked how your shop hunting went and you said orgasmic?" Chatter around me has dulled.

Er, think fast!

"No, sorry. Josie was talking about the chocolate she brought me and I was thinking how wonderful it would be if I could...er...get some. It's been a long day and chocolate would be—"

"Orgasmic," Paisley supplies with skepticism.

"Oh," Josie says, clapping her hands. "I'll go get it now." She jogs back inside and I keep my attention on Paisley.

"Yes, orgasmic."

Paisley flops into the chair next to me.

"Here it is," Josie says after coming back. She dumps an obscene amount of chocolate in my lap; several pieces fall to the floor or on the seat next to me.

"Sweet Jesus." Paisley gives low whistle.

"Praise Jesus," Pippa says and snatches up a dark chocolate bar from her favorite maker. "I don't crave much but this...I long for." Quickly she removes the foil and shoves a large piece in her mouth. "Oh, me, wawd. So 'ood," she says between shoving more into what little space is left.

"In case you were wondering, there was more, but Josie's been working her way through it," Brinn says and takes an elbow to the gut from Josie.

"You weren't supposed to tell," she says with mock horror.

Stacy leans toward me. "Hey, I've been meaning to say thanks. That lady you hired did an incredible job." His voice is low and husky.

"Oh, ah...." Damn my stupid hormones or his pheromones or whatever it is that makes me want to reply "You did an incredible job rocking my world."

"You're welcome." Pippa smiles at him...coyly?

Our one-night replay is forgotten as I try to read my cousin.

"You're the woman Jayne hired?" Stacy says. "You moved some heavy furniture. Did you have help?"

"You rearranged his house?" I ask.

"I Feng shui'ed it," she tells me before giving Stacy all her attention. "I have incredible upper body strength. Watch."

I stifle a groan and Josie laughs as Pippa flips into handstand square in front of him. Should she fall to the side she'd land directly in the fire but she won't. Control and strength are her forte. Unlike me.

She holds the handstand for what feels like an obscenely long time before easing down and sliding into the splits.

"I'm very limber," she says, arching backward. "All upper body."

Showoff.

"Yes, I noticed," he says, mouth slightly ajar. "I mean, at the wedding I noticed. Not that I was staring or anything...."

"Take this chocolate away from me," says Josie as she thrusts a large block at her husband. "I have no self control. I'm unable to tell myself no. You're going to have to do it for me. For better or for worse, remember."

He takes it, chuckling, and pops a small bit into his mouth. "What do I say when you beg for it back?"

"Tell me no. That if I want to do what's good and right I need to cut my ties right now before this becomes a habit I can't break. Can you do that?"

"I can and will," he says before dropping a kiss on her mouth.

"Mm, you taste like chocolate and sin," she says, pulling him closer by grabbing his shirt in her hands and tugging.

"So do you. You sure you don't want to get creative with this stuff later?" We all hear him whisper.

"For Pete's sake," Paisley cries. "Can you two *try* to refrain from such public displays of affection? It's awkward for the rest of us." She turns to me and shakes her head. "I'm going to stop coming here."

"I ignore it," Pippa says as she moves into plank position. "Look at my muscles," she tells Stacy.

And that's when it hits me.

See Jayne get a brilliant idea.

To me, Stacy is like chocolate. Smooth, dreamy, and completely addictive. Aside from his height, he's great with his hands. Well, and all the other moving parts of his body. There's a softness about him that appeals to me. And while that's all wonderful, glittery rainbows and unicorns, starting something up with him is dangerous and ill advised. Outside of the bedroom, what do I offer him? Certainly not a motherly figure for his daughter, I'm not the homemaker type, and, to be honest, I've too much I want—no, need—to accomplish before I begin to contemplate the merits of settling down.

Besides, his fool eyes have been transfixed on Pippa. Perhaps he was unimpressed with our tryst and... No, not going to go there.

Instead, I mentally weigh my idea, sketching out the pros and cons.

Pippa and Stacy. Would it work?

I think it might. She's bendy, as he has pointed out. More

than once. Clearly, he likes that. She organized his home in a manner he found pleasing, even the rearranging of the furniture. She's gentle and loving, albeit gassy, and would love to coddle Cordie.

And I could be their matchmaker. I will remove the temptation that is this tall glass of drink and make two people, no three—wait, four, if you include me—happy.

Who loses?

It requires a more romantic nature than I possess to believe that one night—yes, an incredibly passionate and fulfilling night—equates to anything more than...one night. I've been lonely, busy, and focused on my business; it's to be expected something would be neglected and in this case it was sex. And while I'm still giving all to my expansion, I can't use Stacy as a default to meet my needs any more than I can binge-eat crisps and expect it not to affect my waistline. Besides, I can always *forget* to call the cable company and cancel the free skin channel subscription. During the day, I'm told, they play regular films. If ever I'm home again I might indulge in some of those as well.

But how do I bring him and Pippa together without being so...obvious?

"Pip," I say while leaning forward, snapping my fingers to get her attention. "Thanks for helping out at the pub. I know Mum appreciates it."

"Oh, I love it. Especially helping her cook. Aunt Millie is a joy to be with."

I tell Stacy, "Pippa's a good cook. Should you need anything while you're trying to get sorted maybe she can help you out."

Pippa comes from plank, stretches into a quick child's pose before sliding into the seat between Stacy and me. "I'd love to fill my time. Not that I can work, ahem, legally but doing little bits here and there." She gives a casual shrug. "Who does that hurt?" She looks around the group for protesters and comes up lacking.

Cordie runs up from the beach, a pail and shovel swinging from her hand. "This place is awesome. It's so cool you live right on the beach," she says to Josie and Brinn.

"We like it. You're welcome to come and play anytime," Josie says, stroking a hand down the child's head, smoothing her wind-tossed hair.

"I wish we had a house on the beach instead of that stupid townhouse." She gives her father a pouty look.

"If you were smarter and didn't need to go to school, we could live anywhere, but until that day comes we're bound to live in areas with good schools that can meet your academic needs," he replies sarcastically.

"Jeez, Dad. I thought you wanted me to be 'well rounded' and not just a math nerd like you." Her eye roll tells me this is a standing conversation.

Stacy leans toward Pippa and me and says, "She's exceptionally bright. Likes to rub my nose in the fact that I struggle with grammar. How can knowing what a misplaced modifier is ever come in handy?" His tone is thick with pride.

"How do you like gifted camp, Cordie? Will you stay there for afterschool?" Paisley asks. "My niece and nephew participate in a swim team at their after-school program."

Cordie snorts. "I'm not so lucky. It's awful. One kid put gum in my hair. And I've only been going two weeks. Who knows what else can happen?" she says the last part to Stacy.

"What do you want me to do, Cordie? I'm looking for someone to stay home with you. It's not an easy process."

I elbow Pippa. Hard. Thankfully she gets my meaning.

"But I could do it while you search for someone more permanent," she says.

Unless they fall in love and then she can stay forever. Oh, make that six people I'll make happy. Mum and Dad would love Pip to stay in town forever.

"Besides being a good cook, Pip's great with braids and other cool hair styles," I tell Cordie. Greasing the wheels. "She also likes to play games and is quite fun."

"Oh, I'm brilliant with cribbage, crazy eights, and Uno." Pippa says, the child in her coming out and excited to play. Poor Pip, stuck with me as playmate all her life, and I was more interested in fashion magazines than moving pieces around a board.

Cordie looks at her father; a dolt could interpret her pleading expression.

"Don't make her go back, you awful man," I tease from behind Pippa's back. Nudging him further into the ring.

"Would you be willing, Pippa? Keep Cordie until I can find someone permanent? School starts next week so it would only be after she gets out for the day. It would be a big help." Stacy's pleading expression matches his daughter's.

"Oh, I'd love it. We'll have a fabulous time." She extends her hand and receives a high five from Cordie.

"Great. Can you start tomorrow?" Stacy's wide smile is even and though the dimple in his chin peeks out, it's his crooked grin I like better.

"Fabulous," Pippa says.

"Can you really do good braids?" Cordie asks. "Jayne did mine the other day and it was cool."

"Puh-leez. I'm better than Jayne. Have you seen the side braid with bows?" Pippa raises one brow and I know she's reeling in the child. One thing my cousin has always wanted?

A family of her own. The only child of a mum who would disappear for long lengths of time, Pippa grew up more at my home. The day I left for University was probably the hardest for both her and me. My parents, much to Mum's family's dislike, were moving to America to start their own business and taking Pip with them. She would be starting over in a new country without anyone else to help her plod along the path. Mum, Pip's legal guardian, refused to leave her behind with our aunties, claiming they wouldn't care well enough for the teenage Pippa. But no matter how often we told her how welcome she was and how much we wanted her around, she once confessed to me that she never really felt as if she belonged. I suppose bouncing around from place to place with her mum in her formative years left her unable to tether.

I'd love to see her find her place. If that's with Stacy and Cordie, even better.

"Can you try that on my hair now?" Cordie asks.

"Aye-ya. Come on, let's go through Josie's bits and bobs and get the things we need." She takes the child's hand and off they go.

Now I leave it in hands more omnipotent than mine.

Okay, after a few well-placed nibbles, then I'll leave it be.

I shift so I'm closer to Stacy. "Did I tell you Pippa's fluent in three languages?"

"Really?" He faces me and crosses one leg so his ankle rests on his knee "How've you been? Things working out okay at the shop? You seem pretty busy; I'm glad you're relaxing tonight." He lays his arm across the top of the bench seat, his finger brushing my shoulder.

"Oh, you know me. Career woman first and all that. Everything is as good as I can get it for the moment." I smile as large as I can. *No, this isn't awkward. Yes, I still can smell you sometimes, late at night, when I've got only memories to hold me tight. But no, sadly, I don't think we are suited for more than what we've had.*

"I admire someone who goes after their goals." He plays with the cuff of my sleeve.

"Pippa's the same. I know she seems flighty but she's actually built up quite a clientele worldwide."

"I hope she doesn't find us too pedestrian." He winks.

Drat, not the message I was intending to send I go for broke.

"She personally owns a Kama Sutra book." I wag my brows.

He sits back. Startled perhaps? "I hope she doesn't share it with Cordie."

"Of course not. I was just saying—"

"What *are* you saying?" Paisley asks.

Realizing she was listening, I jump to my feet. "If you'll excuse me. I. Er...I need to wash my hands. Chocolate." I hold my hands out to the group before I drop them to smooth and straighten my sundress.

"Which you just wiped on your dress," Josie says, her gaze narrowing.

"The meat's burning," I say and point to the grill. Then I scurry off while everyone has shifted their focus onto the empty grill.

I hide in the loo and try to gather my wits.

I'm coming out and have no sooner opened the door when I'm pushed back into the small space, the door slamming shut behind Paisley.

"What are you up to?" She crosses her arms.

"Not a thing. What are you accusing me of? Because I washed my hands," I say and smirk.

"You know what I'm talking about. I'm talking about Pippa and Stacy and this...whatever it is you're doing."

"I'm letting nature run its course, bringing two people together who likely should be together." I smile serenely.

"Pfft." She coordinates her words with an eye roll.

"Honestly." I cross my fingers behind my back.

"Because you don't want him?" She levels me with a stare.

"I don't want him the way he wants to be wanted."

"Are you sure about that?"

"Without a doubt." I say with more determination than I knew I had.

"I repeat. I don't believe you." She narrows her gaze.

"No? Oh, all right." I sigh and settle back against the sink counter. "I've decided it's in my best interest to set Stacy up. As I—"

"What? Why? You're crazy. I never thought it would be you who'd be the craziest of us...but it is," she mumbles and leans against the door.

"I'm not crazy. I'm removing temptation. He's like choco-late and as long as I'm able, I'll snack on him. If he's unavail-able, then—"

"Are you sure you want to do that?" Her incredulous expression gives me pause. But it's selfish to want Stacy and it's obvious he doesn't do fly by night (he was recently engaged for Pete's sake) so I steel my resolve.

"Positive."

See Jayne be a good person.

"What if they get married and have tons of babies, because I can see Pippa doing that. And you have to spend the holidays looking at them and their cute children. You know they'd make cute babies, watching them canocdle—"

"Canoodle?"

"And be all...sexual with each other. What would Pippa's version of timeout look like? Would she make them all get into child's pose? Oh, of course Pip's the type to have stick figures on her minivan, because she'd need one for her litter of kids, and she'd have those figures all in some sort of yoga pose. That's kinda cute actually. You're sure you're up for that?"

"I am absolutely one-hundred-percent positive I want to do this."

She presses her lips together and cocks her head to the side, much like a dog who's heard something intriguing, or obnoxious. Could go either way.

Briefly, I press my palm to my temple, hoping to push back a tension headache. "Look at you and Hank. I don't want to go through what you're going through. If I mess around with him, I could muck up a lot."

She blinks several times before answering. "Okay." She pushes off the door. "I'll help you."

"Oh, there's no need—"

"It's a really good idea actually. You're right. When I look at the big picture you two aren't...suited for long term."

"It's not that we aren't suited; it's that we have different life goals," I murmur. "He was engaged, you know. Before moving here."

"Really, how do you know this?" Her eyes narrow in doubt.

"Cordie told me. What more do you need to know that he and I just don't make sense long term?"

She nods once. "I get it now. Hank comes home in two

days and if I can't make him see how much I love him—" Her voice breaks. "Then I, too, will lose a lot. *I get it.*"

"So you have a plan?"

"Yeah, of sorts. I'll let you know." She bites her stubby thumbnail.

"Best of luck." I want to hug her but I'm afraid if I touch her she'll burst into tears.

Suddenly she claps her hands. "Your idea is smart. Oh, I've got three friends we can set him up with."

"Because they're better suited for him than me?" I cross my arms.

She dismisses my words by waving her hand. "It's really you and Cordie that aren't suited. Remember that time you watched Tyler for an hour?" Her raised brow is the sort of condemnation I find quite irritating.

"How am I to know that grapes are supposed to be quartered? Where were those instructions?"

"Good thing Heather came home when she did. He could have choked."

"But he didn't," I point out for the one-millionth time.

"Because you got lucky."

I throw up my hands in disgust. "How was I to know?"

"Everyone knows that."

I narrow my gaze, winging my brows inward. "Well, I guess *not* everyone. I can't believe we're still having this conversation. That was what? A year ago?" I'd leave but she's still blocking my way.

She pulls out her phone and begins to scroll through her contacts. "I'm going to reach out to my friend, Evie. Just in case this doesn't work out with Pippa and Stacy."

"You don't have to do that." I should have kept my fool mouth closed.

"You want him to be happy, right? So much you spoon-feed him your cousin."

"If they're happy, then I'm happy."

There goes her brow again, reaching up into her hairline. "You do whatever it takes to believe that. When you need another setup, let me know. I've got the perfect person and with her you won't have to see them on the holidays," she says, fingers flying over the keypad as she constructs a text message.

"Move," I say and push her out of my way. Let the Stacy diet begin.

CHAPTER FOURTEEN

After parking in my garage, I gather up my laptop, a notebook, and accordion file stuffed with receipts. I yawn three times, and while using my phone's flashlight I search in all the car's crevices for my mobile. Until it dawns on me that it's in my hand, the key instrument in the search. I rest my head on the steering wheel and contemplate sleep. Instead, I force myself from my car, entering my home through the laundry room where I'm greeted by whistling.

Pippa.

It's not that I don't want to be home. I absolutely do.

Pippa's loading dishes into the sink as I come into the kitchen. Likely because she thinks they'll magically wash themselves. She thinks this happens at my parents' pub as well. Even though she's met Cam, the dishwasher, a million times. The tune she's whistling is something upbeat and should be smile inspiring.

But not for me. That's how low I am.

"Things good, Pip?" I sling my handbag and messenger

bag onto a dining chair and head straight for the fridge and the wine.

"Aye-ya, grand. I'm off to the pub in a few." She's drying her hands on a tea towel.

Ugh. The pub. Another topic of failure for me.

"How are Mum and Dad doing? Are they swamped?" I pour a large glass. It's only been two days since I've been in, but it seems like weeks, with the bank visits, appointments with personal clients, and my own shop to keep afloat now that Shara's gone.

"No, it's good. We're managing it."

"Have there been any delays with deliveries or any problems like that?" I haven't shared my fears with Pippa because I don't want to cause an issue where one may not be.

"Nope. Everything's like usual." She narrows her eyes. "Should I be looking for those things?"

I shake my head. "You're a godsend, Pip. Your timing's spot on." I raise my glass in toast of my cousin, who manages to do it all with grace and aplomb. And teal green streaks throughout her hair.

"Nice." I point at her head with my index finger, still cupping my glass.

"Cordie and I did it today after school. Teal looks better on her." She fluffs her hair and smiles.

"All's well there, I suppose." I want to pry, but, not fully having the energy to keep up my end of the conversation much less hear any intimate details about Stacy, I walk away before she answers. That would be too weird, right?

"Aces." She gives me two thumbs up. A horn blares outside and Pip jumps.

"That's me. I'm off to earn money under the table." She

smirks before kissing my cheek and bounds out of the house like an excited puppy.

I lean against the counter and stare at the assortments of takeaway menus stacked next to my fridge while I sip the wine. Which will it be tonight?

Oddly, none sound good. I push away from the counter and fling open the fridge door; inside is cheese and a small opened can of tuna, Pippa's staple.

Stacking them first, I take them from the fridge, kick the door closed, and make my way out the front door where I whistle for that difficult-and-should-be-grateful cat. Setting my wine glass on the pavement, I take his little plastic bowl from under the shrub and dump Pippa's tuna in it. I lay the cheese across the top.

After placing it back in its spot, I call again. And that's how Stacy and Cordie find me, in my bare feet, wine glass in hand, skirt wrinkled, calling for a cat they both know I don't own.

Stacy gives me one of those open-handed waves, heavy with hesitation, as he slowly lifts it in the air while following his daughter from their house. He pauses next to his SUV.

"You have a cat?" Cordie asks.

"Not really per se. There's a rogue little bast...er, rascal of a cat wandering around and sometimes I feed him."

"He could be rabid." Stacy moves to stand next to Cordie. Teal streaks color her hair.

"I like this," I say, pointing to her head.

"Yeah, me too." She looks over her shoulder. "Dad not so much. Pippa says you used to do each other's hair all the time growing up."

"More like I did her hair. Back then it was down to her

bum and she needed it put up. Ask her tomorrow about the time she singed the ends."

With a flash of multi-colored gray and dark fur, he-who-doesn't-answer-to-a-name streaks across the car park and dives under the shrub to his bowl.

I gesture with great flair to the proof that I'm not mad.

"Cool," says Cordie.

"You should be careful with it," Stacy tells me, nodding his chin in the direction of the cat.

"You're not kidding," I say before taking a swig of my wine and glancing at the scar across my knuckle.

"We're going to get something to eat," Cordie says. "Wanna come with?"

"Did Pippa not make dinner?" I only ask because she smelled distinctly of curry and it's not like her to leave them hungry.

Stacy steps away from Cordie, his hand turning a key over repeatedly. "Pippa's great. She really is. But Cords and I are more French fries and burger people."

"And Pippa's making things with kale and quinca?" That explains the curry smell.

"Yeah." He grimaces.

"Are they any good?" I should, at the very least, defend my cousin.

"We only tried the first one." He shakes his head. "Listen, it's hard to get my kid to eat peas. Tofu doesn't stand a chance."

"I see." Sorta. Just make her eat them, I want to say. Besides, who doesn't love a pea? I enjoy them on my pizzas.

"Can you talk to her?" he asks with droopy puppy dog eyes.

"Please," Cordie says from behind him.

"You want me to tell my vegan cousin to make you burgers and fries?" I shake my head. "She doesn't even touch meat when she's at the pub. No, we'll have to find a different solution." I feel guilty that I pitched Pippa's cooking skills to him. I never considered he'd prefer fried foods to healthy alternatives.

"Find it quick. We're starving over there."

"I can't eat any more pizza." Cordie makes like she's gagging.

"Even though I tossed the boxes in the dumpster outside, she knew. Said she could smell it." He briefly looks toward his house and lowers his voice. "It's like she has a camera or something."

To that I laugh. "Not likely, Pippa can barely work a smartphone. No, her sense of smell can rival the best sommelier, and she has a cousin who has a similar palate as you both so she knows the tricks."

"Where is Pippa?" This time he looks toward my house. Is he longing to see her? Was I spot-on with setting them up?

"She went to help out at the pub." I look away, not wanting to see his reaction, to see if he's thinking of her and his face showing the same desire he showed me the night of Josie's wedding. "So you are safe to sneak away for food."

"Have you had anything to eat?" he asks.

"Only this." I hold up my wine glass.

"You're welcome to join us. If you don't have other plans. It would give me a chance to clear up some questions I have about your books."

"Oh?" I step toward him.

"I've been meaning to text. Haven't had a chance." His look expresses nothing. Maybe a wee bit of neighborly friendship. There's no longing etched on his brow. No fidgeting to touch me. The contrast from our night together is staggering. Each kiss was delivered with a hunger matched only to what I was feeling and each time he pulled away it was as if he couldn't bear us to be apart. As if he poured every bit of himself into our night.

He snaps me from my thoughts. "It's nothing, but as I look at the numbers, I could get a better sense of how you want to present them if I knew what the endgame was."

"That makes sense." I'm still in a haze from the memories.

"So?" He nods to the car; Cordie is already climbing into the back.

"Right. Sure thing. Sounds good." I start to walk toward him when I realize I'm still holding my wine glass. I stop and turn back to my place. "Let me put this inside and grab my handbag."

"Don't forget shoes," he calls after me.

I was about to go off with him barefoot and toting stemware.

"Of course," I say over my shoulder.

Cordie agrees to try Indian food. She's promised rice and chicken she'll like. I had nothing to do with the suggestion but am pleased with the selection, and I direct Stacy to my favorite place.

Inside I wave to Amit, who returns my greeting with a chin jut.

"Another visit and it's not even Thursday."

"I'm with people." I say, kinda hoping he gets the wrong impression about Stacy and I.

"Eat in or take out?" Amit asks and smiles at Cordie.

"Table for three." Stacy steps back to allow Cordie and I to precede him, his hand coming to rest on the small of my back. The reaction to his touch, the warmth spreading across my lower back, the instant tingle in my girly bits, and maybe the half glass of wine combined makes me jump and spin to face him. A giggle my other response. Which, I suppose, is better than a moan of desire.

He steps back. "Sorry. An old habit."

From Jill, perhaps? Did his hand fit snugly in the small of her back, too? "No, not a problem. Only unexpected, that's all."

And just as quickly as I turned to him, I turn back and follow Cordie to a booth where I slide into the seat opposite her. He slides in next to her and our knees bump.

First world problems of the long legged. He shifts so his knees are facing away from me.

Amit puts menus before them, omitting me, and I roll my eyes. Two can play this game.

"What's the special?" I ask.

Amit chuckles. "You want extra shrimp in your korma?"

"That sounds lovely; I'll take that then." Because I never order anything else. Because it's my favorite.

"How about we each get a different dish and share?" Stacy asks. Cordie and I nod in agreement.

I might allow a bite or two.

Once they've placed their order, Stacy turns his attention to me.

"Tell me your plan?"

Following a sigh of resignation, Cordie asks, "If you're going to talk business can I play with your phone?"

Stacy hands it to her while nodding with his chin for me to continue.

"I want to expand into a different city. I have a fair amount of personal shopper clients and I studied where most of them came from and am targeting their areas for expansion."

"So what you do here, but there. And Miami is first on your list?"

"It was. But in order to get the right location there, I'll have to purchase a building and lease it out. Which I'm open to doing. I quite like the idea of owning real estate. But I was led to think I might not qualify for the loan." I twist my earring and think about the cold, matter-of-fact tone of the lender.

Stacy nods, lost in thought. Does he see cute little numbers swimming in his head? Do they quickly come together in combinations like outfits do for me?

"What are you thinking?" I ask.

"Let me look at the numbers first. I'll give you a rundown of scenarios once I get through them."

I continue to twist my earring and nod. My fate is in his hands.

"Jayne," he says, pulling my hand from my ear. "Relax, let the numbers be your guide."

My hand is cradled in his. He's a master at caressing; his strokes are perfect, not so light you think it's a bug and not so heavy you wonder if any skin is left behind. I want to entwine my fingers with his. I want to rub my thumb over his knuckles. But I do nothing, committing the feeling to memory for when my naughty free telly subscription runs out.

I wait for him to continue.

"She doesn't get it, Dad," Cordie says without looking up from the phone's screen. "It's a *Star Wars* reference. Dad likes to think he's the Yoda of numbers."

"Ahh," I say, feigning a clarity I don't possess.

"What I mean is that the numbers will give you the direction; they'll empower you."

I slide my hand from his. The act imitates a lingering caress. I quickly stow mine under my leg to hide the quivering mess it's become.

You can't have him.

I glance at Cordie.

"So other than the food, how's Pippa working out?"

"She's teaching me yoga." Cordie flashes me a smile.

"It's impressive how limber she is. Yesterday when I came home she was doing the splits but up along the wall." He runs his hand vertically for added clarity.

"Yes, impressive," I echo. I reach into my bag and pull out a fortune cookie. I'm in desperate need for some direction, and if Stacy thinks it can be found in numbers I think it can be found in a fortune cookie.

"Did you get that here?" Cordie asks.

"No, I carry them in my purse. Sorta inspirational support." I glance quickly at Stacy. "Or for when I'm peckish, like now. Want one?"

I hand one to Cordie and she snatches it up greedily.

"Should you be eating those here?" Stacy asks.

"It's not against the law," I say and crack mine in two.

Cordie waves her around. "It says I'll be rewarded with riches." She beams up at us.

I glance down at mine. It's blank except for lottery numbers on the opposite side.

I sigh with disgust and flick the paper across the room just as Amit steps up to the table with our food.

CHAPTER FIFTEEN

Pippa and I arrive at Heather's with snack food and cocktails in tow. Pippa's made a dip the color of puce and the odor of sweaty socks. She's paired it with sprouted chips and I make a mental note to get the first sample and if it's wretched find a way to *accidentally* knock it to the floor.

Unable to land a sitter and unwilling to miss our bimonthly girls' night out, Heather's invited us to descend upon her place. Tyler will be milling around but we've done this before. We don't get together to get rowdy but more to enjoy each other's company. Heather's house, laid out rambler style, is sparsely decorated, as she's had to split half of everything with her soon-to-be ex, Justin.

She has a warm and inviting kitchen, painted robin's egg blue with white crown molding, white cupboards, and dark wood floors. I've never thought much about the inner work-ings of a kitchen, requiring only a stove to cook things and a refrigerator to keep things from spoiling. Oh, and running water. It's been months since someone used my oven and longer since I have. But something about Heather's kitchen draws me in and I find myself hanging out there. She has a built-in desk as part of her kitchen, an idea I think brilliant. I need one in my flat so when I work I'll be close to the snack food. I imagine if I had the same setup my desk would look similar to Heather's. Covered in newspaper, loose paper, books, and the like. Mine might also have a few used tea mugs and chocolate wrappers.

Within a five-minute span, we've all arrived. Josie is mixing cocktails in the kitchen and I've had my covert sample of Pip's dip. It's so good I've had several more bites.

It just goes to show someone, whose name rhymes with Macy, lacks a refined palette. The food my cousin creates may be unique in presentation and, yes, odor, but quite tasty.

"There's veggies in there. Like cauliflower. You should go easy lest you explode from providing your body with some much-needed quality food," she tells me and dips a chip.

"Hmm, that explains the odor. But I'll suffer through; brave the odds to get in my recommended daily allowance. And real chips would be a lot better but—" I shrug and continue to dip.

She narrows her eyes at me. "Have you been drinking those smoothies I'm making you every morning?"

"Green should not be the color of a smoothie. Smoothies should be pink or purple." At least the ones I get from drive-thru places are and those are wonderfully worth every penny.

Pippa rolls her eyes. "There was one that was purple."

"No. That was a dark, dark, dark poo color." I reach for a loaf of bread someone placed on the counter next to a handful of tomatoes, probably with the intention of making bruschetta. Likely Josie, who's still mentally on her honeymoon.

"It had chocolate in it." She takes the bread from my hand. "It's food like this that keeps that extra cushion on your hips."

By that she also means my arse.

"I like my hips," I say and reach for the loaf.

She steps out of reach, the bag behind her back. "You won't when you're forty."

"Can't I enjoy today, Pippa?" For such a free spirit, she's always had her eye on the next day. Always trying to undo the wrongs of the yesterdays and perfect the tomorrows.

"Fine." She tosses the bread to me. "Pig out. We can share a flat in our single, lonely elderly years and lament on all the things we would have done differently, starting with bread." She spins on her heel and stalks off into Heather's living room, where she drops to the floor and begins to stretch out.

"What was that about?" Josie asks from behind me.

After placing the loaf on the counter, I move away from the food. "I'm not sure." It's a wee bit like a chess match, trying to move the pieces around and not having all the information. I try not to be buggered by how blooming awful I am at chess. "Hey, do me a favor and ask her. Later. After she's chilled out a bit." I slide the tray of drinks off the counter and wait for Josie's response before I set out to deliver them.

"Heather," I say, handing her one light on booze, as she's ultimately in charge of a child once we all leave. "How's the job hunt going?"

"Awful. I've landed nothing permanent. I wonder if it's because I tell them about—" She jerks her head toward her child before continuing. "I mention that we'll be out for a week in three months when he has that brain study. I want to be honest, not surprise them after the fact, but I'm thinking being honest is hurting me." She chugs her drink, finishing it off before I've handed out the rest, and then places the empty glass on the tray.

"Isn't that discrimination?" I ask and we all turn to Josie, the lawyer in the group.

"Only if you can prove it. And in this case, that would be difficult." She walks into the living room with the blender and refills Heather's glass.

Heather says, "It's got to get easier. Really, it has to. I don't know how much more I can take."

"It'll turn around soon. You'll see." Kenley pats her hand.

"Not if my luck continues." Heather stares into her drink.

I arrange the food on the counter and remember when Mum looked as hopeless as Heather does right now. Even surrounded by family and friends, Mum had still required professional intervention. Medication and counseling.

I follow Paisley into the kitchen and stop her by grabbing her arm. "We need to keep a better eye on Heather, makes sure she's not sliding into depression."

Paisley looks over her shoulder to where the rest of our group sits chatting. "Jeez, you're right. I'm a terrible friend. I've been so consumed with my own drama I forgot about how awful it is to be divorced and trying to figure it all out again." Paisley, divorced over a year ago, would know best of all of us.

"Are you all talking about me?" Heather calls from the living room, her teasing tone laced with a crispness that bodes of hidden anger.

"No," Paisley says, her eyes darting to me in panic.

"Paisley was making fun of me," I say, improvising.

"About what?" Josie asks.

Our gazes shift to each other, Paisley and I, each apparently asking, "Now what, genius?"

"Your sign." Paisley points over my shoulder.

I turn to where a small wooden framed sign hangs. It's one of those inspirational mantras posing as home decoration and Heather's hung it over her coffee pot as if the reminder is needed as she starts her day.

It reads: *Making the decision to have a child is momentous. It is to decide forever to have your heart go walking around outside your body. ~ Elizabeth Stone*

"Yes," I say. "She asked if that's why I didn't want children. If I was afraid."

Paisley nods as if she's onto something and says as she faces the group, "Right, but she said the reason why wasn't because of the constant angst but because of the similarity to being pecked to death by chickens." She turns back to me and winks. A few of the friends chuckle, so Paisley and I do as well.

"Your mom has that saying posted in her house," Josie says, pointing a finger at Paisley.

"That's where I saw it," I say and hear Paisley let out the breath she must have been holding.

"That's a terrible saying," Heather says. "There's nothing like having a child and spending every day wondering how you'll make them happy, keep them safe, and get them to adulthood."

"Sounds stressful. Like being covered in chiggers. I spend an unusual amount of time avoiding chiggers," Paisley says.

"Or like being stung, repetitively, by a swarm of bees," Josie adds.

"How about being covered in honey and set out on an ant bed?" Pip says.

Some of us wince before laughing, but the group has deteriorated into giggles and sayings about torture and children. Even Heather's chimed in with a few.

This. This is what a circle of friends is about. Helping one up when they have fallen, sharing laughs, and tears, and heartbreak. I press my hand to my chest, thankful for this eclectic mix of women I call friends and make a silent wish and prayer that nothing comes to fracture this.

As the laughter dies down, Heather turns to Pippa and asks, "I thought you enjoyed children?"

"Oh, I do. I'm not like Jayne. I'd love to have a large brood and a house with a wrap porch and, well, you all know." Pippa looks at her toes, reaches out, and grabs them, pulling herself forward into a stretch, her face buried in her knees.

If I had a lantern that housed a genie who was in the business of dispatching wishes, my first would be to give Pippa the family she desperately longs for. A place she can call her own. My second would be to make sure my folks were set up to live comfortably, and my third would be the for the obvious: three more wishes.

"Are you leaving again anytime soon?" Heather asks, her hand trembling as she takes a drink.

"Well," Pippa says, moving into child's pose. "That depends." She looks at me.

"On what?" Josie sits on the floor next to her, her legs tucked under her.

"On whether I get this job I applied for," she mumbles.

"What job?" Paisley asks.

I wait, wondering if she'll tell them. My superstitious

cousin would never be able to forgive herself if she shared and then failed. Almost always we find out events after they happen and if, on the off chance it's before, it was purely by accident.

Pippa sits up and back on heels. "It's a job at a yoga institute in India. It's where I go every summer." She waves her hands in front of her as if wiping away the words. "But that's all I'll say."

One look at her face is all it takes to see how desperately she wants the position. What I don't tell the group is that aside from my family, the institute is where she found a second home, a place to heal her wounded heart.

I hold up my hand showing my crossed fingers.

Josie wraps an arm around Pippa and hugs her. "Good luck. You'll be a blessing to any employer."

"Yeah, Pippa. Good luck. I hope you're more successful than I've been." Heather toasts her with her glass.

"I'm sorry it's been a bloody headache for you," Pippa says.

"That's okay. But if you get this other job, do you mind handing me over the one you have now? I'm thinking working for Stacy might be just the thing."

"Sometimes it doesn't amount to more than fifteen hours a week. And can I say here that they are the pickiest of eaters? They wanted mac and cheese so I made them mac and cheese."

"With nutritional yeast," I tell the others.

Pippa transitions to lotus position. "Can I help that I want the gastrointestinal tract of my fellow man to be healthy?"

"Seriously though, Pippa. If you get tired of the job...."

"What's this about?" Kenley asks Heather point blank.

For a woman so gutted it is quite admirable how Heather keeps her composure long enough to put her glass on her coffee table before bursting into tears.

"I'm sorry. I'm sorry," she wails, hands over her face. "I'm a pathetic mess."

At the first sob, we all descend upon her. Kenley, sitting closest, is next to her rubbing her back.

"Heather," Paisley says, crouched at Heather's knees. "Going through a divorce is awful, awful, awful. Doing it with a child has to be even more difficult. Add in that your son has medical issues... Hon, you need to give yourself a break."

"I can't. I just can't." Her sobs increase and we all look at each other. Josie, ever practical, gets up and makes more drinks. The sound of the blender gives us the moment we need to collect our thoughts. I search for encouraging words.

"I'll text Doug and let him know I'm staying here tonight," Kenley mumbles under her breath.

When Heather looks up, her face tear ravaged and puffy, Josie says, "We have some serious business to get to and it looks like it's going to need liquid courage. Before this night is over, Heather, I guaran-damn-tee you'll have a plan."

"But I needed a plan yesterday." She looks at Pippa.

Pippa, with her teal streaks fading, her demeanor just as soft, says in a matter-of-fact voice, "Heather, if I believed letting you take the job with Stacy would improve your current situation, I'd let you take it. But Stacy's hoping after Cordie adjusts more, makes some friends, and starts to click then he'll put her in aftercare. He wants her with friends. He doesn't want her hanging out at home alone."

"I thought he said he was looking for a nanny of sorts," I say.

She shakes her head. "That's what he tells Cordie."

"I still want it," Heather says, her words hitching now that her cries have eased.

"Heather," Kenley says. "What good will it do you if you only have the job for a few days?"

"It might be longer." She crosses her arms and sits back, looking away from us all.

Right, so things have gotten seriously weird here. I look to Paisley for guidance because she's the one with the closest experience. But she's looking at Kenley, who is related to Heather. Even if it's by marriage.

Kenley's looking like a deer caught in headlights.

Oh for the love of God.

See Jayne take charge.

"Heather, love. You seem...er...focused on this situation with Stacy, though it doesn't sound like it could really work out. Aren't you doing temp work? Isn't that steady?" I swear I try to probe gently.

To everyone's surprise, Heather leaps from the couch "But don't you see? It's perfect. Cordie needs a mom. I am a mom. I love children." Her face is still red and puffy from crying, but the slanted inward pull of her brows speaks of her fierceness. "I need someone to help me get on my feet. To be with me. I've tried this love thing, twice, and it hasn't worked out." Her voice wobbles with the last bit and my heart melts.

"Dax?" I meant to say it in my head. Not intending to push her when she's out so far already.

Heather snorts and shakes her head. "Ha, Dax." She stares off and whispers, "Lord I was crazy about him. But he wanted his career more than me." She looks at Paisley.

I take in all my friends and wonder if they have hidden

heartbreak like Heather. Likely so. I suppose we all do on some level. And look what it's done to them. To all of us.

Fear. That's what this is about. Fear of being alone, of not being chosen, and fear of wondering if she has what it takes to go it alone. For Heather, putting the pieces back together has to be one of the most difficult tasks, much like wandering a pitch-black hallway looking for the missing pieces and the way out.

"Oh, hon," I say and turn her to me. "Being with Stacy, or any man for that matter, isn't going to make it perfect. It's only going to complicate matters. What you need to do is figure out what it is you want and where you want to be this time next year. Take it in steps. One day at a time."

"But don't you see? He's just like me."

"What? How?" Josie's confusion comes through in her tone.

"I overheard him tell Brinn that some girl really worked him over good. His ex, I suppose."

"Jill?" I ask.

"He didn't say her name. Just that he thought it would be easier to get a mail order bride than go through waiting for her to come around." She places a hand over her chest. "I could do it. We would make good partners. Raising kids together. It could work." She looks at all of us.

Paisley moves closer. "The best piece of advice I was given was to not do anything drastic for a while. That's why I took the year off. I tried not to make any major decisions or hasty ones. I'm giving that advice to you."

Heather shakes her head; her lower lip wobbles. I pull her into a hug. "I think Stacy was being facetious when he said that. But picture yourself a year from now. When things have settled down. You've a job, a routine that makes sense.

What if pushing into Stacy's life is not as good an idea then as it seems now?"

"It's so hard," she says into my shoulder. "I'm sorry, everyone. I'm a terrible friend."

"We all have our days we act like a mad bitch. Today is yours. Embrace it," I say and laugh. "It will get better. It has to."

"I can't get a job." She wraps her arms around me, holding tight, possibly for dear life. "I can't do the simplest things in life like, you know, buy food for my child. I'm dependent on Justin and even then money is tight."

And then it hits me. "How do you feel about clothes?"

"I don't"—hiccup—"understand."

"I'm asking how you feel about helping people pick out clothes. Offering them suggestions about what might work and not work. How do you feel about working in a clothing shop?"

She pulls back and looks at me. "I don't need a pity job," she whispers.

"I've lost my best employee and the one I have left *has* to go." Actually, the more I process the idea, the better I like it.

"But I'm not anywhere near as skilled as you with clothes."

"Pft." I wave my hand. "Every time a new outfit comes in I photograph it with several suggested accessories. A cheat sheet if you will. But what I need is someone responsible. Someone kind. Who actually knows math. I open after Tyler goes to school, so you could take the morning shifts. I open late on Wednesday. And you can work on the weekends Justin has Tyler. If that's all right with you. Also, I pay more than minimum wage."

Heather hesitates then says, "Why not Pippa?" Her gaze

leaves my face to look over my shoulder where I assume Pippa is.

I laugh. Pip will appreciate this. "Because she can't stand to be around clothes. Likely from all those times I made her dress up and be my model. I must have stuck her with a pin several times a day when I went through my fashion design fad. What's that disorder people have when being in a certain situation causes them stress?"

"Post-traumatic stress disorder," supplies Paisley.

"Yes, that. Pippa has that."

"Too right!" Pip says from behind me.

"Are you serious?" With large, wide eyes likely from hope, Heather scans my face.

"Absolutely. You can start tomorrow if you want."

"Oh, Jayne," she cries and pulls me back into a hug. "Thank you, thank you, thank you."

CHAPTER SIXTEEN

Hiring Heather has to be one of the best moves I've made this year. She stepped into the position with ease. I worried, but her quiet confidence, a trait I realized now had been missing since her marriage with Justin imploded, appeared and wowed more than me.

Leaving the shop, feeling more secure with Heather and her first-day inexperience than my half-wit employee, I make the mad drive to Stacy's to pick up Pippa so I can deliver her to the pub. I'll have to rush back home to make my meeting with Stacy about the state of my books.

The vague text that he used to arrange this get-together leaves me worried and fearful that I won't be able to see my dreams come true.

Before I can press a heel to the horn, Pippa's out of the flat and jogging to the car.

Her teal streaks have been replaced with pink tips.

"Hallo." She buckles her seatbelt.

"Playing dress up?" I shift into reverse and slowly back out. Having Cordie in the neighborhood makes me more cautious of looking for children. Not that I haphazardly and ignorantly pulled out before, I'm just more mindful.

"She's a good child. Easy to be around. She needs a mum." From her large gypsy bag, Pippa pulls out an apple and shines it on her shirt before she takes a bite.

Perfect opening. Pippa's been tight lipped about what goes on at Stacy's house.

She's not indicated one way or another if she fancies him. I only know she adores Cordie. And makes them meals they don't enjoy. I'm curious to know if my matchmaking machinations have borne fruit.

"You'd be a good mum," I say.

"Only because your mum was a good example. Mine, not so much." She continues to work her apple.

"Which says a lot about you. You're amazing, Pippa. You know that, right? Cordie would be lucky to have a mum like you." I slow to a stop at a red light, my attention on the signal a ruse I'm using in hopes of conveying my nonchalance.

"What are you about?" She rummages through her bag, then pulls out a brown paper sack that she uses to store the core of her apple.

"Nothing, only wondering if maybe there might be…er…sparks between you and Stacy." I shift into first, pretending that task requires all my focus as if I haven't been driving a manual for oh, the last ten years.

"Are you bloody serious?" She faces me. I can feel the penetrating stare bore into me.

"Er…."

"You have a one-nighter with the guy—which I've kept to myself, mind you—get your fill and then pass him on to me? This is a new one for us." She faces the window.

"How did you…I mean, nothing—"

She quickly faces me, her anger clear by the deep blush to her cheeks. "Come off, Jayne. I saw you two leave together. And the next morning you were rosy cheeked and walking tall. What I don't know is why you keep it a secret from the others?"

"Because I'm afraid of all the complications. What if we date but it ends horribly—as all my other relationships have ended, you know this. And then it causes problems in the group? Between me and Josie or Stacy and her. I don't want people to have to pick."

When she looks at me, I'm acutely aware of how deeply I've hurt her. "So you decide that I should have him. That pairing us up is suitable enough and who cares if any or all that stuff happens between me and the group? Which is a stupid reason by the way. Paisley wants you to hook up with him and I haven't heard Josie argue that you shouldn't. So come again with the truth this time."

"Honestly, Pip. I wasn't trying to hurt you." I adjust in my seat, feeling the restrictiveness of the seat belt.

"It feels like that," she mumbles.

"I'm sorry. I only thought that he was a lovely man who might benefit from someone as wonderful as you. Both of you would."

"What's the real reason, Jayne?"

"That *is* the real reason," I say.

Her eyes narrow further.

"Partly. Mostly it's because I do want you to be happy. And I thought he might be able to give that to you."

"You like him, don't you?"

I pull into the back lot behind the pub and idle, setting the parking brake before I answer, "I could like him, I think."

"And that scares you," she says, her voice low and gentle. "And your frightened heart."

"You know how it goes. Look at how unsuccessful the women in our family have been. You were too young to remember the devastation after Robert left Mum but it was awful." I refuse to call my biological father by anything but his given name. His other daughters, women I don't know, nor have ever met, are welcome to call him something more familiar.

"Yet look at her now with Uncle Thomas. She seems to have done well the second time around."

I snort. "It hurt watching her."

"Scarred you deep, it did."

"Even the small flings I've had left an ache when they ended. I'm not sure I could bear to give up a part of me only lose it. It would be bloody awful. You know how I get after I end something. I would avoid him at all cost, which means I would be avoiding my friends, too."

Our gazes meet. I know she understands. It was her mother, after all, who took her around the world while chasing after one man or another. Only to deposit Pippa on our nana's doorstep and disappear for months at a time. Mum couldn't stand the thought of little towheaded, blue-eyed Pippa being forced to hang with the geriatric crowd and moved her in with us.

"I'm scared, too," she whispers. "I've not had a long-term relationship. Ever."

I search my memory, wondering why I paid that small fact no never mind. "Me either." That reality is a lonely truth. I was far more giving with my virginity than my heart, and perhaps now I see why it should have been the other way around.

These last few years I've been more removed, playing my personal life casual but in my defense, I was building a business. Who has time for more? I still hold firm to the belief that love comes on quickly and bursts just as suddenly a few months later. It's just something in the way Stacy kissed me, like he needed it as much as he wanted it, that begs me to wonder if there's room for more.

"We're a sad lot," I say and take her hand.

"Too right. Our mums messed us up thoroughly." She squeezes my hand and smiles.

"Oh, I'm going to tell Mum you said that. I'll use anything to get her attention off you. She loves you so."

Pippa's smile wobbles. "Speaking of mums. In a few Saturdays is—"

"I know." I squeeze her hand. It'll be nineteen years since the yacht Pippa's mum was holidaying on capsized and sank off the coast of Majorca. "The usual, yes?"

The tradition started the first year I came here to visit, on holiday from University. I knew the anniversary of her mum's death was difficult for Pip. Compound that with being in a new country and an awkward teen there was no question I had to do something special for her.

Even after growing and striking out as a young adult, Pippa still comes here on this significant date. Wherever she may be in the world, whatever it is she's doing, she stops and comes homes. Sometimes just for a few days, often with a glib just-popping-through ruse. But I'd wager it's more to remind her that she does have a home, a place to go back to, where family is excited to see her. Unlike her own mum who barely gave her the time of day.

I misread the situation that first time and thought to distract her from the date by taking her to a film. The second year I got smart and paid attention to the signals she was putting out and let her guide us. We ended up at the beach under a midnight moon where we sat in companionable silence. The third year I took rose petals for Pip to toss into the sea; she forced me into doing yoga. Now, it's our annual ritual and one of the handful of times I'll assume downward dog, because being an uncoordinated giraffe trying to strike graceful poses does nothing for my confidence. But in the shadows of night, I have no qualms.

"Yes, I like what we've done. Don't you?" She squeezes back.

"I do."

Using the cuff of her shirt, she wipes her eyes. "Thanks, Jaynie-girl." She flashes a quick smile and is getting out of the car when I stop her by grabbing her elbow.

"I love you, Pip. For all the teasing I give you I thought I should tell you." My sweet cousin who's more a little sister to me than anything.

"Pish, I know you do."

I laugh and release her arm.

Once out she bends so I can see her face and says, "But not half as much as I love you." She slams the door and, in her usually bouncy, carefree steps, bounds into the pub.

Agh! Damn her. Just once I'd like to have the last word and it be sweet and loving and altruistic.

CHAPTER SEVENTEEN

The alert I've set on my phone tells me I have ten minutes to get home if I want to meet Stacy in time. I pull into my garage with one minute to spare and am entering through the laundry room when a pounding on my front door has me scurrying to look as if I'm not rushing. I kick off my heels while flinging my messenger bag on my dining table.

"Coming," I say in what I hope is a voice that sounds like I've been lounging on the couch and can't be bothered to get up.

Damn I wish I'd put gloss on in the car.

I open the door and am instantly confused.

"Amit, what?" I stare at the takeaway in his arms. "I didn't order food." It's from my favorite Chinese restaurant, but Amit owns the Indian place. I try to work it all out but the pieces aren't lining up. Though it's a fabulous idea and the rumble of my stomach, a sound both Amit and I are privy too, indicates I want the food. Only I didn't order it.

"But you own the Indian restaurant." I point in the general direction of his place.

"My cousin owns the Chinese place. His wife is having a baby and I'm helping out." He shakes the bag.

I focus on the problem before me.

"I ordered this?" If that's the case, I'm instantly going on a holiday. When one forgets something of this nature, one is losing it.

"No, a deep-voiced lady named Stacy did and asked to send it here. It's paid for." He shrugs before handing me the large order.

Over his shoulder, I see Stacy and Cordie coming out of their place. Cordie looks both ways before running across.

"Yay, food. I'm so hungry." She skirts around me and enters the house.

"Hold on, I'll get a tip," I tell Amit. But Stacy beats me to it and Amit's off before I can find my handbag.

Cordie's made herself at home and is setting out several cartons and Styrofoam containers.

"Gads, how many people are coming to eat?" I don't expect an answer. From my cupboard, I take the soy sauce, red peppers sauce, and other condiments I like to add to Chinese food. Then I get cups for everyone and chopsticks, and set forks out for the inexperienced.

Both Cordie and Stacy reach for the chopsticks, as do I. "What did Pippa make for dinner?" I open the carton closest to me and sigh with delight at the sweet and sour chicken that greets me.

"Something she creamed in our blender and is trying to pass off as a sauce over... What kind of noodles were they?" he asks his daughter.

"Buckwheat. It smelled like moldy underwear," Cordie says.

I'm pleased to say she uses her chopsticks like a pro.

"Cordie, that's not nice," Stacy scolds, but it's hard to censor a child when laughing.

She ignores him and continues to shove food into her mouth.

"Cauliflower," I say. "She puts it in everything and it has the misfortune of smelling like a fart in any state but raw."

Cordie laughs. "You know, you and Pippa aren't anything alike. Until you say something like that."

"We did grow up in the same house together. Some things are bound to rub off."

Cordie hands me the Styrofoam container of my favorite, black mushroom in oyster sauce, and I'm in heaven.

"Can I try?"

"May I try," Stacy and I correct in unison.

"Jeez." She rolls her eyes with such severe irritation I'm envious of the skill. "Whatever. Never mind."

I wave the container under her nose. "Are you sure? It's very, very good." I tease her much like I used to tease Pippa at this age.

"*May* I try," she says.

"Of course." I hand her the food. "So, we've taken this hiding food thing to a whole new level. I feel awkward." I pause for dramatic effect, place my hand over my heart, and shake my head with mock disappointment. "Complicit really. How will I look my cousin in the eye and be expected to lie should she ever confront me?" I look at them both, wiping away a non-existent tear.

Following a laugh, Stacy gives me a slow, sarcastic clap.

"Nicely done. By chance any theatre experience in your past?"

I smile. "No. None. Just a natural."

"Name your price," he says then looks at Cordie. "Could be anything."

But for me, it's always about food or clothes. Sometimes sex. I sneak a peek at Stacy under my lashes.

Speaking of sex. Okay, better not.

"There's a gelateria in the plaza with the grocer. Some incredibly wonderful flavors. We could start by going there tonight."

Cordie's face shows the excitement I experience thinking of sweets, particularly gelato.

I swing my gaze to Stacy and raise one brow in question.

"Okay, tonight's easy, but am I to expected to pay out every day?" He raises one brow in a silent challenge.

"Shall we take it on a week-to-week basis? Tonight's payout will remove all memory of this meal. Should I have to harbor you food fugitives again, we'll decide on that occasion. Deal?" I extend my hand, hoping I don't look goofy but coquettish.

"Deal." His grip is warm and strong.

At first contact my pulse races. A warm tingly feeling fires up my arm and reaches straight for my girly parts, which raise their hands, waving madly to be touched. I start to pull my hand away, noticing that his lingers, as if he doesn't want to part, so I let it dawdle.

I have a small, quick fantasy about shoving the food from the table, crawling across it to him and letting him have his way with me right on the teak surface turned bed. I wouldn't mind if the legs gave way to our passion. I'd shop for a newer, sturdier table with pleasure; perhaps I'd make our sex be the litmus test of table quality.

"Okay then, I'm done. I'm saving room for gelato," Cordie says, pushing from the table.

Child alert! Child Alert! My brain screams.

Dear Lord! I've just had a sex fantasy with a child in the room. And it was about her father.

I gulp.

"Are you two going to work or just sit there and hold each other's hand?" I jerk my hand from his, clasping mine together.

"Why don't you go watch TV?" Stacy turns to me. "That's okay with you, right?"

"Oh, sure. The er...thingy is on the...er—"

"Remote is on the table?" Cordie looks between her father and I, likely wondering what's wrong with me.

"Yes," I say relieved that not all basic language has escaped me.

She walks the few short feet to my living room and throws herself on my couch. Her hair, pinked tipped like Pippa's, reminds me how lonely it must be for her having no mum. I spent a few years without a Dad but losing him was less impactful. I never wanted to talk clothes with a man, or boob issues, much less puberty and the always poorly timed and never welcome period.

Too bad Pippa has no interest in Stacy. Who better to mother a motherless child than a woman who was one herself?

"So." Stacy clears his throat in a husky, scratchy manly way. Sure, other men have cleared their throats in my presence before, but they've been the nasty boogie clearing variety. Not the raw, carefully bridled sex way Stacy does.

Or so that's how I choose to interpret his throat clearing. I'm also going to assume his desire for me leaves him choked up. I'm not going to question what he thinks of my height, or the width of my hips. Or that we can't do anything about this powerful sexual tension between us. I'm going to ignore, briefly, that a child's emotions are involved. Instead, I'm going to bask like a goddess in the sun, embraced by the warmth being desired and wanted brings.

All this from a handshake. I'm a pathetic sod.

"About your business." He takes the container I've been eating from.

And...moment over.

Back to the realities of the cold truth that makes up my days.

I try not to glare at him, instead watch as he eats directly from the container. The familiarity of it actually causes a prick of pain. This is what people call the *Small Things*. This is what broken-hearted women lament once their lover has moved on.

"How's it going?" This conversation requires sustenance of weight. I forgo the basil spring rolls, reaching instead for the fried version.

"You've done a great job of keeping records on the shop."

"Really?" Yes, I'm surprised. Bookkeeping is my least favorite part of owning a business. It's drudgery. Healthy eating, exercise, bookkeeping, and sex with a man at least six inches shorter than me are also ways I define drudgery. To name a few.

I have avoided it at all cost, doing my books only when I had to. Read: when quarterly taxes were due.

Stacy chuckles. "Yeah. You should give yourself more credit."

Curious as to his meaning, I stop dipping my egg roll in the sweet and sour sauce and look at him.

He holds up his hand, prompting me not to say anything. "All I'm saying is you're great with clothes. And you know it. I'm case in point." He taps his chest. "I would have never thought I could put on a shirt with pink in it—"

"A hint of pink," I correct. He's wearing a white T-shirt with the palest of a blue, green, and pink pinstripe. Not overly manly on the rack but on a form like his, delish.

"Yes, a hint of pink. As I was saying. I never thought I'd wear *this* and still be comfortable and feel like myself. You did me right." The right side of his mouth lifts and becomes his adorably crooked smile.

It's powerful, that smile. Only men like him and Mr. Darcy possess it. Commonly mistaken for their normal everyday expression of pleasure, it's oh-so-much more. It hints to something underneath, something delightfully wicked or mischievous.

He continues. "You are so good at clothes; it's reflected in your numbers. Which you've done a great job of keeping...for the store."

Wait. I cease focusing on his smile and play back the last few words he said.

"What do you mean, for my store? That is my sole business."

He shakes his head. "No actually, the personal shopping should be taken out of the store finances. They are two different beasts. And you haven't done as good a job keeping those numbers." He sets his chopsticks down, likely expecting to have an intelligent, articulate conversation about what he just said. "All I can give you right now are the numbers for opening a business similar to the one you have here."

"Right. That's all I need." Why do I feel as if the rug is about to be pulled from beneath me?

"Don't kill the messenger." He shifts in his seat before pulling out a piece of paper.

"These are the numbers your business, the brick and mortar store, makes. My best guess is it's bringing in twenty to forty percent of your revenue. Probably closer to twenty."

I shake my head. How can that be possible?

Did he just tell me that my store only makes a twenty percent profit? "Tell me in a different way."

"I'm saying that when I look at your profit but tease out what's from the store versus the personal shopping, it looks to be about twenty percent of your income. That's going high, to be honest."

"Hang on, you just said up to forty—"

"Yeah, you had one month that was high and I used that to ease the pain." He grimaces.

"So my store isn't profitable?" I blink slowly, processing the info.

"It is. It's just not the bulk of your income. Any chance you have kept a different log for the other portions you do?"

"You mean the personal shopping?" I'm still reeling.

"Yeah and the photos you send. I noticed you charged people for that."

"In a way. I've been meaning to sort it out and get it plugged in." I gesture to the computer.

"Can I take a look?"

I swivel the computer to me and pull up my emails. "They're all in here. I can do a search for bills and print them." I reach into my messenger bag that hangs on the back of the chair. "Here's more." I hand him a notebook bound by a fat rubber band. Papers stick out from all sides.

He takes the book. "I'll go through this." He faces me again. "Are you determined to open a second shop?"

"I am." It's been my life's dream. I picture Mum's goal thermometer. I see the OVERDUE stamp on their bills

"Then based on what I have in front of me, this is what you can afford to finance, unless you want to take on a partner." He turns a paper toward me and I search for the number, scanning the sheet.

I gasp. "I don't want a partner."

"I wouldn't suggest you get one either. Just shift your focus."

"But...."

"If you want to expand here, in Daytona, there are lots of small business loans that can help you do that. But a new location? That's your hurdle."

My gaze falls on the number he's referring to. It's shockingly low. It's two-thirds less than the number I had established. I can't buy a building with a two-thirds cut. I can't rent something reasonable with the one third left.

I blink.

I blink again. My brain can't compute and staying true to my fashion, I look for an escape.

I find it with Stacy.

CHAPTER EIGHTEEN

HE SITS BACK AND RESTS HIS ARM OVER THE CHAIR'S
back, his t-shirt pulling taut across his yummy swimmer's
chest and I instantly go somewhere else. A place with sheets
tangled between legs and hands caressing flesh. A place that
brings me happiness and not grief.

"I've lost you, haven't I?" With his free hand, he takes an
egg roll from the carton and stretches ever so slightly to dip it
in my bowl of sauce.

I can't stop staring at his long fingers, remembering what
they felt stroking my flushed skin. How eager he was to
touch me. How he'd tell me he wanted more after I'd just
given him everything.

Inadvertently, because I was daydreaming, I drop the
remains of my egg roll into the sauce; splashing it all over his
hand and roll.

"Oh dear. So sorry," I say and in my haste to grab a
napkin, I knock over the bottle of soy sauce. Stacy, in the
process of reaching for his own napkin, is leaning forward
at the same moment the soy sauce bottle bounces against

the table, on its side, spraying soy on his shirt with each bounce.

Now, I've done it.

See Jayne be a klutz.

"Bloody hell, I'm awfully sorry. You better go home and spray that shirt right away if you want those stains to come out." Profusely, I feed him napkins and go so far as to make one awkward attempt to dab at the splatter.

"I don't have stain remover. I keep forgetting to get some." He's wiping the sticky orange sauce off his hand without any sense of urgency.

One crisis at a time I suppose is his motto. Though I do want to scream that he needs to hurry before the stain sets.

"Here, hand me the shirt. I'll spray it and try to get the spots out. You can go grab another." I stand and wait with my hand out.

He blinks once and smiles before pulling his shirt off by reaching behind his head and grabbing it from the back collar.

The rippling of his shoulder muscles begs me to run my hands over the hills and valleys and maybe tangle my fingers in the small smattering of his chest hair.

Cripes, he's yummy.

He places the shirt in my hand and I jerk into action, rushing to my laundry room. I'm spraying the special stain mixture I make at home, taking care to get each of the little spots, when he says my name.

Startled, I squeal. Having not expecting him to follow me into the room, I jump as well and clutch the spray bottle to my chest.

"Bloody hell you scared me." I take a deep breath, forcing my gaze to be anywhere but on his naked chest.

"I only wanted to say you don't have to go to all this trouble." He steps into the small room. The only way out is either around him or back into my dark and dusty garage.

"It's no bother. I should have this worked out by the time you get back from getting a shirt," I hint.

He closes the door behind him. Would it send the wrong message if I dashed away through my garage and ran the ten plus miles to the pub? I'm not sure I can be in this space with him without compromising myself.

"Jayne," he says in a low, husky whisper. "I was wondering; do you think of that night we shared? I know I said I didn't but...."

I stare up into his blue eyes. And involuntarily step toward him. "Sometimes." My voice is breathy and the word quivers off my tongue. I lick my parched lips.

"Me too. Or more often than that." His nostrils flare slightly.

I fling the shirt and bottle to the floor and leap on him like the starving woman I am. I want to lick him from head to toe. Binge eat until I can't stand another taste and then I want to do it all again.

He wraps me in his arms and hoists me so I'm able to wrap my legs around his waist. In two steps, he has me against the washing machine and is pushing the hem of my dress up while simultaneously sliding his hands up my thighs.

I moan, cup his face between my hands, and kiss him with all I have, sweeping my tongue against his.

"Jesus, I want you," he says when we come apart, and he roughly tugs my hips forward, grinding me against him.

"One more time," I propose. "What harm is one more time?"

"No harm. None whatsoever," is his answer before he spreads sucking kisses down the column of my neck.

I caress his chest, rubbing my thumb over his scar and have one of his nipples between my thumb and index finger, ready to pinch the way he likes, when a small voice calls from the other side of the door.

"Dad? Are you in there?"

No sooner does Cordie's question penetrate my brain do I shove him away.

"I am," Stacy says, raking his hands down his face before tugging at the crotch of his jeans.

What is wrong with me? We shouldn't be doing this. The reasons why are numerous.

Hmm, let me count them, and in the meantime maybe my common sense will return.

One: Cordelia. She's an innocent who eats at my house, hangs with my cousin, and is struggling with adjusting to a new school and friends all without the guiding hand of her grandmother, who she's had up until now.

The last thing she needs is someone to cause more havoc. Namely, me.

"I dropped the spray bottle and your father's getting it for me," I say and shrug. I'm so lame.

"Or you're making out in there," she calls through the door before mumbling, "Cause that's what I need."

The child's headed for a Mensa membership; clearly she's not buying any of this.

I jump from the washer and smooth my dress before picking up his shirt from the floor. Stacy picks up the bottle, holds it over his crotch, and then swings open the door.

I try to hide behind him.

"Is there something you wanted?" he asks her.

"To go get the ice cream." Her expression says it all: irritation but also a bit of fear. I saw it on Pippa's a million times when she was younger. Born from the uncertainty of not knowing how or where you fit in.

"Why don't you two go? You can bring me back something; drop it off on your way home. I need to stay here and look at those numbers you were telling me about." And maybe finish what he started or else there'll be no concentrating on anything, much less numbers.

I'm a rotten old slapper thinking these things in front of a child. His child.

"Fine with me," Cordie says. Drawing the metaphorical line in the sand.

"They have a nocciolo that is my favorite. It's hazelnut." I try to smile in such a way that's friendly and not threatening.

"I'm allergic to nuts," is her retort.

"You are not." Stacy places a hand on her shoulder. He turns her around and pushes her to the door. "Why would you say such a thing?"

"I could be allergic to hazelnuts. When was the last time I had any?"

"This morning when you put Nutella on your toast."

"Oh," she says in a smallish voice.

"Thanks for dinner." I hand Stacy his shirt.

"Let me know if you have any questions. We can go over the numbers in more detail. I have some thoughts about your business." He gives Cordie's shoulder a squeeze and turns her toward me. "What do you say, Cords?"

"Thanks for letting me watch TV." She keeps her gaze on everything but my face. "It was really interesting. Educational. Though I'm confused about what a tossed salad is."

"Anytime," I murmur automatically. "Wait, what did you say?"

"A tossed salad." She crosses her arms over her chest and finally looks at me.

Stacy glances at me, puzzled, and I check my watch. It's minutes after nine.

"Er, by chance were you watching The Food Network?" I pray fervently that she was.

"Nope, something called Babs and the Football Team. I like football, right, Dad? But this didn't make any sense. One minute they're in school and the next he's pushed her against the locker asking if she'll toss his salad. I want to go to a school that offers salads."

"Jesus Christ." He spins his daughter on her heel. "You know better than that go to any other channel than the ones you are allowed to watch."

"It's a naughty channel, right? Jayne watches naughty TV," she says over her shoulder.

I cringe. Meeting Stacy's gaze, I say, "I'm so sorry. I forgot to mention it. It's a free subscription and—"

"I have to get her home and bleach her eyes. If you want to run by your business ideas with me, I can give you the pros and cons. But I'm not sure a second shop is the best move for you."

He hustles her to the door, talking to me over his shoulder. But I don't hear anything. All I can think about is how his child watched soft porn at my house and once the girls catch wind of this it'll go on my Jayne's-a-bloody-awful-pseudo-parent list.

Once they're out the door, I lean against it and try to catch my breath.

This is not good. NOT GOOD. What might happen

between Stacy and I, how it affects Cordie, all of it is nothing more than trouble. And I mean trouble so large it's made from one of those bold and puffy fonts used to scream its meaning from the page.

TROUBLE.

More determined than ever, I know what needs to be done, and if it requires more alone time with the personal assistant I bought at Kenley's sex party a few months ago, so be it. I'll get over my craving for him, eventually.

Maybe find a kick-your-man-habit boot camp printout on Pinterest? I can make a board for it. Outfits and accessories that help a woman beat her addiction to a certain man.

Laughing at my own idiocy, I dig my phone from my purse then send a voice memo to Paisley saying, "Pippa's out. They aren't matching like I thought they would. Still interested in helping me set up Stacy? You mentioned a friend? I'm open to suggestions on how to bring them together. Let me know."

Within seconds she responds with a text: *Leave it to me.*

An hour later, I receive a second text from Paisley: *Two Saturdays from now. UF football game. All of us. More info to follow.*

Operation Kicking the Stacy Habit has begun.

I crack open a fortune cookie only to find this stupid-arse message: *The fortune you seek is inside another cookie.*

CHAPTER NINETEEN

Atlanta—Buckhead actually—my once- contingency plan, has skyrocketed to the top of the list. I developed a business plan for the trendy, well-coiffed mum-town because Miami is officially off the table. Holding onto a lost cause will get me nowhere. It helps that I've had a recent increase in personal shoppers from the area and am developing a reputation.

Jayne Grandberry is not a dummy. At least I try hard not to be.

I sip a lovely cup of iced green tea and wait for a client's highly recommended estate agent. Apparently this gent is a prodigy when it comes to finding the perfect property and right now I need something, a sign to tell me I'm on the correct path.

But it needs to be a clear sign. Like a strong wind blows me into the right building or a bank gifting me money. Jesus, or some other divine entity, should pay a visit and simply tell me what to do and since I'm taking a command, I'd happily accept accompanying instructions.

Or a winning lotto ticket. I could set Mum and Dad up. They could take off "dead week" guilt free and go mourn the passing of Elvis with the rest of the fanatics who secretly believe he's still alive.

Oh, how I really want to give that to her.

Swirling the ice in my plastic cup, I tune out the chatter around me. Pippa would hate this place, as coffee is her soapbox. Last week she tried to replace Stacy's coffee with an alternative and reported that she'd never seen a man's eyes look as if they were going to pop out of his head. She said the vein that runs up his neck to the side of his head was pulsing and throbbing with such intensity she believed he'd stroke out right in front of her eyes.

The story from Stacy later that night, as he and Cordie grilled steak and potatoes behind my flat, was a similar retelling. Throbbing vein and all. Stacy and I somehow moved past the embarrassing child-watching-TV-porn-whilst-we-snog-in-laundry-room evening—or maybe we're ignoring the awkwardness—and now their visits were a pleasant custom I've come to depend upon.

"Jayne?"

Looking up, I'm surprised to find a tall, towhead, sharp-featured yet strikingly handsome man standing there.

"Yes." I stand and continue to look upward.

What? Have I found another man taller than me? It appears I have.

I look into warm gray eyes and smile. "Yes, I'm Jayne."

"I'm pleased to meet you. Our mutual friend speaks highly of you and it brings me great pleasure knowing I'm a part of helping you actualize your dreams. I'm Fitzwilliam Davis."

Fitzwilliam? The same fist name as Mr. Darcy? It it

possible? Is that a sign? Could it be? I want to stomp my foot in frustration and rail to the clouds above, "I said a clear sigh. This isn't clear."

I hold out my hand and he takes it, his grasp warm and light and soft. As first impressions go, it's a good one, professionally speaking. He's skillfully puts me at ease without getting overly familiar.

"Fitzwilliam?" He doesn't have an accent unless one could consider his southern drawl.

"My mother was a lifelong fan of Jane Austen and *Pride and Prejudice* in particular." His voice, though deep and masculine, is quiet and everything about this man is...gentle. If he were a preacher, he'd swindle the life savings from a gazillion women, easy.

"Aren't most women?" I say.

He straightens his jacket. "Everyone calls me Davis. I've brought several options for you to peruse." He reaches into his soft leather briefcase and pulls out a bundle of pristinely bound paper, held together with one of those plastic coils.

"Er...thanks. I'm curious about the options." I gesture for him to take the seat next to me, my thoughts on signs and interpreting their meaning.

"Do you mind if I get some joe? May I get you anything?" He has an easy smile.

"No, thank you." There's something intriguing about him. His form is quite lovely, lithe, and he moves with an easy grace. Everything he does is with gentleness. No pulling out a chair and scraping the feet against the floor, it's as if the chair glides away from the table on its own. There's no slinging his bag onto the seat, it's placed with care before he slips off to place his order.

He's exactly the sort I envisioned I'd end up with.

And yet I feel no attraction whatsoever. Is the universe saying, "Clear enough?"

It sure feels like a sign. Or a lesson.

I'll admit that I've been thinking more about the personal life of Jayne and less about the business. And with that comes a heavy case of guilt. Slowing my pace is an option that I've ruled out. Not because I fear my Mum's wrath or the potential of being haunted by my debt thermometer. Truth is, I want to make that stupid thing all red. I want to be the subject of another brilliant young entrepreneur article. I want my parents to know I've got their back. Getting distracted by a guy is the last thing I need.

With forced enthusiasm and heart, I flip through the pictures and brief descriptions of empty buildings. I don't dare look at the costs. I come up short when my gaze lands on a picture so charming I coo. Walls lined with wooden shelves; stained glass windows, many arched; and a large wooden door with antique brass handles.

I'm in love.

"That used to be a book store. The owner passed unexpectedly. It's been a real loss to the community." He eases into a chair, having come upon me like a ninja.

I want to take a snapshot of him and sent it to Josie with my Wickham list. To show her relatively attractive and successful men do exist and that not all of them would be settling. But she'll want to dissect and compare and I'm afraid I wouldn't be able to provide an argument as easily as I could have in the past. I'd likely agree with most everything she'd say.

"I love it. The character would suit my shop well." I fade into a quick fantasy. A second shop using books themes when displaying clothes. Maybe dresses donned by beloved famous book characters? Would I be able to find some mannequins that look like regency period women and others who evoke visions of highland lasses and men in kilts? Mentally, I've left the coffee house and am on a plane to exciting locations to shop for unique outfits. I could get Cordie a scarf in her family tartan, Stacy a tie.

"Would you like to see this one first?" Davis brings me out of my fugue. With a sigh, I tuck the daydream away.

See Jayne be a responsible adult regardless of how much it sucks.

I scan the page for the price. "It's to own, correct? Not let."

"That's correct. The family who owns it want to finish up with the owner's estate and divide the funds. This is the last to go and, I'm willing to speculate, they might come down on the price."

It's then my gaze falls upon the price and I involuntarily gasp.

"Don't freak out." Davis scoots closer to me, his hand covering the numbers on the paper. The nutty aroma of his coffee and the lack of urgency in his voice woo me into a relaxed state.

"It's more than I wanted to spend," I say in the same dulcet tone.

"Let's go see it. It's right around the corner. We can sip our drinks and talk. There's no commitment and I'd like to get to know you better." His voice drops at the end and the shift in his tone is subtle, of course, but my woman instincts kick in.

I'll need another sign, obviously, but I think he was flirting with me.

I wait for the rush of excitement that comes with first-time flirting. Nothing.

When my focus shifts away from the potential of the bookstore building and onto the potential of what is sitting in front of me, I say, "I'm not the sort to tease myself with what I can't have. I don't want to see the building if there's no chance I can get it."

"Do you have a budget?" He sips his coffee.

Ugh, a budget.

"I do." I focus on the remains of my iced green tea, shaking the ice. Silently cursing Stacy and his calculator. Not that he uses one. All his gray matter is what I should be angry with. I know people say that numbers don't lie, but how is it a second shop wouldn't turn more profit? Riddle me that.

"If you're looking for backers, I have a list of investors that are always looking to support small, local businesses."

"I'm not sure I'm ready for—" Stacy had discouraged the idea of an investor.

"Silent partners. Never interfere. You run the business; they foot extra capital and take some of the profit. Some are willing to do a fade-out partnership." He sits back, giving me space and breathing room and allowing the opportunity between us to plant, take root, and sprout.

"Fade out?" I push my tea away before taking a notepad and pen from my purse.

"Yes, are you not familiar with it?" He scratches his chin. "Well, I suppose it's not common practice. It works like this." Pulling a pen from inside his jacket pocket, he gestures to my notepad. After my nod, he slides it toward him.

"I'll use whole numbers because they're easier. You put up this amount." He writes a number less than my budget.

"The backer puts up the difference." He writes the number I thought I was playing with all on my own. "You set terms and it's simple math really, interest is added and you pay the loan back in the given time." He adds the number together, does a quick addition of interest that I make a mental note to ask Stacy about, and divides it by seven years.

"Why seven?" I ask.

"I just picked it at random. You could do two if you wanted or twelve."

"What if the shop doesn't work out? What if I have to close it?" I won't deny there are alarm bells. But I also won't pretend I'm not intrigued. If I can get terms less than a bank without having to jump through as many hoops, I'd consider it.

"You will have to pay pack what you borrowed with interest. But do you really think you'll fail?"

"And you think this could be less?" I slide the paper with the picture of the shop from under the note pad and touch my finger to the listing price.

"Significantly. It's a lot to think about, but why not see the building in person? You'll be more informed. You might find it doesn't suit." He tips his empty coffee toward me as if to say the timing couldn't be any better.

"I do have a bit of time before my flight." Where's the harm? There's no commitment and if one is going to dream why not dream big? Mum has always taught that the smart business is in the tangibles and this building has tangibles I like. It's the same dream, really, taking on an investor. Only a modified version. Maybe I shouldn't hold so tightly to every specific detail to my plan. Be more flexible.

Davis stands, smooths the creases in his heavy linen trousers, and straightens his jacket. Normally, I find something arousing about a man who knows how to wear clothes...and pick them. I'm surprised to discover that I prefer a pair of well-worn jeans to Davis' crisp linen pants.

He then extends his hand to help me from my seat. "It's an easy stroll. You can tell me about what brings you across the pond and I'll bask in the sensual tones of your accent."

Sensual tones? Most decidedly flirting. I glance at him and wonder if I could date him for longer than my standard six weeks. How would he fit in with my circle of friends?

"Did you want another drink for the walk?" I gesture to the bar.

He shakes his head and indicates I should precede him. He guides me from the coffee shop, his hand on the lower portion of my back, and moves silently at my side, the door gliding open before I've had a chance to reach for it.

"How does one go about finding these private investors?" I ask, more curious than hedging for an opening. Josie has always offered to be a silent investor. Heaven knows she has plenty of money, having come into her trust fund last year. But I'm not a fan of borrowing from friends or family and being beholden to someone long term, someone who is unpredictable or might have a different agenda, is a situation I've avoided. Yet, here I am. It was setting the terms for a buyout that intrigued me.

"Through networking mostly, investors with property looking to diversify. What makes you want to open a business in Buckhead?"

"I have a shop in Daytona that's doing well. I get a fair number of clients from this area and Miami. Expanding into those markets makes sense." I don't bother spewing Stacy's belief about the personal shopping because without the shop to bring the clients in, however would I find them to personal shop for? One begets the other.

"We would love to have you up here. I think you'll really enjoy the atmosphere. It's great for singles."

He stops quickly and ducks his head briefly, almost boyishly, looking up at me with what I interpret is an apologetic gaze. "I'm sorry. I didn't mean to assume you're single. I don't see a ring, and maybe it's wishful thinking on my part but I leapt to the conclusion that you weren't married."

"I'm not married."

"Dare I hope?" He places both his hands over his heart. "No someone special?"

I shake my head. "Not this week."

Immediately the apologetic expression is gone, replaced by the easy, light one from the coffee shop.

"Wonderful news," he says briefly clapping his hands together. "Hopefully, I can convince you to fall in love with our city, woo you away from the bikers and spring breakers of Daytona, and introduce you to the tennis players and wine-tasting groups we have here."

Ugh, doesn't tennis require exercise? Has the video universe of YouTube ever documented a graceful giraffe? Do cartoons ever depict them as tennis players? I think not. I'd take a biker over that any day. But the wine tasting sounds lovely. I know how to sip gracefully and am accomplished enough to do so without spilling on my clothes.

"My mum and dad are in Daytona. Leaving them would be difficult." And I leave it at that. I like these moments, where one's fantasy is better than the reality. Davis thinks I might be the tennis sort. It's a better fantasy than the stag-gering realities of the non-exercising, bean-and-bagel-consuming glutton I am. Remain a mystery. Perpetuate the myth. All repeat advice one can glean from reading any geared-toward-women-and-knows-better-than-you magazine.

There must be some truth to it I suppose.

We walk in silence a short block before Davis begins to whistle a floaty tune that makes me think of Cary Grant and Katherine Hepburn films.

This is nice. And though I struggle for something to say, his whistling is the perfect reason not to say anything at all.

I glance up, finding his gaze on me, and smile. Without breaking stride or stanza, he slows and gestures to the building ahead by two doors.

Situated one block away from the high end shopping of Peachtree Road is a row of older brick stores, the one I'd fallen for in the middle.

"No wonder the price is so high." From where I stand I can see the signs for Buckhead Village, Jimmy Choo's, and French cuisine.

"Yes, but this block has yet to be renovated. It's obvious that Buckhead Village will do all the work for you with finding clients. Come inside." He fits a key in the lock and pushes open the heavy wood door.

It's better than I imagined and more than I could hope for. Instantly I take a step back.

Nothing good comes from wanting something you can't have.

Only heartbreak and insatiable longing.

Davis softly presses his hand to my lower back. "You're just looking. Not buying."

And, as though I've seen a waiting lone chocolate éclair on a shit of a workday, my self-control is out the window and I'm cramming the goodness and comfort of chocolate and cream in my face. Yet, this is solid pine floors, hand carved glossy white medallions with trim chandeliers so delicate and round they look made for a cotillion.

Large built-in shelves, once cradling first edition books (or so I like to hope) would showcase one of a kind jewelry and scarves from the four corners of the world. I run my hand along the wainscoting that wraps the room.

"Come see the back. There's an office with a window."

Two French doors with porcelain knobs divide the front from the back.

After a walkthrough of the rest of the space, all presenting with the same handcrafted charm of the main room, Davis asks, "You love it right? It seems meant for you."

I sigh; part with determination and part sadness. For years to come I will remember this building and the business I could have built here.

As if sensing my thoughts, or more accurately reading my sigh, Davis says, "Location. Location. Location."

"Which is really good. Off from the main flow a wee bit but that makes the traffic slightly lighter and easier to get to it." I look around one last time and dig deep for that steely reserve I know is in there somewhere, looking in the same place I pull from when I have the overwhelming urge to lick Stacy like an ice cream cone.

"It's out of my range, Davis. There's no point entertaining it any further." I'll have to rethink Buckhead. And that thought only brings forth the disappointment and frustration I felt with Miami. I have the mental image of the empty debt thermometer exploding.

"It doesn't have to be." Davis doesn't move. Not his hands in his pockets, no coins jingling, and not his shoes across the floor. He's relaxed and his lack of urgency could nearly blind my senses, much like a seventy-five percent off shoe sale does. But I would need a second mortgage on my flat. I would have to make concessions I never imagined.

"I've never had an interest in a partner. Silent or not." I swing my bag onto my shoulder, tucking the bulky part under my arm and gesture toward the door with my head. "Shall we?"

I don't wait for Davis before leaving the building.

"I hear what you're saying, Jayne. Honestly, I do. So I ask this with trepidation. Would it be all right if I send you some dossiers, if you will? You can get a feel for what the investor is like, what they're willing to spend, and their philosophy."

"Er...."

"I love my community. I want to see if grow and flourish. I think you would be a good fit here, from what I know and have learned about you. That's why I—"

"Push?"

He ducks his head but continues to look at me. "Yeah."

The ease at which he presses his agenda is quite smooth and non-threatening. Had I been a less cynical person, I'd not notice.

But he got you inside to see the building.

Point taken. I step aside, closer to the curb, and scan for a taxi. As luck would have it, one is coming toward me. As I raise my hand to flag it I say, "Thank you, Davis. But I'm not confident that's the best plan."

"Just give it a look. I'll get something to your email before your plane takes off. If nothing else, think of it as medicinal, the tool to help you sleep through your flight." His laughter is just as light and breezy as his demeanor and I'm laughing with him before I realize it. There is no affront. No force. Just a suggestion to keep an open mind and that I can do.

Right, I do it all the time when selecting clothes to purchase or outfits for my clients.

I extend my hand. "Okay. I appreciate your patience."

He clasps my hand in between both his and gently squeezes. "I hope we see each other again, Jayne. Even if it's not about this building."

The taxi slides up to the curb, causing my skirt to dance in the wind. I feel womanly and desired and the combination, something I first experienced with Stacy, makes me lightheaded.

Funny how there is little threatening about this man before me. If I held him to my Wickham list, he'd likely come away a winner. Yet in a moment of clarity I admit that my list has changed, practical must haves replaced with those driven by desire and passion. Davis would have been a winner on the old list. But on the new list, one with several blanks, he'd never get passed the first entry.

Must make my pulse race.

It's uncharacteristic of me to put something this incorporeal on my list.

But I like the way it feels. The way it makes me feel. Even if it will fade with time. Perhaps if it was once present it can be found again?

CHAPTER TWENTY

Stretching out my legs, I appreciate the wisdom in Stacy's choice of vehicles, as he favors the SUV varieties.

"Do you guys go to these games often?" Stacy asks, one hand draped lazily over the steering wheel, his other arm resting on the center console.

"I know that Paisley and Josie have but I've avoided them for the most part, to be honest."

Happily, I leave all thoughts of the shop behind. My attention on Stacy. Well, not in the lustful way. I mean I must hook him up with someone soon, because in the week that I've been home he and Cordie have had dinner at my house three nights, we've played one board game (I did not get bored like I did when Pippa and I played as children), and I've had six erotic dreams about his taut stomach, broad shoulders, and those long fingers of his.

He's got to go. A girl only has so much self-control.

Last night, while sharing a carb-rich meal of pasta with loads of meat (veggies pushed to the sides of both mine and Cordie's plates), and several rounds of bruschetta, I found myself staring at Stacy's hands. The way he held the tiny bread so as to not lose any toppings or how strong they looked as he held his beer. I caught myself mooning over how sweet and endearing it was to see him stroke Cordie's head, tangling her locks between his fingers before dropping a fatherly kiss to her forehead.

Soon, I'll need an intervention, but Mum would be the only one to show up.

"Are you a football fan?" I scan my phone for the few tidbits Paisley gave me about her friend, Evie, who is the latest in Operation Jayne Hates The Idea Of Sex With Hot Men, as Paisley has so eloquently termed it.

Even though I do *not* hate sex with hot men. Particularly Stacy. But no matter how much I protest that casual sex between us is a guaranteed, to borrow a term from Paisley, clusterfuck, my words fall on deaf ears. Josie shakes her head and laughs at all my reasons.

"I'm not a big college ball fan. Having grown up outside Seattle, I'm a Seahawks fan—"

"SEAHAWKS," Cordie yells from the back seat and pumps her fist.

"That's my girl!" Stacy lifts his hand and they high five.

Cordie comes between our seats. "Can I play Minecraft now, Dad?"

"Yeah, but know that this is eating into your screen time. Wear the headphones. If I hear that music anymore I'm going to go berserk."

"Thanks, Dad." She's gone in a flash, headphones on and face buried in a tablet.

"She's a good kid," I say without thinking. Because she is. More like a miniature adult than a child.

"She is. Moving here, not having my mom around, and

adjusting to this new routine has been difficult but she's done a fantastic job."

"You've done a fantastic job."

"We've had our struggles. Learning to be just the two of us, without my parents, has been good for us. And all the vitamin D she's getting now has probably helped with her mood and made that transition easier."

I chuckle. Having grown up in overcast Oxfordshire, I can relate. To this day I'm not sure which climate I like the best, as there are attributes to both I love equally.

Then it dawns on me. Stacy and Cordie learning to be a family was not something I had considered when I made the blanket assumption they needed a woman in their lives.

I'm reminded of that common adage about the word assume.

Undoubtedly, I've made an arse of me. Hopefully, though not of Stacy.

And all this while driving to a football game where set up number two is waiting to meet the lovely single father and his equally adorable child.

"Er...may I ask a personal question?" Like I'm not going to anyway.

"Sure." He turns slightly in his seat toward me.

"She told me about her mum. Do you know where she is?"

He glances in the rearview mirror before shifting closer and saying in a low voice, "Yeah, she'll send cards occasionally. Honestly, I think the day is coming soon where Cordie will want to meet her. Though I'm not sure Karen will ever be ready for that. Guilt's a terrible thing."

I shrug because the truth is guilt is only a terrible thing for people who have a conscience. I doubt my biological father has ever once given me a second thought. The one time I accidentally shared space with him on the tube, heading back to University from Nana's house, he showed no recognition whatsoever when he caught me staring at him. Me, unable to close my mouth or look away. Him, annoyed by the stranger who didn't have the wherewithal to avert her gaze.

"Does she want a mum?" A question I might have wanted to know the answer to before I thrust Pippa into their path.

"I don't think she noticed she didn't have one because she had my mother. Until now that is." Whether he wants me to or not, I interpret his smile as a wee bit sad.

"How are your parents?"

"Great. They're in Istanbul. It's my mom's every wish to travel and see the places my dad has and now she is."

"Being a photographer, your dad must have seen some amazing places. Sounds wonderful," I murmur, trying to think of a way to bring our conversation back to what I need to know.

He's dressed in a short sleeve gray and maroon college t-shirt with MIT in bold athletic font.

"I see that the movers didn't lose this." I finger the fraying hem of the sleeve. When my knuckles graze the top of his arm I want to giggle as touching him makes me feel like a sixteen-year-old virgin excited to be so close to such a divinely arousing specimen of a man.

"Lucky, right?"

"I suppose. I'm sure they sell these online."

"Yeah, but I've had this one since the first week I started college. It's my good luck shirt." He moves ever so slightly and the result is more of my hand coming into contact with his skin. Firestorms of desire shoot up my arm and course through my body setting me aflame.

I let myself get lost in the momentary fantasy of unclasping the safety belt, climbing over the console and straddling him. I can feel his hands on my ribs moving upward while the car magically drives itself safely down the road.

When I snap myself from the brief reverie, (remembering Cordie's in the back seat was all it took), I find I'm caressing his arm, stroking his muscle with my index finger. Coyly scraping my nail across the peaks and valleys.

"Jayne," he says gruffly, dragging out my name, weighing it down with need. The deep timbre of his tone makes my girly parts squeeze with hope.

I shift as far away as possible, press myself against the door, and wrap my hands under my knees in hopes of making them behave.

"I'm sorry. I don't know what came over me. I think we should stop for food. I feel a bit light headed." Heat radiates off my skin and I swipe a bead of perspiration from my brow.

"Did you eat?" He glances between the road and me.

"A bit," I lie, thinking of the bagels, bacon, and bowl of cereal I had before we met in the car park to begin our trip to Gainesville.

"Jayne," he says again. This time the need is replaced more with frustration. "What's happening between us?"

I twirl my earring before I speak, hoping I've selected the right words. "Chemistry, perhaps."

"Meaning when my O_2 mixes with your O_2 we get combustion?" He gifts me with his adorably crooked smile.

"The end result of combustion is devastation." I glance back at Cordie before continuing. "You know I'm more like a big sister to Pippa. As she lived with us from the time she turned six."

Stacy shrugs. "She mentioned something about that."

"Did she also mention that Mum worked long hours in our family's tea shop so I was often in charge of her and frequently forgot to feed her or pick her up from school or—"

"Weren't you a kid yourself?"

"Last year, Tyler, Heather's son, asked me if he could play with some of my Sharpies. I gave him some paper and told him to knock himself out. He colored all over his legs, arms, and face. With a permanent marker. You caught that part right?"

Stacy coughs discreetly but gives over and lets his laughter free; briefly looking away from me, I assume, to gain control.

"My Sharpies were pink, blue, purple, and black. He looked like his skin had a bad tie-dye job."

Stacy rubs his hand over his mouth. "What did Heather say?" His lips twitch.

"She didn't talk to me for two months. She was that mad. It also took that long for the color to fade."

"We all have moments we aren't proud of—"

"I'm not good with children, Stacy. It's not fair to the kid. You hear people saying things all the time about how some people shouldn't have children." I lower my voice. "I've never wanted any. Never. And knowing that, potentially taking on a child, would feel much like a huge injustice to the poor child."

"You're hard on yourself." The twitch in his lips is gone, replaced by the puzzled, thin pressed lips look.

"These are the formative years," I say quoting something Paisley has said a million times.

The silence that resides between us is laden with unspoken words, but to continue the conversation further to try to tease out a solution so we might have mad crazy sex against my washing machine will only take me on the one-way trip to heartbreak hotel, to borrow the term from Mum's one true love, Elvis.

I've got to turn the conversation back to the confirmation I seek, is he looking for something long term? But jumping right into it would add more to the awkwardness we're trying to avoid. In a flash of brilliance, I go for what works with most men.

"You think I'll draw any attention with this shirt?" I've worn my Oxford United jersey in defiance of the two teams playing, the Florida Gators and...oh, who am I kidding? I only know it's the Gators because of how many times Paisley has said it. I haven't registered the other team's name. Nor do I care to. I pull out my jersey. "After all, it's the original football whereas what you all—"

Stacy clasps his hand over my mouth. "Is something you should never say in public, at a stadium, packed with Americans who worship the pigskins as much as they do Jesus."

I push his hand away, laughing. "That serious, you say?" I ease from the door.

"Without a doubt. Have you been to a game before?"

"No." I shake my head for further emphasis. Had this not been the venue of a setup I would not be going at all. I don't understand American football. Nor do I understand painting one's face in team colors. It looks itchy and hot and the beads of perspiration across nearly every painted hooligan's face tells me I'm correct.

"Paisley says they're a blast," I say, mimicking Paisley's accent, which causes Stacy to laugh.

"They can be if you're in the right frame of mind." He eyes my jersey and I guess he's meaning my attitude toward real football and the American version.

So begins the gentle probing. "Speaking of Paisley, she mentioned she's bringing a friend. Sounds quite lovely. Evie, I think her name is. Isn't that a lovely name?"

Stacy gives me a puzzled look. "I hadn't given it much thought."

"She went to therapy school with Paisley, which means she's a good caretaker. Has that gene that enables her to self-lessly give to others in a meaningful way." I clamp my teeth together to shut my mouth. Gives to others in a meaningful way? What's that shite about? Who says that other than a person trying to set another up? Why not tell him what my intentions are? It would be easier.

Briefly, I close my eyes and try to picture the list Paisley sent me about Evie, searching for my next teaser, but when I open them Stacy is casting me curious glances.

"By that do you mean I'm to assume you're selfish?"

"Oh, terribly. How do you feel about redheads?" I hope my action of digging in my purse makes it seem like its casual conversation and not probing.

"I guess they're okay. I've never dated...wait a second. What's going on here?"

He jabs me in the shoulder with his long index finger. "Is this Evie a redhead by chance?"

Dammit, how do I get out of this? He knows I've never met her, so how am I to know if she's a redhead? I shrug and purse my lips as if I'm trying to recall but can't. Do I feign ignorance and then when he sees her claim happenstance? Or should I come clean?

I hear an imaginary clock ticking loudly as if my delay is about to time out.

"Er...." I twist my earring hoping, praying for inspiration when it hits. "Paisley might have mentioned something in passing." I shrug one shoulder. "But all this talk of mum's and children and I did the math, so to speak. You can appreciate that. What are the odds of you meeting an eligible, lovely, child-friendly woman? Hmm, answer that. You should—"

"You forgot willing," he says deadpan.

"I beg your pardon?"

"A willing and eligible, lovely, child-friendly woman. You forgot willing."

"Who wouldn't be willing after one look at you? You're a catch. A fantasy. And what you do with your hands is...oh my word...should be illegal." I open my mouth and insert both feet without thinking about it. I should keep snacks there as my feet are often visiting. Stacy stops at the red light. I know I shouldn't look but I'm desperately curious to see his reaction.

He breaks me with his unwavering glacial blue-eyed stare. "You're not willing."

I lean across the console before I say quietly; overly cautious for fear Cordie might hear. "I'm willing in the carnal sense but what good would that do us? How would that work out for Cordie?"

"Can't I be the judge of that?"

It's a relief when he turns his attention to the road and I ease back into my seat.

"So you want to set me up with Evie of the redheads?"

"I thought maybe it should be something to consider. You mentioned you were just out of a relationship so I'll understand if you aren't ready but...you do the math on the odds of meeting someone."

"And if it isn't right? Are you going to set me up with another friend? And then another? What about Pippa? How about her? You gonna add your own cousin to the list?"

I don't require a mirror to know my face is aflame. I can feel the heat wafting off me.

"Jesus, Jayne." He glances over his shoulder at his daughter then back to me. "We've had sex," he says before looking back at the road, shaking his head. "You really can deliver a hard blow to the old ego."

"It's not like that. You're perfect. I'm—"

"Don't give me the old 'it's not you, it's me' line, and don't tell me that if Cordie wasn't here and I pulled this truck over, reclined this seat, and pulled you on top of me, nothing would happen."

He's got me there.

CHAPTER TWENTY-ONE

All it takes is one remark from him about pulling me across his lap and I'm gone.

Just imagining makes me salivate.

As wide as the seats are in his SUV, I think it could work. There'd be enough space for both our legs and if not then the seats in the back lay down and....

I'm a pillock.

Cordie's in the back seat. I know we'd never do any such thing with her around. But why am I always picturing her not being around? Quite endearing of me, how I'd like to make her disappear much like my father, my biological father, did me. All for my own selfish reasons.

It's the reality check I need.

I once had a fortune cookie that read: *Your reality check's about to bounce.*

But not this one.

I try to pick my words carefully. "I won't deny that I'd have a difficult time walking away from that opportunity. But should lust be acted upon every time? Aren't there other issues to consider?"

He says nothing.

"We live across the street from one another."

"I'm aware of the arguments." He ends his statement by clamping his mouth closed, the small muscle in his cheek popping intermittently.

"We need a buffer. Like an electric fence between our places." Shock treatment is what I've been reduced to.

"So you figure if I'm dating other people that might act as a buffer."

"I don't poach." It's true. If he were dating others I might still be strongly attracted to him but I wouldn't find myself on my wash machine with his hand between my thighs.

He shakes his head and we both turn away from one another. The stadium looms in the horizon so I text Paisley our location.

It's going to be terribly awkward trying to set him up with someone if he's not talking to me. Rather, I suppose the whole thing is moot anyway. Silver lining to telling a guy he's only wanted for his body? That his kid is the reason you want to avoid him? He'll dodge you like the plague, rendering the problem solved.

I'll miss their company over takeaway meals and Graham Norton. I'll have to remember to give Cordie the how-to magazine I picked up for her about various braids and styles.

Without taking his eyes from the road he says, "So tell me about this Evie."

I let out the slow breath, my hands still clutching my phone. "Thank you," I whisper.

"I'm not doing it for you." He says without so much as a glance. "I did the math and you're right. The odds of finding a keeper are slim so I should take this chance. Find a good woman, make a good life, and raise a nice family. American dream and all that. Where are we meeting them?"

When he faces me, I expect to find a steely glint in his eyes, a checked anger but I come up lacking. I show him the map on my phone all while trying to discern what this means and more importantly how I feel about it.

"Cordie, we're here," he yells and reaches back to wave his hand in front of her tablet.

"What?" she says.

"We're here. Look there's Josie." He points over my shoulder to a parking spot that's currently being emptied of the lawn chairs our friends used to save the space for us. We're quickly settled and out of the car, Stacy moving away from me.

"Great timing," Paisley says, coming to stand next to me. "We just got situated and the grill is warming up." She looks blissfully happy and I see Hank standing near the men. I nudge her with my elbow and she gives me a side hug.

"I'm starving. Are there hot dogs?" Cordie asks and flops into a lawn chair next to Josie, tablet still in hand.

"Put that up. Time to talk to real people," Stacy tells her before moving to shake hands with the guys, Brinn and Hank.

I take a seat opposite of the person who can only be Evie, leaving the one next to her empty.

"Hallo, I'm Jayne." I wave to the lovely creature with her ginger hair pulled into a large fat braid and large sparkling brown eyes. She's exactly what I'd expect for Stacy, the kind of girl who'd look adorable driving a minivan, would never swear, always exercises, and knows not to give young children Sharpies.

"Hi, I'm Evie."

"Stacy," I call over my shoulder. "Come meet Evie." A delicate little bird who'll tuck nicely against his side and he can protect until the end of time.

I really have no right to be jealous. This was my idea, after all. Couldn't she just be knock-kneed or walleyed or something? Does she have to be so bleeding perfect?

"Oh, let me introduce you," Paisley says. "Evie and I went to high school together and occupational therapy schools as well, though she's a couple years older than me."

"It's nice to meet you, Evie." Stacy eases his long form into the lawn chair.

Does she notice how the jeans I bought him fit his bum so well? She can thank me later.

He continues, "We just moved here and it's nice to meet new people, hopefully make some new friends." He bestows that woman-killer smile on her and I turn away, desperate for a distraction, needing something for my hands. I catch Josie's eye and signal for a drink, as she seems to be the one handing those out.

"Where did you move from? Your daughter seems to be adjusting well," she says, looking at me.

"We're not married and that's not her daughter," Stacy says, waving a hand dismissively in my direction. "She's my neighbor. We carpooled here."

I've been reduced to sharing petrol and a filling an empty seat. Well, I asked for it, didn't I?

"Oh," Evie says. Then, "Oh" again only this time facing him. "Where did you say you were from?"

I turn away, my job, for the most part, done. Now it's in Stacy's capable and talented hands. I force myself to focus my attention on the others and plaster a broad (at least I hope it's large) smile on my face.

"Eight years I've lived in American and I've never cooked off the back of a tailgate nor have I eaten in a car park." I sip the lukewarm lemonade Josie handed me from an orange Solo cup.

"You lie," Josie says.

"Lie about what?" The oppressive fall heat leaves me wilty in my lawn chair, the netting sticking to the back of my legs.

"I watched you scarf down a chili dog in the parking lot during Bike Week last March." Josie tucks a sucker in her cheek, letting it protrude outward, and turns to Paisley. "Do you remember?"

Paisley, decked out in orange and blue sans face paint, though her ginger hair is the perfect complement, plops in the chair next to me. "It was two hot dogs. And she chugged a beer afterward."

"Give over." I turn to the group. "It was hot, I'd been working at my parents' pub serving fish and chips all day, and that was the first chance I had to eat." Some blooming friends I have.

"A chili dog sounds good right now," Paisley mumbles.

Her now-it's-official-boyfriend, Hank, a hot guy in his own right if one likes the military sort, is working the grill and laughs.

"All food sounds good to you." He delivers her a hot dog wrapped in a bun and follows it with a kiss.

"Can I get one?" Cordie looks up at Hank with the same crooked smile of cuteness her father has.

"After you're done eating, you want to paint your face?" Paisley waves some tubes in the air.

"Yeah, can I, Dad?" She bats those big eyes at Stacy, who is heavily engrossed in a conversation with Evie.

"Sure, honey."

Evie looks like she's about to melt out of her seat at the sweetness of it all.

"It must be hard being a single parent, a dad with a girl. I raised my sister for a few years and had the advantage of being the same sex to help me figure her out. But it was exhausting. I admire you," Evie gushes.

"I'd like my face painted," I say to Paisley. The agony of heavy makeup and a sweaty and itchy face is the distraction this moment calls for.

Paisley turns to me surprised. "Okay," she says before dropping her voice to the lowest whisper. "You all right?"

"Absolutely." Deep down I know this is the right thing to do. Deep down my girly parts weep. I hold my Solo cup up and give it a shake. "Josie, love. Got anything adult for this?"

CHAPTER TWENTY-TWO

A week later, Pippa and I hit the beach.

The night couldn't be better had Mother Nature herself planned it. The air is cool but not so that we need wraps and the moon large and full shining down enough light to guide us. And by us, I mean me, because to this day I still have to watch Pippa to understand the yoga moves.

A yoga pants wearer does not a yoga master make.

We've been careful to select a beach spot that won't interfere with the sea turtles that are hoping to make their grand adventure into the ocean. We've a cooler with some water and trail mix, I brought a large sack of rose petals for her to throw out into the ocean, and Pip is smoothing out a spot for us to get our yoga on. She spreads out the mats so they face the moon and the water.

With hopes of showing Pippa how she belongs with us, I invited Josie on the down-low and sent her a Find Friend alert to our location.

Even though it's almost midnight, the traffic along the

road is loud and busy, a distraction I always have a hard time blocking out.

"Okay, ready?" Pippa looks up at the moon.

"Er, don't be upset, but I invited Josie and she's three minutes out." I twist my earring and wait for her reaction.

She slowly looks from the moon to me. "She's going to come?"

It's hard for Pippa to see her value but she needs to know how much she is loved. "Of course, she didn't hesitate."

"I thought about asking but I wasn't sure if anyone would be interested in this. It's good karma to have such positive energy here when we do this. Thanks." She hugs me.

"Yeah, Josie will cancel out all my negative shite." I hug her back.

With a short shrill whistle, Josie alerts us to her presence. I look toward the pier, over the dune, and can barely make her out, waving an arm in the air. Thankfully she's dressed in light clothes like Pip and I. Behind her are others in light clothes. I count five heads; one is shorter than the rest.

"Well," I say.

"The others have come too," says Pippa, clasping her hands together gleefully.

"Hi, Hi," says Paisley. Her arms are loaded with towels. Each of them has a yoga mat slung over their shoulders.

"I hope you don't mind that I asked the others." Josie drops a larger cooler next to ours. Cordie by her side.

"No, no. I—" Pippa breaks off and covers her mouth.

"She's happy you all came. She would have invited you herself but she wasn't sure anyone would be interested," I interpret. "Aren't you up late?" I point to Cordie.

"She really wanted to come and Stacy said it was all right." Josie slings an arm over the child's shoulders.

"My mom's not dead, but she's gone and I'd like to..."

Pippa rushes to her and folds her into a hug. "Of course, darling. You deserve to be here. Let me explain the purpose. It's not so much a tribute to my mum as it is a way for me to let go of the hurt and anger I feel. Of not letting all that hold me back. It's my way of cleansing my soul and purging out all the extra junk I'm holding in there that's unhealthy."

"I'm really mad at her, my mom," Cordie whispers. "And my Mimi too. If she didn't want to travel, then we wouldn't have moved here." Her voice breaks at the end and the fracture matches the one in my heart.

Bless this child and her broken heart.

Josie squats before Cordie and says, "You all were moving here regardless of your Mimi traveling or not. It's because the job was here. But I know for a fact that your Mimi emails you every day and you all get to Skype once a week, right?"

Cordie nods.

"That means that even though you aren't together, she is always thinking of you. She misses you just as much," Josie says.

"It sucks here."

Pippa kneels next to Josie and takes Cordie's hand. "I know the feeling. I came here when I was a teenager. I felt like I was from a different world. That I didn't fit in. But it got easier with time and the same will happen for you. You will find the people you click with. You will find things you love and one day when you're older and you move away you'll realize that you miss it."

Heather swarms her as well, cooing and rubbing her back.

Because the child's near tears, I go for distraction. "After we leave here we go eat. You ever had a sundae after midnight?" I appeal to her stomach because in that way she is like me.

"And french fries?" She looks at me.

"Of course."

"That sounds awesome."

"Don't forget to thank your dad," Pippa reminds her. "All right, spread your mats next to ours or behind ours. Cord, you're next to me." Pippa directs us with the tone of an infantry officer. "Get in place."

Once we've all lined up, Pippa raises her arms up toward the moon. We follow suit and she lulls us with instructions. Why we're here, what we want to let go of, how to find the calm within ourselves, and though I've always come with an open mind, I've never had an open heart. But today, I try. Today I let go of my fears of failing Mum and Dad. Of not opening a second shop or making my monetary goal before thirty. I let go of what I thought my business expansion would look like and open myself up to other visions.

I follow Pippa's lead, bend in ways my long form finds awkward, but I'm thankful I'm not top heavy like Josie, who manages to make yoga look easy nonetheless. At the end, Pippa has us lying on our backs looking up and breathing. The tide is coming in, which means we'll be done soon. Something about the exercise and quiet is peaceful and in this moment everything is dandy. Soon we'll all go home to bed and in a few hours rise ready to face the day's challenges. All the questions and uncertainty that come with tomorrow are currently not present, and now I understand why Pippa is so keen about yoga.

Maybe I should give this more than a cursory attempt.

Add it to my lifestyle. Quieting the brain is a lovely experience, to be sure.

"Who's hungry?" Heather asks.

"First we throw rose petals and then we have food," Pippa says, rising from her mat and stopping to offer Cordie a hand.

I roll to the side, push up, and then quickly walk to the two silk shoe bags I'm using to store the rose petals. With them in hand, I walk back to the group and hand one bag to Pippa and the other to Cordie.

"Each of us will get to toss some petals into the ocean. I like to make it a wish when I do," Pippa tells Cordie, shrugging slightly. "But that's up to you."

Without having to be told, we line up behind either Cordie or Pippa and wait our turn. Each of us in our private moment making a wish or a prayer.

When I step up where the water thins against the shore, my toes sinking into the sand, I scoop the last of the petals and, while holding my breath, set them free. I wish for clear guidance. The others wait for me by the coolers, mats rolled and ready to go.

Excited, I say, "Let's eat."

The vibe is different, less melancholy. Having the others here has reminded me that we all struggle; we've all had loss that has shaped us into the people we are. It has reminded me that I'm not alone, not the oddball I might sometimes think I am.

The ride to the diner is less weepy than it's been in the past, more laughing. When we pull into the car park, Brinn and Stacy are waiting for us.

"Aw, the womenfolk," Brinn says, arms wide, waiting to

collect his wife. "Did you bay at the moon? Become one with yourself?"

"Hush." Josie elbows him in the stomach.

"It was *awesome*, Dad. Amazing." Cordie says, bounding around Stacy like an excited dog.

"So you had a good time?" He catches her by the elbow and slowly pulls her to his side. Pushing hair out of her face, he says, "I think you've gone over the threshold past being too tired."

"No, it's that I feel good. I'm not as sad as I was. I set it free into the ocean with the rose petals." She tugs free.

"Throwing flowers into the ocean made you less sad?" he asks.

"No, it helped me let it go." She stares up at him. But his blank expression tells her, and us, he doesn't get it. Cordie turns to us, arms up in question, shoulders in a shrug.

"Don't bother, hon," says Josie. "They'll never get it. But that's okay. On some things they need to be left in the dark."

"Who wants french fries?" Stacy asks as he falls in behind us.

Once inside we settle at a large table and order all my favorites, anything fried or dipped in cheese. Even Pippa breaks her strict diet rules and has a large three-scoop sundae covered with copious amounts of whipped cream. That much dairy will not agree with her tomorrow.

Cordie and I select smaller versions.

"So, Stacy," Paisley starts as she dips fries into a bowl of ketchup. "My friend Evie thought you were nice. Did you two switch numbers or anything?"

I glance at him and just as quickly away. I hadn't told Paisley that Stacy was in on the matchmaking. An oversight I hadn't recognized until right this moment.

"No. Was I supposed to?" He uses a spare spoon to scoop a bit of Cordie's ice cream.

"Ah, I suppose not if you didn't want it." Paisley looks at me and I shake my head slightly.

A peek at my watch shows I'm past my threshold too. It's going to be difficult enough getting up. "I'm afraid I need to go. Pip, you want a lift?" I ask while looking for quid in my handbag.

"Aye-ya, need to be at the pub early tomorrow." She looks at her watch and giggles. "Well, today that is."

I throw notes on the table and rise. Stacy stands up as well.

"Can you give us a ride home, too?" he asks.

"Right. Sure, I can." I look at Cordie, whose face is split in half by a wide yawn.

Brinn leans across the table and hands me the notes I threw down moments earlier. "I've got this. You all know my mom passed when I was a kid. It's because of that I'm the man I am today. Consider this my part in tonight's event."

Josie wraps her arms around him and says, "For that I will forever be thankful to your mom." Then plants a loaded kiss on his lips.

"Well, time to go," Paisley says, jumping up. "I'm so glad I insisted on driving, because we would be stuck here forever now that this has started up."

And she's not kidding. Josie and Brinn are whispering who knows what to each other, paying no never mind to the rest of us.

"It's exhausting, really." Heather pushes away from the table. "I'll meet you at your car, Paisley."

"It's gross," Cordie says and yawns again. "Dad and Jill used to do that all the time."

Stacy springs into action. "C'mon, kiddo, time for bed." He lifts her out of her chair then flips her across his shoulders like a wet towel.

"Dad, I'm too big for this," she cries as he begins to walk out of the diner.

"You're never too big for your dad," he says and spins back toward me. Only I was right behind him and his sudden change causes me to slam into him. The shock of impact fires up every nerve ending with tingly loveliness. "Maybe I should drive. You're dead on your feet."

"If you insist." I hand him my keys.

Both Pippa and Cordie climb into the back and when Stacy slides into my seat, he cuts his eyes to me and sighs before making a production of sliding the seat back a few notches. As if his knees were behind his ears or something. But it's bloody adorable and I'd laugh if I weren't thinking of him and this Jill snogging all the time.

Stacy backs out and when he looks over his shoulder, that adorable, crooked, chin-dimpled grin is on his face and I force myself to look away lest I spontaneously caress him everywhere...while in the car...with his child and my cousin in the backseat.

"Dad?" Cordie yawns again.

"Yeah, Cords?"

"I'm sorry about you and Jill. I was really mean to her before we moved."

"It's all right, kiddo. It's in the past," Stacy says, his eyes darting between the road and me. I turn to look out the window, hoping to lighten the awkwardness.

"I mean, you should be happy, too. I'm going to be happier." Another large yawn. "And I'll be a better kid." Her voice fades at the end.

"Listen, Cordelia, you're the best kid in the entire world. I'm the luckiest dad to have a kid like you. You understand me? You make me happy and are not to blame for anything that happened in Seattle before we left. You hear me?"

Cordie laughs softly. "I love you, Dad."

"I love you more, kiddo."

"So if you want to marry Jill, I'm okay with that now."

I look over my shoulder; Cordie is snuggled up next to Pippa, her head on Pip's shoulder. Her eyes are closed and a slight smile on her lips.

"Cords—" Stacy starts but I touch his shoulder, stopping him, and press my fingers to my lips.

"She's asleep," I whisper.

"About what she said—"

I hold up my hand. "It's your life. I'm not a part of it. I mean, in that capacity."

He glances at me, his smile gone, before returning his attention to the road. I don't know what to say. And as my normal custom, instead of staying quiet, I prattle about, wishing I could quiet my own mouth or stick my foot up my arse.

"I'm sorry Eve didn't stick," I say.

"Evie."

"I beg your pardon?" Because confused is also a normal state for me.

"Her name is Evie," he says with bite.

"I apologize." I shift away, leaning against the door.

"What is with every woman in my life trying to set me up? You, Cordie, my mom, and even Josie. Is there something about me that says I can't get my own woman? I know I have a girl's name, but I can promise you there is nothing girly about me," he says with such passion I'm startled.

"Again, I apologize and ask for your forgiveness. I will cease from matchmaking from this moment forward."

He sighs heavily. "Why do we fight in cars? You ever notice that?"

I shake my head, refusing to look at him.

"Maybe I'd like to be in charge of finding someone for me."

"We were only trying to help. And Cordie, she wants you to be happy." I look at him now. He's got one hand on the wheel and the other is adjusting the mirror, I assume looking at his child. Do I tell him what she shared tonight? When does it become a parent's right to know? I suppose not having the answer to this question points to my non-existent maternal instinct.

"I know. I thought she'd be happier here. I'm glad she had a good time tonight."

"She really did. You're a good dad for letting her come." Does he have maternal instinct? Or is he limited to his paternal guts? We're pulling into the car park and I gesture for him to pull in front of my flat rather than go around to the garage.

"She needs to make friends her own age. Outside our group. She's becoming too dependent on Pippa and Josie. I know it's because she wants a mother but she's not going to find it there, and the sooner she starts doing things a nine-year-old does instead of hanging out with adults, the less she'll be aware of what she doesn't have."

I turn to him, mouth agape as I search for the proper words. "If you think that's true then you're a bit of a punt, aren't ya? Nothing will make this child less aware of being one parent short other than filling that void, and even then it's not a hundred percent."

CHAPTER TWENTY-THREE

It's been over two weeks since the football game and now that I've promised not to matchmake anymore, I'm flat out of ideas on how to deny myself Stacy.

I'd ask Paisley for recommendations but now that everything's worked out between her and Hank, her suggestion of jumping his bones is counterproductive.

As he promised, Davis delivered a dossier of potential investors, only not to my email but to the shop, bound professionally, the spine a coil that allows the thin book to lay flat when opened. I've been carrying it around in my messenger bag for a week now, having not cracked it open after the initial glance through.

Another girls' night, and again I'm the designated driver for Josie and Paisley. And three seconds after settling in the car, they started complaining about the limited head and legroom in the back. I hoped Pip would join us but she begged off, claiming an appointment, and said she would meet me there.

Thankfully, the drive from my house to the pub is relatively quick and we are entering said establishment the same time Pippa gets out from a cab. I point to the yellow eyesore. "What's this?"

She does a finger wave to Paisley and Josie.

I narrow my gaze. "What goes on here?" I say. My typically dressed-in-only-tunics-and-yoga-pants cousin is wearing one of my flowy peasant blouses with a skirt and boots.

She pays the driver and ignores me completely.

"Seriously, Pip. You know I'll come get you anytime. Anywhere." There's a secret being kept and I want to know about it. When she gets close enough I lean toward her and take a whiff, but she doesn't smell like anything unexpected such as sex, cigarettes, or pot. She smells like Pippa. Bergamot essential oils. Five Thieves when she's sick

"Mind your own," Pippa whispers.

"Are we going to stay out here all night or are we going in?" Paisley motions to the door.

"In," Pippa and Josie say in unison.

I walk in behind them all, still trying to figure out Pip, seeking a clue that might lead me down the path to my answers.

We aren't two steps past the hostess station, making our way to the tables that flank the bar, when Pippa stops, folds in on herself, and sneezes with such vigor I'm sure birds outside have flown away in fright.

When she straightens, a clear, gelatinous half circle blob the size of my hand drops to the ground, catches the tip of her boot and bounces like a skipping rock ten feet away.

"What in the hell was that?" Josie says as Pippa, who has just figured it out, gasps in horror and clutches her chest. Or, more specifically, the right portion of her chest.

"A chicken cutlet," I say.

"A what?" Heather asks, coming up alongside us, a tray of drinks in her hand.

Paisley covers her mouth, a poor attempt to disguise her laughter.

"A chicken cutlet," I say again as Pippa runs off to try to retrieve it. Seconds before she's able to scoop it from the floor an unknowing patron accidentally kicks it.

"I thought she was vegan," Heather says, still holding the tray, her brow knitted in confusion.

This renders Paisley a mess as she dissolves in laughter, but she's cut short when the cutlet, also known as a silicone bra insert, is launched into the air by another kick, tags an older gentleman along the side of the head, bounces off, and, quivering in the air, arches downward, coming to rest once again with a resounding plop on the floor.

Josie and Paisley lose it. Overcome with hysteria, they lean against each other and laugh.

Pippa lurches forward, scrambling to snatch it off the ground.

"Oh," Heather says. "*That* type of chicken cutlet."

No sooner are the words out before another patron, this one a biker with heavy boots, clomps right on the tip of the gel pack, the force of which is too great, and the silicone gel squirts out, all over Pippa's (my, actually) shirt.

She freezes. Heather and I gasp. Josie and Paisley nearly fall onto the floor— they've given way to the hilarity of it all— and biker man continues obliviously on his way.

Pippa turns and beelines straight toward us.

"I could murder a drink," she says through gritted teeth and clinging gel. Small beads of gel glisten in her hair.

"Look, Pippa," Heather says, holding up an aperitif glass

of limoncello, a yellow opaque liquid. "This is made with lemons. So technically it's a fruit."

"Too right," Pippa says before tossing it back in one swallow, slamming the tiny stemware on a nearby table. "I need another one. Now."

Heather springs into action and so do I. Residing deep within my cousin is an impressive temper. It takes a tremendous amount for her to display it but when she does its scary. I try to force the beast back.

"Aw, love. It's all right." I wrap an arm around her, careful to avoid the silicone.

"Come, let's get you cleaned up."

"What's the point?" she says tersely. "Why does it matter?"

"Hey," Josie says, her laughter instantly gone. "What does that mean?"

"Look at me. I'm a mess. This is why I wasn't chosen. I'm not good enough."

Josie crosses her arms. "This sounds like someone needs to be taught a lesson. Point me in their direction and I'll do some teaching. Can I sue them? Use self-defense? Because that's straight up bullshit, Pippa."

"Come on, let's go sit." With my arm around her shoulder, I guide her to a back table where Kenley is waiting, her face buried in her phone. I settle Pippa in a chair and after taking the napkins from the table, proceed to clean her up.

"Start with deep breaths." I demonstrate my meaning by doing the yoga breathing she taught me.

She pulls out her phone and stares at the screen. One lone tear courses down her face.

"Pip?" I say.

"I didn't get the job," she whispers.

"Oh, Pip." I toss the napkins on the table, slide into the seat next to her, and wrap her in a hug. The others have rallied in closer.

"Those...those...those—"

"Fuckers. You can say it. It'll make you feel better. Add a mother to it." Josie coaches.

"Those motherfuckers. I gave them years of my life. I remain flexible for them. I take all the additional course work they *suggest*. Not recommend but *suggest*. And I still don't get the job." She stares at her phone's screen.

"Why don't they want me?" she looks at me, her eyes glassy with unshed tears.

"Because they're jackstupid," Josie says. She reaches over and begins to rub Pippa's shoulder.

"I'm really sorry, Pippa," Paisley says.

"Who did they hire?" I ask. Because who could possibly be better than my cousin? No one I tell you. No. One.

"That large-chested, superficial cow, Cynthia. She can't do downward dog without toppling over she's so top heavy. Half the positions she assumes are modified because her teats are dragging on the ground. But I bet they want her for their new marketing plan." She turns to me with wild eyes, spewing anger, and reaches into her shirt, pulling out the mate to the now-decimated cutlet and slapping it on the table.

That explains the chicken cutlet, but not where she was.

"Like couples are going to travel from the four corners of the world to take lessons with her? What woman would want that? They're so stupid. And I hate them. And I'm never going to do any more work for them forever," she says, ending her rant by stabbing the other cutlet with a knife causing the others to sit back a few inches. "I should have never mentioned it," she adds.

"And this?" I point to the cutlet.

"I applied for a job here, in a local studio, and they said I wasn't a good fit." This time the tears break free and unintelligible words follow.

"Oh darling, what would you tell me if our roles were reversed?" I hand her tissues from my purse.

"Stuff it," she says between tears.

"All right then. Let's be angry. Let's get you drunk," Josie says. That's Josie; she works well in an angry place. A few weeks before her wedding she talked us all into vandalizing the car of a guy who'd manhandled Paisley.

"Gimme your phone," Paisley says, before snatching it from Pippa's hands.

"What? Why?" She uses her palms to wipe away her cheeks before dabbing the tissue to her nose.

"Because booze and phones don't mix. A few drinks later you're tapping out a strongly worded email calling that guru guy, oh, what's his name?" I snap my fingers trying to remember what she told me. "Anyway, calling him some Yogananda hack or wanna be—or worse, actually—is something you'll regret tomorrow."

"He is an insult to Yogananda," she says before blowing her nose. A sound equal to several geese honking.

"And that's why we've taken your phone," Josie says when Pippa stops her impersonation.

"Do you want to stay or leave?" I ask patiently. "I'll do whatever."

She gives an adorable hiccup breath. "There is something better waiting for you. Be open to receive it. That's what I would say if our roles were reversed."

I pull her into a tight hug, squeezing her full of love. Josie wraps her arms around us, then Paisley.

Needing no further words, we finish our group hug then settle around the table. Since Kenley arrived first she ordered appetizers and an assortment are ready for our dining pleasure. Pippa goes right for the bowl of crisps—not on the menu but surely delivered by Mum, as she knows these are my favorites. They're also something Pippa never eats.

"Think of your gut." I say in her ear before she can get the flaky, oily delight to her mouth. "Is that asshole in India worth upsetting your digestive system? Is it worth comprising your values? You know, I read in a travel magazine that they weren't in the top ten best studios."

"I love you, Jaynie-girl." She stuffs the chip in my mouth. "I'm righted now. Let us carry on with the girls' night." She wipes her eyes and smiles.

"You sure?" I ask.

"Positive."

I pull the bowl of crisps closer.

"Please no one feel they need not share something wonderful because I just had a wee bit of a fit," Pippa says.

"And assaulted an elderly gentleman with a silicon pad," Josie adds.

"Oh, dear. Did I really?" Pippa claps her hands to her cheeks, mortified.

"I don't think he knew what hit him," Paisley says and we all chuckle.

"I registered for college," Heather says in a rush of words.

The group erupts with cheers and congratulations and I'm elated for Heather. I really am. Just a few short weeks ago she was drunk flirting with Stacy. She was crying on her couch wondering how she was going to get through the next day. Now, she's registered for college and has a plan...and I'll once again be short a reliable, smart, forward-thinking staff member.

This is truly the worst part of owning a business, staffing it. Well, that and not making any money.

"Any chance you're going to study fashion or clothing marketing?" I ask.

Heather reaches across the table and takes my hand. "It's because you gave me a job that I'm able to do this. You gave me back dignity or self-respect or whatever it is that I needed to push me into being proactive. Thank you, Jayne." She squeezes my hand and looks around the table at others. "I had Tyler when I had only a year left of college but instead of trying to finish it with a newborn, I dropped out. I've decided to go into teaching. In two years I can get my my teaching degree and if I add on another year, I can be certified in special education. I think that's what I want to do."

"Yay! We can work together when you get out. That would be so amazing," says Paisley, a pediatric occupational therapist therapist who works in special education.

"That would be awesome but until that happens I'd like to stay at Jayne's shop." She swings her gaze to me. "If that's all right with you. For the most part I can work my classes around our schedule and Tyler's." Her expression is radiant with excitement and hope.

"That's a HUGE relief." I lean across the table hug her. "Having you at the shop is tremendously valuable to me, Heather, as I try to figure out my plan for expansion."

"Not going well, is it, Jayne?" Pippa asks. She's been nibbling on the lettuce Mum uses as garnish for her pot sticker appetizers.

"You and I will have to be patient so we can see what's meant for us," I say.

"Whatever it is will certainly want you to be yourself," Josie adds and sticks her finger in the gelatinous chicken cutlet.

Suddenly, from the back of the pub comes a loud crash of several dishes and Mum yelling "Thomas" in a voice that sends goose pimples across my entire body.

Frightened.

Mum sounded frightened.

Or worse, terrified.

CHAPTER TWENTY-FOUR

Pippa, Josie, and I dash through the pub to the kitchen. For once I am eternally thankful for my long legs as I reach the area before the others. Mum's bent over Dad, who's lying on the floor. A quick assessment makes me think he collapsed from his chair. His eyes are closed and he's not responding to Mum's repeated calling of his name or to her shaking his shoulders.

"Auntie Millie, move please," says Pippa, gently pushing Mum aside. She begins to check him, bending her head to listen for breathing. That one simple move is all it takes for Mum to burst into tears, panic etched across her face.

"Mum." I swoop her into my arms, moving her away to allow Pip some room. "Tell me what happened."

I hug her to me, forcing her to face away from the sight of her husband, colored the same chalky gray as the concrete floor. A quick glance at Josie, who's on the phone, reassures me emergency services are on the way. I force myself to be removed from the situation, holding back the panic that's clawing to get out. But I won't be more of a problem; I can fall apart when I get home.

"One minute we were talking about planning a holiday. Doing something different this year and the next he's on the ground."

Thankfully the pub is close to a firehouse and in minutes we're surrounded by a blur of people: emergency works, staff, and friends. We get Mum and Dad off to hospital. Josie, a natural leader, has already mapped out the plan. She stays behind to help and has put a call into Jeff, Mum's part-time assistant. Paisley drives Pippa and I to hospital in my car.

Once there we're forced to wait with Mum as Dad's rushed back for tests.

"He'll be fine, Mum," I say hoping my words don't sound as hollow as I feel.

"Daft man," she says, popping up from her seat. "Said he wasn't feeling well. Told him to go to the doctor, I did. But he said he wouldn't take a day off unless I did. As if seeing a doctor is a holiday."

"Mum."

"I will have that man raised from the dead so I can give him a piece of my mind, I swear to you I will." She's pacing the short length of our waiting room, clenching and unclenching her fist, and I know I shouldn't smile but this is not the reaction I expected from her, given her past experience.

Of course I realize Dad's not lost yet. The awful could happen and Mum might then truly lose the plot. As anyone would.

"Mrs. Grandberry?" A young man steps into the room, wearing scrubs, a longish white lab coat, and a stethoscope around his neck. It's Joe, the doctor Amit suggested setting me up with.

"Yes," Mum pauses her rant and pacing, her hands going to her chest.

"I'm Doctor Lynch. I was assigned your husband's case."

"Is he alive?" she whispers.

"Yes, ma'am. Very much so." Dr. Lynch gestures to the seat. "Why don't you rest a moment while I discuss your husband's condition?"

"Oh, dear Lord. He's going to die, isn't he?" She collapses in the chair next to me.

"Auntie Millie, perhaps you should let the good doctor speak," Pippa suggests.

I pick up Mum's hand and hold it between mine, hoping it gives her some comfort.

"Please continue," I say.

He squats in front of Mum, a lovely gesture to be sure, but undoubtedly causes her anxiety to rise as she's now clutching my hand in a vise grip.

"Your husband appears to have fainted—"

"Crikey, that's all?" Mum's voice rises.

"Mrs. Grandberry," says Doctor Soothing Tones. "We'd like to rule out possible heart problems as the culprit, if you will. Your husband's blood pressure is low, which normally isn't a concern, but...the best way I can describe it is to say that it's not pumping as well as it should be."

"You think there's something more," I say, and squeeze Mum's hand, choking back the tears of fear that threaten to escape.

"We're keeping him overnight for observation. He took a knock to the head when he fell, but we'd like to do a stress test tomorrow and go from there." He nods, waiting for Mum to respond.

"Might we see him?" Pippa asks.

"Of course. He's getting a room as we speak. But he's a bit agitated and well, frankly, I need you to take him in hand. If you can?" Challenge extended.

Brother, this doctor has Mum's number right off. He's good. No one can bring Dad around better than Mum and nothing gives her more motivation than being in charge. I'd laugh and congratulate him on his astute observations if the mood wasn't so serious.

"I most certainly can. Take me to him." Mum leaps up from the plastic chair, nearly knocking over Dr. Lynch.

"He's going to be difficult. He's a little confused and says he's hungry—"

"I'll straighten him out," Mum says.

We follow the doctor to the door that separates the doers from the wait-ers and Dr. Lynch pulls it open for us.

"You single, Dr. Lynch?" Mum says.

I nearly faint myself. "Mum, seriously?" I glance at Pippa.

"I am." He faces us.

"Jayne here is a business owner, savvy and responsible. Good genes. Oh, don't think she has her father's genes because Thomas isn't her real father. Her real father comes from very strong stock."

Dr. Lynch looks at me. Or, up at me, as I'm easily three inches taller than him in flat feet. Today I'm wearing a modest heel and feel as if I could cuddle him in my arms like a wee babe, as he's likely forty pounds lighter than me as well.

Either I look like the hearty stock Mum alluded to or he's

frail. I'm going with frail. In a healthy, only-eats-lettuce sort of way.

"Er... Just ignore her, Dr. Lynch. Shall we go see Dad? Eh, Mum?" If I knew where I was going, I'd push past them all and lead the way.

But alas.

Paisley elbows me and when our gaze meets, she rolls her eyes. She totally gets it. When she and Hank started dating her mother sent her a list of baby names that went well with Lancaster, Hank's surname.

But this is a first for Mum. She's always been the opposite.

"If your father has heart problems it might come in handy to have a doctor in the family," Mum whispers.

Without further embarrassment, we follow Dr. Lynch to a different floor marked Cardiology and Mum fairly swoons when she sees the sign, gripping the nearest person, Pippa, to hold her steady.

But when we walk into Dad's room, he's sitting up in bed, a bandage near his right temple and a cross expression on his face.

"Christ on the cross, Millie, tell these people to let me go." He wags a finger at a nurse who's messing with a machine that subtly beeps Dad's heart rate. I'm thankful for that line and try not to guess what it might indicate.

"We're happy to see you looking well, Uncle Thomas," Pippa says, effortlessly skirting the force field of anger around Dad as she drops a kiss on his cheek.

"You look lovely, Dad." I say, ignoring the wires that run to his arm and chest.

"For a stubborn ass of a man," Mum adds and steps closer to his bed. "You listen here, Thomas Grandberry. You gave me the scare of a lifetime earlier and I will not have that again. I burned the fish."

Looking chagrined, Dad says, "I'm sorry, dear."

"You will be staying overnight. I will be staying with you. You will do as these people say because this cannot happen again," Mum demands as she sits herself on the corner of his bed. She takes his hand and clutches it within hers.

"All right, dear. If you say so." He leans his head against the pillow. Before my eyes, time speeds up and I no longer see him as the young man, a sudden father, who embraced me as his own. Gave me his last name when my own biological father wanted nothing to do with me anymore. Now, I see a loving face that's aged with wisdom, life, and laughter.

I step next to the nurse and quietly ask, "Can she stay?"

"Yes, ma'am. The chair opens out into a sleeper. She'll need linens and a pillow is all." The nurse finishes whatever it is she was doing and steps from the room.

I turn to Paisley but before I can ask she says, "Just tell me what to do. Of course I'll do it." She rubs a hand down my arm.

"Can you take Pippa home—"

My cousin swings around to face me, saying vehemently, "No, I'm staying to help. I'm family."

I lower my tone like Dr. Dulcet the Master and say calmly, "You'll need to go by the pub first and check on Josie. Make sure all is well and that Jeff has it under control." I hold up a hand to stop her from interrupting and glance at Paisley. "Then go to my place, get some linens and a pillow so Mum can stay overnight."

Pippa shakes her head. "We'll go by their house and get them both a change of clothes. Something Auntie can be comfortable in. I'll get some linens there."

I nod. Pippa has a key, so that's taken care of and my only obstacle is Pippa not knowing how to drive. It's times like this where it would come in handy. "Can you bring my car back?" I ask Paisley.

Paisley nods.

"Can we bring anything else?" Pippa stifles a yawn.

I shake my head. "But, Pip, it's okay to stay home. You and I'll be running the show for a bit, so maybe being well rested should be high priority?" I shrug my shoulder as if to say I'll understand if she doesn't want to stay away.

"We'll be in touch through text, okay?" Paisley wraps me in a hug.

I nod, as there's a lump in my throat, a buildup of fear and relief blocking out the words.

Pippa hugs Mum and Dad, her eyes glassy with unshed tears. When she passes me, we reach for each other's hand, tangle our fingers, and squeeze. To do more than that would reduce us to tears.

While waiting for someone to return with my car and Mum's clothes, I run errands. Coffee and light food for Mum, step out to ring dad's sister, Auntie Sheila. I field a few texts from Josie about the pub and make a call to Heather about my own shop, thankful more now than ever I have her. The value of a good employee (though she is my friend first) is essential in times such as these.

I'm sitting outside Dad's room, giving my parents privacy, and staring down at my chipped nail polish, named *Pinking about You,* a lovely light color more appropriate for spring, when my mind wanders to Stacy. I can no longer look at my nail polish and not think of the first time we met.

As if conjured from my mind he slides into the plastic

chair next to me and tucks a large overnight duffle on the ground between our feet.

Stupidly, I ask, "Are you really here?" I'm awfully knackered and wouldn't doubt for a moment if my mind were playing a trick on me.

He looks over his shoulder then back at me. "I think so. Do you not see me?"

I touch him, stroke his cheek. It's warm, my fingers caressing the bristle of his five o'clock shadow.

"I've brought both your car and the items requested. Though you're gonna have to give me a ride home." His blue eyes are gentle and soft and fill me with warmth that escaped the moment Mum screamed.

"Where's Cordie?" I try to soak in his heat.

"Paisley's with her."

"I can't leave." I desperately want to lay my head on his shoulder. Instead, I drop my hands to my lap.

"Where are you going to sleep? Out here?" He scoots closer in the chair, wrapping an arm around my waist.

"I hadn't thought about it." I'm surprised to find my voice quivering only to then notice my legs are trembling as well.

"Hey," he says in that husky voice I've come to dream about. "It's okay. He's okay."

I nod, only I'm not so sure if it is because I am agreeing or the trembling that has taken over my body forces me to do so. The lump in my throat rises up and pushes out tears, one escaping down my face.

He folds me in his arms, hauling me close and says, "Aw, babe. I gotcha. Hold tight to me."

CHAPTER TWENTY-FIVE

Hold tight to him, he said.

And I did.

I let him wipe my tears, hold my hand on the drive home, and tuck me into bed where I fell into a deep sleep before he pulled the covers over me.

The next day, Stacy was there, standing quietly behind me, his hand on my shoulder when the doctor came in to give the results of the stress test and Dad was scheduled for some serious work: a stent, a pacemaker, and a valve replacement. They said his heart had the wear and tear of a much older man. It explains the fatigue he'd been complaining of. It might also explain the fall that broke his leg. There was hope that the first two procedures might do the trick and Dad could avoid the valve replacement. I crossed my fingers *and* toes. Though he will need a new valve in the future, undergoing three separate procedures puts him at risk for several other issues. I lost focus after the doctor began listing them.

The day after, Stacy sat next to me while Dad had his first of three procedures, the stent put in and we encountered our first complication. Initially, they couldn't get Dad's bleeding under control and he required a blood transfusion. This pushed out the pacemaker procedure and only increased our anxiety.

On the third day, Mum lost the plot and cried all over me when I popped by the pub to help her sort out the schedule, only to find out they were still delinquent on bills. I tabled the conversation as Mum was in no state for a discussion and I paid the invoices from my own accounts.

Afterward, I found myself seeking Stacy out, calling him, needing his strength as reinforcement. When I drove home, I went to his house before mine. He pulled me inside and I had my first solid night sleep on his oversized couch, wrapped in his arms.

There's something about Stacy that balances me. When my brain is cluttered from everything, when the weight of what I want to accomplish staggers me, it's talking with Stacy that breathes in the calming oxygen I need. Everything gets all sorted or, at least, my plan of action does.

It's astounding really. How it seems as if he's always been around, helping me keep it together. I wouldn't have made it without him. With back-to-back meetings himself, he's insanely busy, yet each night he works on my books, feeds me takeaway, and holds me until I fall asleep.

The last two weeks have passed in a flash and feel more like forty-eight hours then days stacked on end. Pippa's been running the pub; I've been personal assistant to both Mum and Dad while going by the shop every chance. Thank heavens for Heather.

Now, sitting next to Josie's fire pit, the afternoon sun is warm enough that Cordie and Tyler are splashing, knee deep, in the ocean. I want nothing to do with work, only to put Dad's impending heart surgery, their life after said surgery in regards to the pub, and Pippa's ever-increasing broodiness about the job loss out of mind, if only for a few hours.

One last bit of work and I'm going to shut down. Everything but being here can sod off. Even today's fortune from a new cookie can get stuffed. It read: *Life will be happy until the end when you'll pee yourself a lot.*

Responding to Davis' reminder email about the investor packet is last on my list.

I answer it with a brief one of my own, hoping he'll let the matter rest, but when my phone rings and his number pops up I groan loud enough that the others look at me.

"Hello, Davis," I say, unable to disguise my annoyance.

"I do apologize for calling you, Jayne. I'm sorry that your dad is sick. I hope the situation gets better soon."

"Thanks," I murmur while watching the kids splash about.

"I hope you'll forgive my interruption but one of my investors—I sent you his profile—is very interested in your store. He has an opportunity to invest in something else but would prefer to go in your direction, and while I don't enjoy rushing these things, I was wondering if you might be interested. I'd hate for you to miss out on this. You'll have to make a decision in forty-eight hours." He poses the question in his light, airy voice.

It's magic really. How he keeps from sounding pushy. He's a marketing marvel because at the mention of losing out on this opportunity I'm sucked in. I don't want to miss out on something that could change my life. Desperation to push the red of my thermometer to the top clouds my judgment.

I school myself.

Mum has always told me to not let need come before sense. I try to apply that here. "I'm not sure I can make a decision that quickly."

"But you can try? Give it some thought. Spend some time mulling it around. I could come down and be a sounding board if you'd like. It would be a shame to lose this opportunity because you didn't give it a glance rather than deciding it's not for you."

I sigh. The dossier is in my messenger bag in the car and, to be honest, with covering some of the pub's expenses, I'm even more in need of an investor than before if I want to launch this shop.

"Want me to come down?" he offers again.

"No, there's no need." I press my hand to my temple and close my eyes.

"So you'll give it a look?" His tone is a mixture of excitement and hope and who can say no to that rich sweetness? Certainly not I.

"Yes, I'll give it a proper look."

He tells me which investor it is. "Call me with any questions. There's no limit to how many times either. I'm here to guide you."

I nod. "Okay. I'll get back to you." Hopefully, Josie still has extra chocolate around. I might require a brick or three.

"Thank you, Jayne. Thank you."

As if I've just made him the happiest man in the world. And damned if I don't feel like rushing right to my car to get my bag.

"I'll be in touch," I say, hoping I sound as compelling as he does.

"I'll be waiting. The offer stands for me to come down. I could take you to dinner—"

"Thanks anyway. But I doubt I could get away for a quick cup of tea much less a meal." It's not really a lie, as sitting here with my friends is not "getting away." I'm in standby mode.

We disconnect and I press the end of my phone to my forehead while taking in deep breaths as Pippa taught me, trying to push back the panic that comes with being over-whelmed.

"Here," Josie says, nudging my arm.

I open my eyes to find she's holding a bottle of lemon-flavored seltzer water, my favorite, two aspirin, and a bar of chocolate.

"Bless you," I say and work my way through the gifts.

"Was that smooth-talking Davis?" She plops onto the bench next to me.

I glance at the men, who are overly engrossed in a foot-ball game on the telly, before I answer. "Yes. He really is that, isn't he?" I shared my impressions with her one morning when we met for breakfast. "He wants me to look at an investor who has a timeline." I break off a one corner of the chocolate and offer her the other.

She shakes her head. "You know I'll invest. I've said it before. If your instincts tell you to run from him then run."

I truly have the best friends in the entire world. And I plan on keeping it that way. Borrowing from her could end all that.

"I know. But I'd rather not have an investor at all if I don't have too. Davis brought it up. And it's not that I distrust him. It's that I can see his primary objective is to broker a deal."

"And if he has to hit on you to make it happen?"

"That's the thing. I couldn't tell if Davis was sincere with that or not." It had been something I'd thought about a lot, honestly. Not that I was interested, because I wasn't.

Yet still. Was he the sort to do such a thing?

"Who's Davis?" Heather asks, coming to sit across the fire from us.

"I didn't tell you?" I say.

She purses her lips in thought before answering "Maybe but I can only absorb so much." She grimaces. "Sorry."

"Davis is Jayne's Mr. Darcy," Josie supplies. "Well, the Mr. Darcy she's looking for."

I groan.

"Oh, tall, dark, and handsome is he? How did I miss this conversation?" Heather, as always, is completely engaged in the chat with one eye on Tyler. A skill I'm sure is inherent with those who received the motherhood gene, as I'd no sooner looked away than I forgot they were out there.

"No, actually. Quite the opposite. Fair, blond hair." Josie did an identity check on him from her law firm.

"What makes him Mr. Darcy then?" Brinn asks over his shoulder, attention on the game. "He is overly prideful?"

I flick a questioning look to Josie and raise my hands with the same message.

She shrugs. "Heightened senses. He *is* a pilot." Is that all she has to offer?

"No, not prideful," I say. Not in the way I think he means. Not in the way Colin Firth came off in the film. "And he's not my Darcy. Not like that anyway."

"So he's prejudice?" Stacy briefly glances at me over his shoulder. "Really, Jayne? That's your type?"

"Good Lord." I groan again.

"It's because he fits her Wickham list," Josie says and

takes a shove to the shoulder from me. "It's not as if it's a secret, really. The girls know about it."

But that doesn't mean I wanted the guys to know. Duh.

"What's a Wickham list?" Stacy twists off the top to another beer and watches me. I don't want to have this conversation. Ever. And I certainly don't want to have it with Stacy.

"Wasn't he the bad guy?"

"Where's your daughter?" I say, partly to challenge his "maternal instincts" and to deflect.

"She's building a sandcastle with Tyler," he answers without so much as hinting he needs to look to reassure himself.

"It's her man-must-possess list," Josie says and I chuck the last bit of chocolate at her. Aiming for an eye.

This causes the guys to turn away from the game and focus on us.

"I've heard of these lists. 'Must have sense of humor' is always on them. Even seen them mentioned in some of those magazines you have, Josie," says Brinn. "Did you have one?" he asks his wife.

"No," she says.

Hastily, I add, "That's not true." Why should I be under this bus alone? "Yours was what you didn't want instead of what you wanted. Like mine. You used a list of sorts to avoid relationships—"

"Whereas, your list is to determine if you want to be involved with someone," Stacy says, leveling me with a hard stare that has me shifting my attention to Heather.

"I have one." She raises her hand. "Mine's a combo of both. Traits I want and those I don't."

"Should someone check on the kids," I suggest.

Josie arches up, looks out to the beach, and gives us two thumbs up before plopping down.

"What's on your list, Jayne?" This from Stacy.

Brinn's brow arches. "I'm interested in knowing as well. I think women are too vague about what they want."

"I have good dancer on mine. My ex was such a lump on a hump." Heather rolls her eyes; the others look expectantly at me.

"Oh, all right. Good dresser is one. I am in fashion after all. Shoes are important to me." Boy, does that make me sound like a punt. I hadn't thought so when I wrote it out those many years back.

"That's what I mean. Too vague. How would you define that? Only Hugo Moss?" Brinn says.

"Hugo Boss," Josie corrects then chuckles. "Clearly, you don't make the cut. I think cargo pants and aviator vests disqualify you."

"I suppose socks with sandals is out," says Brinn.

Stacy nods. "They say 'clothes make the man.'" He looks at Brinn. "But some might say they make him soft."

Everyone but me chuckles and the guys fist bump.

"Come on, Jaynie-girl," Stacy says. He slid into calling me my nickname after that night at the hospital. "Give us another."

"No way. I'm not a daft boob." I cross my arms over my chest and stare over their shoulder at the telly.

"Chicken," says Brinn, needling.

Josie is bristling next to me. She loves a challenge.

"Of course she'll want someone intelligent," she says, unable to contain herself.

The guys nod in unison.

"That's a fair one," Stacy says.

"Thank you," I murmur.

"But not a true answer. That's on everyone's list—" begins Stacy.

"Because who says they want a partner dumber than a box of rocks? No one." Brinn finishes the sentence.

This time they clank their beers together. If the jesting wasn't directed at me I'd likely enjoy this display of two half brains coming together and working in unison. But no matter how much *fun* it is to see this once-in-a-lifetime event, which we should be filming for scientific purposes, the fact remains that at their core these men are knuckle draggers.

"He can't have a history as a player," I say and instantly regret it.

"Been there. Done that," adds Heather.

"The kind of guy who tells you he loves you to get you in bed." This from Stacy. "That's another fair one. Not that any man will admit to being a player."

"Unless he's in a room with other men. Then it might happen." Brinn shrugs as if to say a man's behavior around other men is unpredictable.

"Keep going," Stacy encourages.

I hesitate but come up with one they can't find an argument against, Brinn being an entrepreneur and all. "He'd have to be a man of his own making. Not one waiting for jobs to come to him. A go-getter."

The guys nod.

Then Stacy says, "My last two jobs came to me and I'm appreciative of the opportunity." They clank bottles again.

"Slacker," Brinn says to him.

"Sounds like a workaholic to me," says Heather. "That's not on my list."

"You have to make sure he knows how to stop and smell the roses," Stacy says, leveling me with a stare.

Oh please, as if my life hasn't been a bleeding mess these last two weeks. I smell plenty of roses otherwise.

"I take enough time for you and the roses, don't I, babe?" Brinn asks Josie, nodding toward the henna work that's beautifully scrolled down her body and comprises a variety of vines and flowers, many roses.

"Yes, you do," she says.

"Just last night I paid tribute to those fabulous roses. Smelled them, licked them."

"Enough." I cup my hands over my ears. Josie, light pink tinting her cheeks, fans herself.

"I miss sex," Heather mumbles and inspects her cuticles. "Anyone interested?"

That large elephant stands in the room...and farts. Who could she possibly be propositioning if not Stacy? Me? All of us?

"Let's have another," Stacy says. Does he sound almost desperate? Or am I confusing that with laughter?

"Jayne?" Brinn prompts.

"I'm sorry," Josie says to me under her breath. "I don't know what's gotten into them."

"Make it stop," I plead.

"Half time is over guys," she says.

"It's a stupid game anyway." Stacy flicks his hand toward the TV. Neither turn back to the telly, more engrossed in this conversation than ever.

I cave under their penetrating stares. "Family oriented." Stuff that, boys.

It's as if time pauses, their brains searching for something. Anything.

"We got nothing," Brinn says.

I can't seem to make myself shut up. "I'd also like a cultured man. Someone who knows the bouquet of wine. Knows the fruit used in scotch."

"Ah, yes," Brinn says, attempting an accent like mine. He takes a whiff of his beer, swirls it once before saying, "I smell moss, apricot, yeast—"

"Rubber boot and musty rain," finishes Stacy. "I'll concede that point. I have no interest in dissecting booze—"

"Only drinking it. Cheers," Brinn says and they clank their beers, again, and proceed to chug them.

Neanderthals. Both of them.

"It would be nice if he were taller than me," I say and try not to look at Stacy. "And if he were sensitive. That would be a bonus."

"Cried last week when the Seahawks lost. Does that count?" Stacy, after finishing his beer, gets up to deliver the next round and pours Heather a glass of wine.

Of course Brinn can't be left out. "Me, too. Only it was because *The Dirty Dozen* was on—"

"That scene when James Brown dies gets me every time," finishes Stacy.

"Yup. That's the one. Or how about *Lonesome Dove?*"

The shake their heads, feigning sadness. Brinn goes so far as to wipe a pretend tear from his eyes.

"Stop, man, you're getting me all depressed." Stacy turns away, his hand raised to block out Brinn.

"You two are hilarious," I say drily and stand. "But all this willy jostling is too much for me." Granted, it's not cock swinging at it truest form but this entire vignette came about when Josie mentioned Davis fit my Darcy list. I've had enough and if I'm going to look at that proposal Davis sent, now's a perfect time.

"Aw, come on, Jaynie-girl. Don't go. We're only teasing you," calls Stacy.

I flip him two fingers and a smirk before I skirt around the outside chairs and leave them behind, ignoring their guffaws and blustering. I force myself to retrieve the dossier from the car. Pulling it from my bag, I stare at the simple and elegant cover Davis used. Pretty as it is, it feels as if it weighs a thousand pounds. Reinforcements will be required to take on this task. Maybe I can get Josie to funnel me some more chocolate. And wine.

CHAPTER TWENTY-SIX

Stepping back into the house, I'm thrown from my chocolate plotting when someone grabs me by my arm and pulls me into the guest room, away from the patio where everyone is sitting.

Stacy closes the door behind me and backs me up against it.

"You aren't mad, are you?" He braces himself by resting both hands beside my head, against the door.

"Angry? Over that nonsense?" I roll my eyes and clutch the dossier to my chest. He smells a little of the fire and a lot of raw man-sex and...beer? There's a wee bit of dried strawberry jam, from the sandwich he made earlier for Cordie, stuck to his sleeve, and his t-shirt, though old and worn around the hems, isn't as manky as one of the first shirts I saw him in.

Perhaps a smart dresser should not be on my list; instead I could replace it with a man who knows how to wear his clothes. There is no question this applies to Stacy.

He looks good enough to devour, with the shirt

stretching across his broad shoulders, and I don't care that some crazy cartoon character adorns it with a math saying I've no clue how to interpret.

"It's nice to see you relax." He thumbs the dossier. "Why don't you leave this for another day."

"I have to make a decision soon."

"May I help? Whatcha got there?" He shifts so that his face is in front of mine, and any request by Davis is forgotten.

"You've been a good friend to me these last few weeks." How would I have made it without him?

He nods and brushes back hair from my forehead. "I'm glad you're letting me help out. I like being your friend."

Problem though is, of all my friends, he's the only one whose form I'm keen to jump. I don't fantasize about my friends touching my girly bits. Only Stacy.

I'd like one example of friends who had casual sex and went their separate ways without fallout. How does one avoid having their heart trampled on? Already I get a dull ache in my chest when I think about him finding a new Jill and moving on.

"I have a list too, you know," he says, dipping his head toward mine.

"You don't say?" My surprise is genuine as I assume men never gave it much thought outside of physical attraction. Not very open-minded of me.

"Maybe it's because I have a girl's name. Made me do it." He drops his gaze to my lips.

"There's nothing girly about you." I resist the urge to devour him like the starving lady at the buffet bar.

"You want to know what's on my list?"

"Do tell," I whisper, clutching the book with such intensity the spiral binding bites into the palm of my hand.

"Well, she should be tall. One day I'll be too old to stoop and bending over to kiss her will be difficult. I can't have that because I'll want to kiss her until the day I die."

"Foresight. Very clever." I lick my lips.

"She also has to be curvy." He runs one hand down my side and over my hip, sliding it back to cup my bum. He steps closer and at the same time, he pulls me toward him and all the important parts line up beautifully.

I quiver then moan when he moves against me.

"Jayne," he whispers.

"Yes." My eyes flutter closed.

He nips my chin, his teeth grazing across my jawline, and I fantasize about throwing the book across the room and winding my arms around his neck, lifting my legs to wrap them around his waist. I get lost in the dream of being ravaged good and proper by a guy who found my hot spots the first night and seemed to commit them to memory.

Instead, I tilt my head to the side, allowing for greater access, and pretend I'm playing hard to get.

"Jesus, you're going to kill me," he says, blazing a streak of white-hot kisses down the column of my neck.

"Wait." I move to the side, my eyelids springing open. "Friends shouldn't do this."

His breath is on my neck, and when he chuckles it reverberates through my body. "Jayne, friends do it all the time. Josie and Brinn, Paisley and her guy, and—"

"That's not the same and you know it." My palms are sweaty, desperate to clutch something other than this stupid report.

"Sure it is, they just added more to it. Listen, Cordie and I are still getting used to it being the two of us. I'm not looking to add a mommy for the sake of it, and Cordie knows this. She knows I want to date and that she has a voice in relationships."

This snaps me out of the mood, my weak knees find strength, and I straighten up and turn to meet his gaze.

"Seriously?"

"Yeah." He pulls back and drops a hand to push back my hair, damp from my restraint, off my forehead. "It's always been Cordie, me, and my folks. This is the first time we've had to do it on our own. Adding another adjustment might be too much for her."

"Hmm." Because that's the only thing a twit like myself can say. What an imbecile. I never once considered he might not want a relationship. I only thought about what I didn't want. What I was afraid of. "I'm actually quite embarrassed. Trying to set you up."

"Don't be. It was fun. Kinda." He briefly lifts a shoulder. "I thought I better say something before Heather was served up. That might lead to complications."

My eyes go wide. Yes, I can see he might be right. Especially in light of her earlier declaration.

I grimace then say, "Sorry."

"Jayne, look at us. This is ridiculous. There's something between us. Why are we fighting it? I like spending time with you. I think you like spending time with me and with Cordie."

"You know my thoughts. Sexual attraction alone does not mean action should be taken."

"True, but we're both interested. We're both willing. We're both unattached—"

"We both want different things."

"Right now, all I want is to taste you."

I moan. "Oh, Lord. This is bad news."

"Why?"

"What's the end result here?"

He's playing with the neckline on my dress, his fingers grazing my collarbone, my knees wobbling. It's astonishing I'm able to have a coherent thought much less string the words together to make sentences.

"Do you always ask that question?" He bends to kiss the hollow of my neck.

"I usually know the outcome before I begin anything." The folder slides from my hands down the front of me, and falls to a soft thud on the floor, freeing up my arms to wrap around his neck.

"They all have an expiration date?" He undoes the top button on my dress, sliding it open to kiss the top of my breast.

"Yes. There's no time in my life for more than something casual." I borrow a page from his book and run my hands up under his t-shirt, touching all that I can.

"Why can't we start there?" He looks up from my breast, one brow quirked so adorably I'm ready to throw him down right now.

"You're saying you think we're ill-suited for long term?"

"I'm saying I want to stop fighting this."

"Out of curiosity, on your list is there something about a mother for Cordie?" When it comes time to settle for the long haul, I wouldn't meet his list criteria, curvy hips and height don't carry the significance a mum would have.

"And on your list is no children," he says, looking away. "We've established this."

It should give me comfort that we aren't each other's ideal mate. But it doesn't.

We're still, only our chests dare rise and fall. Suddenly, he lets out a slow breath and straightens only instead of stepping away he steps closer. He's pressed against me, my arms trapped between us.

"You feel that?" he asks.

Beneath my palm his heart races, thudding energetically. I nod.

"Yours is doing the same. I can see it jumping right here." He lowers his lips to the pulse point on the side of my neck and drops a light kiss. "And there's this." He licks along my collarbone where a light coat of sexual-tension-induced sweat has popped up.

He has it too. On his brow, down his throat.

"I don't know." I whisper and meld between him and the door.

"You don't know how you feel or you don't know what you want?"

"There's more at stake," I argue but return the rubbing.

"Only if we let it. I want you, Jayne. I want your friendship and I want to take you right here on my friends' guest room floor. But this job with Brinn will grow and my job with it. Will I be here in a year? Hard to say. There's so much you haven't accounted for."

He kisses me then. A good one. Hard and fully loaded. It's a real knee buckler and when he pulls back I've a two-fisted grip on his shirt.

"What do you say?" He kisses me again, this one light and airy.

"To the shag on Josie's floor? I say hurry please." I rub

one leg up the side of him, the hem of my dress rising up, exposing my unmentionables.

Stacy lets out a deep, guttural moan and slides his hand up my thigh. "I mean about you and me avoiding this. Can't we just have this?" He lifts the edge of my panties and I almost come on the spot. All the nights he's held me have done nothing to cool my attraction for him.

Being with him would do me right. I run the argument through one more time and it sounds tired and old. I simply want this. I want to be touched and cherished. I want to be chosen. And Stacy is choosing me.

"I say it's too bad you can't come home with me."

"Cordie is staying with Josie tonight. They're all going to Sea World tomorrow. Heather included."

"You aren't?" I wish we'd shut the hell up and get to what really matters.

"I have an afternoon meeting with Brinn and another investor. I have all night and all morning."

Pippa's staying with Mum tonight so there's no need for me to be there.

"Are we going to do this here or my place?" I say and shudder from the anticipation.

Gently, he lets go of my panties, but rubs the palm of his hand over me before lifting me up and pushing me harder against the door. "I don't know if I can wait."

"We can make as much noise as we want at my place."

He drops me suddenly, stepping back, and rubs his hands over his face before dropping them in front of his crotch. "I'll give you a ten-minute head start. It's going to take at least that long to get control of this."

CHAPTER TWENTY-SEVEN

I must have caught all the lights and Stacy none. He's not but a few minutes behind me.

We come together in a rush of pend up need, our restraint breaking and setting us free.

We didn't even make it to my room. No sooner was he in the door were we undressing each other and having our way. I'm pleased to say my table actually did hold up. Though I didn't dare test it more than the one time.

"I'm starved," he says propped up on his elbows as he hovers over me.

"For me or food?" I tease.

He pretends to give it thought. "At this moment, food. But only because I want to build my energy up fast. This next time I want to do everything again, only slower this time."

"I might have cheese and crackers," I offer. I want him to eat so we can get down to what he just propositioned. I've never looked forward to something so much. Sounds like heaven and a spiritual event I'm meant to have.

We partially dress. Me in a my slip, Stacy with his jeans pulled on my not fastened. I load a tray and gesture for him to sit on the sofa. I sit next to him with my legs folded under me.

"Do you feel guilty?" He did leave Cordie behind.

"Nope. Cordie's having fun and so am I." He winks then feeds me a cracker with cheese folded on top. "Do you feel guilty?"

I ponder, searching my feelings. "Hard to say, right now I feel satisfied."

He tugs me to him, setting the tray I put between us on the coffee table. "I think I need to do it again, I want to know if a person can max themselves out on sex. Mathematically, what are the odds?"

I laugh. "I'm game to finding out."

I stretch forward to kiss him. Loving his taste combined with cheese. Loving the closeness between us. Loving this.

"You're going to kill me," he moans.

"And here I was the one who initially thought you the killer." I bring up our first encounter.

He laughs. "Imagine where we'd be tonight had things gone differently back then."

"Well, if I'd been right I'd likely be dead right now."

"Not funny," he says. "But had we had a normal meeting that night maybe we'f have had tonight before now?" He quirks one brow.

"Maybe. Maybe not."

Look how far we've come. I trust him to the end of the earth and back.

A shattering realization, no doubt.

And I think we'er here now because of how the events have lined up.

"Do friends like to eat cheese of their friend's body?" I push him back and dangle a wedge of Gouda over his navel.

"I think this is the weirdest sex fun I've ever had or even heard of. Chocolate, whipped cream, even popsicles, but never cheese."

I place the wedge on his belly and lick it off. Then I chew. Once I swallow I say, "Yes, Now I see why cheese is not the go-to. Quick dissolving is an essential quality needed in the food item."

He laughs. Then threads his hand through my hair and pulls me close.

"Jayne," he says, his lips close to mine. "Thank you for tonight."

And the loving begins again. He rolls me so I'm under him and slowly eases my slip from me. I help him slide his jeans off. And we explore. Like we had the night of the wedding. We rediscover familiar and find new. We take our time, joining and easing our way to the precipice. And when we let our selves fall off the cliff, we do it together, holding on to one another. Together creating a moment, a memory, I never thought possible.

CHAPTER TWENTY-EIGHT

"Wʜᴀᴛ's ᴛʜᴇ ᴍᴀᴛᴛᴇʀ?" Pɪᴘᴘᴀ ʜᴀɴᴅs ᴍᴇ ᴀɴ ᴀᴘʀᴏɴ.

I blink several times and force back the exhaustion. The hot kitchen and six pieces of fish I'd inhaled ten minutes earlier haven't helped.

"Nothing. What are you going on about?" I slip the apron over my head.

"Because you've yawned about twenty times in the last two minutes. And you put the apron on inside out."

I look down, yawn, and forget what we were talking about.

"Oh, my God, maybe you're deficient with vitamins. I have a pack here. Take two doses." She rummages through a hemp hobo bag and pulls out a large brown bottle with no label.

"I'm not deficient. Just tired." I plop on to Dad's stool and stretch my legs in front of me.

I've gone barmy from getting my end all night long. And I don't feel like a dirty slapper who's had a leg over on her neighbor. I feel satiated. Balanced. Like I can breathe.

I smile, rest one arm on the counter, and lean into it. Then I sigh and wink at Pippa, whose mouth falls open long enough to net a fly, and then, I suppose, she figures it out.

Pippa claps and lunges at me at the same time, startling me to where I almost fall off the stool.

"You slept with Stacy!" She throws her arms around me, taking me off the stool.

Praise the yoga gods that she has such amazing upper body strength as she manages to balance us enough that our fall is more graceful than I could ever execute. Needless to say we land with an oomph and Pippa on top.

"You're mad," I say as she straddles me. It reminds me of our childhood when she'd ask me to spot her in some gymnastic pose or something of the sort before she found yoga. The end result the same, me on my back and Pippa on top.

"Good for you, you daft hen," she says, hands on hips.

"I beg your pardon?" I push her off and roll over.

"You're boffing Stacy." She rolls her eyes. "And you tried to set us up. Crikey you're a lost cause." She scoops up a handful of flour and tosses it at me.

"Let's not share this with the group. It could end tomorrow, so why get everyone worked up?"

"So long as you get worked up, all is well." She wags her brows at me.

I scoop up my own handful and blow it in her face. "Oh, no! You'll melt. It's not organic flour," I say and toss a second handful.

"Get stuffed, you manky slapper." She tosses two at me.

Within moments we're covered in flour and once again hugging each other.

"I'm a mad cow, you know," I say, wiping a heavy streak of flour from above her brow.

"Why so? Because you're shagging someone you *really* like instead of someone you tolerate?" Even covered in flour, she sets about finishing the scones.

"This is going to hurt when it's over," I say and plop back onto Dad's stool. "Sometimes that's all I can think about and it's terrifying."

Pippa stops, staring at me, her mouth working to find the words, her hands still deep in dough. She sighs, shifts, and looks away, her gaze fixed on something other than me.

It was a secret I'd been holding on to. A fear I was afraid to give weight to with words and now that I have, I wish with all my being I could take them back. Having my fear out there leaves me vulnerable and scared and wondering if perhaps I should schedule another trip out of town. Far out of town, like on a different continent. Only I can't leave Mum and Dad or the shop and that only makes the panic more present, a tiny buzzing in the back of my mind.

"I'm sorry," she finally says and takes her hand from the dough, crosses her arms and levels me with a stare. "For once in your life you have a chance to feel something wonderful. Something magical and yet you sabotage it. One night and I bet you've looked at flights to Italy."

"And you know this how?" I attack her because it's safer. She'll love me no matter what.

"Because I watched Josie fall in love, I see Kenley and Doug, and now Paisley and Hank. Because I believe in love and its healing powers. Maybe I'm a romantic. Maybe I'm a realist and the rest of you are all cowards because you all go kicking and screaming but me...not me. I would rush into love's waiting arms and hold on until either forever or it unravels in my hold, whichever came first."

I lay my head on the counter, covering my eyes with my arm. "What about Cordie? She might get the wrong idea. Might think something permanent will come from it," I say from between the folds of my arms.

"Maybe something great will come from it. You aren't the first woman he's dated or slept with and you might not be the last."

I send her a glare.

"But embrace this, Jaynie. Make good memories for all of you. Love rewards the brave," she says, never wavering in her stare down.

Love rewards the brave.

I'm not being so brave right now. A bit of a prat actually.

I smile up at Pippa.

"All done are we? Can I put the pram away? Going to be a big girl now?" She says, her smile broad.

"Sod off." I sit up again. "I can be brave."

"Trying to be brave is enough, too."

"When did you get so clever?" I ask and hand her the cutter for the scones.

She smiles and turns back to the dough, punching out the round shapes. "I've always been. Question is when did you get so clever that you finally figured it out?"

I toss back my head with laughter. "Too right, Pip." I'm cut off from saying anything further by the ringing of her phone.

"Answer that, please." She turns her backside to me so I can take out her phone.

I show her the screen that reads *Logan Ikert*. Pippa

freezes, hands pushing down on the cutter, her face suddenly pale even under all the flour.

"Pippa Clarke's phone," I say while staring at my cousin. I kick her softly on the side of the shin to spur her into action.

"Hello," says the richly deep male voice.

I arch a brow at my cousin.

"Hallo," I return.

"May I speak with Pippa, please? Tell her Logan Ikert is calling."

"One moment, please." I press the mute button. "What's happening here?"

Covered in flour from head to foot, she calmly washes her hands and dries them before taking the phone from me. "Logan owns one of the most popular yoga studios in the states. He modeled it after the one in India. That's where we met. Travel magazines everywhere rank it as either the best or second best in the world."

Impressed, I ask the next logical question, "What do you think he wants?"

She shrugs. "Let's find out." She takes the phone and taps the mute button and then speaker and holds the phone between us. "Hallo, Logan. I have you on speakerphone because I'm working at my aunt's pub. I hope you don't mind. I'm surprised to hear from you. It's been how long—"

"Two years since we saw each other last, but three months since I sent you that email about the spa in India. I just saw their press release about the new hire. I'm sorry, Pippa. When I found out they had an opening I thought you were sure thing. They're dumbasses for not taking you on."

Briefly, Pippa purses her lips. "Thanks, Logan. I won't lie and say it didn't hurt."

"Do you still work for them?" He's an American, his

accent is more northern if I'm correct, and whoever he is has Pip all flustered. She's wiped her brow four times already.

"No, I gave notice last week. They asked me to come for the holiday season and I resigned." Her eyes dart to mine and I cover my gasp with my hand. In the madness of all our family drama, Pippa was giving up her dream.

I want to weep on the spot.

"Fabulous." We hear him clap his hands together.

"I'm sorry?" Pippa says with such an air of indignation, Logan Ikert is scrambling over the line. We hear him fumble the phone and sputter.

"Christ, I didn't mean it was fabulous you quit. Well, that's not true. It is fabulous that you no longer work for them. All I meant was that you being a free agent and all, forgive the sports analogy, that means I can extend an offer I've been waiting two years to do."

"I'm afraid you've left me confused, Logan." She looks at me and rolls her eyes.

"I want you to work for me. I want you at my retreat. I want to give you what they were too stupid to do."

Pippa staggers and plops onto my lap. "Work for you?"

"Does that offend you?" He's quick to ask.

She's just as quick to respond, "Absolutely not. I just...it's just...."

"You've blown her mind," I say into the phone, taking it from Pippa's hand. Fat tears are rolling down her cheek. "Hallo, this is her cousin Jayne. I apologize for eavesdropping but it looks like it's come in handy as my cousin has been rendered a mute."

Logan laughs. It's a nice, easy laugh. "So you think she's interested?"

Like a manic bobble head, Pippa nods.

"Oh, I'm quite certain she's interested."

"Can she start in two weeks?"

I raise a brow, looking at Pippa. The struggle is clearly written on her face. Cordie, Mum, Dad, and the pub have all become part of her day, where she's needed. I know she wants to say yes and I know she wants to say no.

"Well, there's the issue of her work visa."

"If she can get me her specs, I can get my lawyers on it today," Logan says.

"Specs? You mean her information and the like." The businesswoman in me wants everything to be clear.

"Exactly."

"How about three weeks?" I say making an executive decision while mentally scrolling through the calendar.

"My uncle's ill. He's having a surgery tomorrow and possibly another surgery in two weeks," Pippa finally chimes in. "I want to be here for that."

"Absolutely. The schedule will be very flexible. Even afterward, you can take time off as you need. Welcome to the family, Pippa. I've been wanting to say that for a long time."

I take the phone off speaker and hand it to Pippa. I squeeze her hand before I leave her alone to finish out her business. Once out front in the restaurant, I make a list on my phone of things the pub will need to have in place before Pip leaves and a second one to organize her going away/congrats party. I text Josie the specifics.

Her response: *Let's make the party happen Wednesday. My place. 8.*

Then I unwrap the fortune cookie I tucked on my skirt pocket this morning after Stacy left.

Some inspiration would be welcome. It reads: *Don't be grumpy, be grateful.*

CHAPTER TWENTY-NINE

When we arrive at Josie's, it looks as if the event has been planned for ages, not two short days. Chinese lanterns in various colors hang from the arbor. Flickering candles light the way around the fire pit and reach out to the beach. A buffet of food, all healthy, is spread on a long table that rests against the house on the deck.

I stare down at a veggie tray, my stomach growling, but nothing looks enough to feed my hunger.

"There's cheesecake in the fridge inside," Josie says in my ear.

"I see a spinach dip that I might be able to choke down, but must I only have celery sticks as the mode for which to deliver it?" I load my plate with celery and carrot sticks because the truth is I want some of that dip. The stress of everything, Mum, Dad, Pippa, and even Cordie and Stacy makes me want to wallow in the goodness of junk food. I want biscuits with chocolate, onion-flavored crisps, and chips saturated in malt vinegar. With Pippa staying at my flat, I've had enough vegetables to hold me for the year.

Josie reaches across me and puts out two plates, one of fried rice and the other sweet and sour chicken.

"Bless you," I say and scoop the veggies back onto the tray. I feel safe in doing so as I've not touched them with anything but the tongs Jo set out next to them, and I need the room for the rice and chicken. I load my plate and find a quiet corner where I can devour it in peace.

Time has sprinted away at a breakneck speed and I need a moment, a long one, to process everything that has happened. Dad's pacemaker surgery went well with no complications. Hallelujah! Unfortunately, the two procedures weren't enough and though we'd hoped to avoid it, Dad was scheduled for his last procedure, the valve replacement. After which Pip will pack her hemp and cotton clothes and be gone again. I know I should find comfort that she'll be in the same country but part of me wonders if having her in town takes off some of my burden with Mum and Dad and that's why I want her to stay.

See Jayne be a bloody awful selfish person.

I've cleaned my plate without realizing it and glance to the buffet only to find Stacy there with Cordie. How had I missed them coming in?

He glances up at me as he's loading a plate for her and winks.

Cripes, my taste for food has been replaced by my craving for him. He's wearing a ball cap, has it pulled so it shades his forehead but not his eyes. He's in a Henley I picked up for him on a whim, figuring if he were from the Pacific Northwest he'd like it. I'd been correct and the fit was spot on. He moves with the grace of mountain cat and for a guy who I likened to nerd quite early in our acquaintance, he's shown me that people are more than the one thing we first think.

I mean, I knew that. Everyone does. But mostly people don't think nerd and mountain lion in the same context, yet that's Stacy. Because out of his back pocket sticks a small notepad and pen, tools I've seen him use to jot down thoughts or equations. The dichotomy is as much confusing as it is attractive.

Sweet heavens it is oh-so-very attractive.

That's when I know why I waffle the way I do. Why he's not cut and dry for me.

If he were an outright player, the score would be known. The outcome understood and expected. If he were a hundred percent a sweet pliable bloke, again the outcome would be known. But the predator in him, the trait that makes him a sharp business man, not only has me fantasizing about him long after he's left my bed but shaking with want to my very core.

Needing space, room to stretch my thoughts, I toss my plate in the rubbish bin and escape the group through a side door, hoping Josie's cheesecake has been pre-sliced so if I nick one now no one will be the wiser.

The thankfully assorted and sliced triangles are in the fridge and I select one with chocolate. I strip away the thin sheet of parchment, lick that clean, and stare intently at the slice, trying to decide which way is best to devour the scrumptious morsel of courage. All at once or in small bites? Either way, sustenance gives me strength.

"Hey," Stacy says behind me and I turn, cheesecake in hand. Heat climbs up my neck.

"Hallo," I say.

He steps closer, his smile large and inviting, and lowers

his head for a kiss.

BAM! The bill of his hat collides with my forehead.

"Yowl," I say and lean back.

With a swiftness I've come to read far more into than I should, he flips the hat backward, steps one space closer, and goes for the kill.

And it does kill me. Sends shockwaves of pleasure through my body. Makes me forget about all things like cheesecake (impressive) and financial worry. I want to rest my forehead against his shoulder and let that feeling of being more than one fill me. It's better than sex or cheesecake. It's better than when takeaway arrives when you're the hungriest. It's feeling safe from all the elements set about to break you.

Because he's the one that makes me feel the safest, I know I've given him the ability break me. Break me like Hank did Paisley when he walked out. Like my bio-dad did Mum when he left.

"How was your day?" He pushes away an errant strand of my hair.

I shrug. "I'm moony for Pippa," I say and squint, looking closer at his eyelids, which, depending on how he moves his head, sparkle. "Are you wearing eye shadow?"

Stacy chuckles and ducks his head. "Maybe."

My lips twitch with amusement. "Is there something I should know?" I can't wait to hear this tale.

"Cordie had a half day so I worked from home. Apparently, she and Pippa do quite a bit of girly things. Like each other's makeup. I had mine done today. I learned that I am a 'winter'." When he says it, his brows raise up. "So I need to stick with jewel tones."

"Hence the blue," I say and wipe away a smidge of

shadow with my free hand, (the other still cradling the cheesecake). "It's very nice."

"Nice enough to share your cheesecake with me?" He bends forward and presses a kiss to the pulse point in my neck.

"Never, get your own," I whisper, ready to give him not only the dessert but all the quid in my bank account, my secret stash of cupcakes, and well...that list is endless.

I roll my head to the opposite side and relax my body into his.

"What are you thinking about more? Me or the cheesecake?" he mumbles.

"Hard to say."

He chuckles. Even his laugh is damn sexy.

"Jayne?" Josie calls. She's coming down the hallway toward the kitchen. "You better not be in my cheesecakes."

I push Stacy away with such force he actually staggers backward and has to catch himself on her kitchen table. I shove half the cake into my mouth and start chewing.

Surprise then anger flashes across his face and it dawns on me how it must seem. That I'm embarrassed to be with him. I want to correct him, to apologize, and explain that I'm not ready for our friends to know we're fooling around. But I've this mouthful of cheesecake that tastes more like mud than chocolate bliss.

Josie whips into the room, finger already extended. "Ah, ha. I knew you'd be in here. And I knew you'd be eating."

I shrug as if to say "busted" then return my focus on Stacy, who will not meet my gaze.

"What are you doing in here?" she asks him.

He nudges his chin toward me.

"Ah," she says and opens the fridge. Taking out the tray

of cheesecake slices, she cuts her eyes to me. "I feel as if I interrupted something."

I shake my head and swallow. "Only me about to murder this dessert."

Josie looks to Stacy. "How's Cordie taking the news of Pippa leaving?"

He rubs a hand down his face and briefly pierces me with a wounded look before answering, "Pippa asked that I not tell her. But she's going to take it hard. Pippa was exactly what Cordie needed. Someone waiting at home, braiding her hair, and making cookies. Even if they were made from chick peas."

"That would explain why they just took a walk down the beach," Josie says.

"I better go wait for them." He stands, flips his ball cap around, bill shadowing his face, and leaves me alone with super-intuitive Josie.

"Just sleep with him already," she says matter of fact. "And if you have, do it again."

"It's not that easy," I say and put the cheesecake down on the counter. No longer hungry.

"Everything is that easy." She leaves me standing alone in the kitchen.

I follow her outside to the deck where everyone has gathered and is eating and chatting. Cordie and Pippa come up from the beach holding hands. Both of their faces look a little ravaged from shed or unshed tears, I'm not sure which.

I'm not privy to the exchange between the three of them but Stacy ends it with a hug to both, and poor Pip, her face contorts briefly as she tries to hold back the tears.

"Hey," I say stepping up to them. "Can I borrow Pippa for a minute?" I don't wait for a response but grab her hand

and tug her behind me as I make my way through Josie's house, ending at the guest room where Stacy and I made out a few days ago.

"All right?" I say.

To which she nods and promptly bursts into tears.

I wrap my arms around her and let her fall apart. After a good spell, she pushes away from me only to slump back against the wall.

"I'm going to miss that child," she says between staggered breaths.

"But you'll see her again. Likely more now than if you were still working for that company in India."

"Except this job is the real thing. Full time. No more coming home and staying for weeks." She wipes away fresh tears.

"You don't know that. It sounded like there would be lots of flexibility once things were established."

"Things are changing, Jayne. Aunt Millie and Uncle Thomas might not have the pub much longer. You might be in Atlanta or some place. Where will home be then?" Her voice quivers.

"Wherever we are, that's home, and you will always have a place there. Or maybe you become our center. But regardless, we'll always be a family. That will never change."

Following a chuckle, Pip pushes from the wall and wraps her arms around my neck. After she ends the hug she says, "And who thought I'd be the one to have all these issues with change? That's more your expertise."

"Hey," I say, slapping her arm. "I'm great with change."

"Controlled, heavily plotted out change that happens slowly, sure. But seizing a moment and making it yours? Not so much. At least, not until Stacy showed up."

CHAPTER THIRTY

Dad's surgery was a success. Not only did he do well under the knife, so to speak, but there were no further issues and the doctor beamed when he told us how pleased he was with Dad's performance.

Well done, Dad.

Mum though. Not so much. Finding a groove has been difficult with the frequent hospital stays and complications. She'd get him home for a week or so, things would start to go back to normal and then they'd have to go back to the hospital for the next procedure. The cycle would begin again.

For her, the wheels fell off after the doctor left us with the grand news following procedure number three. I think it was when he reminded her Dad needed to learn to manage his stress better and reiterated he *had to* make some serious life changes. My guess is she was hoping things could go back to how they were prior to all this and suddenly realized that was not the case. They'd just begin down their new path.

Pip and I had to peel her off the floor; change is hard for her. When my parents decided to move to America, it took three years to bring it to fruition. Mum required that much time and even then stumbled some as she made her way to the plane that was to take her to her new life.

Never mind trying to get her to make fast decisions about the pub. It's as useless as tits on a bull, to borrow a phrase from Paisley. In the interim, Jeff is making all the decisions with Pippa and I acting as the sounding board. But he's got such a firm grip on what the pub needs that when we discuss things I drink my tea and nod when required.

And write the checks.

With Pippa standing watch, I deposit Mum at home, in bed with a sedative— praises to the doctor who saw that need —and I pull up outside my flat with plans to devour whatever I can find in the fridge for a late lunch, change my clothes, call into the shop, and try to catch my breath. The afternoon and evening promise to be just as exhausting.

Stacy's car is parked outside his place. I'm getting out of my car when he comes out of his place carrying a box that looks strikingly like a large pizza.

I ponder the odds of being able to nick that from him. I'm that hungry but I'm more tired and the energy required would take all that's left in my reserves.

"Hey," he calls across the lot. "I was just coming to see you at the hospital."

We were texting most of the morning and I realize I forgot to respond to his last text, inquiring as to my plans, as I was busy peeling Mum from the floor. Though at quick glance nothing's changed, yet things haven't been the same since I pushed him away at Josie's. I can't put my finger on what's different except to say it feels like a gap between us. A space that before didn't exist. We haven't talked about it. He hasn't mentioned it once. But I know we should.

I sigh. "Sorry, had to get Mum home." I focus on the box. "Is that a pizza?"

"It is." He's coming across the car park and I swear I can smell the melted cheese and sauce.

"What do you have planned for the pizza?"

"I plan on feeding it to you. Figured you didn't really eat and comfort food would go a long way." He's dressed in dark wash jeans that make his legs look miles longer. A heather gray V-neck sweater covers a white t-shirt and I can't decide which looks yummier. Stacy or the pizza

May I have both, please?

"I may have snacked on vending food but it's hard to really do that with Pippa there telling you about all the crap that goes into such wonderful food."

"Where is Pippa?" He steps closer and there's a small nick on his chin where he cut himself shaving. I gently brush the spot with my finger.

"She's staying with Mum. Can you believe she leaves in three days?" He takes my hand, the one touching his face, grasps it around the wrist, and brings my palm to his lips.

Following a soft kiss, he says, "You're going to miss her." I nod and bite my lower lip.

"Look at us, young entrepreneurs with the flexibility to be home in the middle of the day. No Cordie. No Pippa. And a pizza. What shall we do?" He winks.

"We should definitely go inside." I step back and he follows. Sliding his hand into mine, he spins me around and pushes me toward my house. I fit the key with fumbling hands and just as I'm about to turn the knob, I hear a rustle in the shrubs.

Meow.

"Bloody hell," I say. That arsehole cat has impeccable timing.

"Here, give him a slice." Stacy lifts the box and I select a small sliver, placing it in the bowl under the bush. Then I push the door open, drag Stacy in, and boot it closed.

"Pizza now or later?" he asks, but is already kicking off his shoes.

I roll my eyes and work the side buttons on my sailor trousers as nimbly as my fingers will allow. I slide them off, stepping out of my shoes as I do.

I stand before him in my lacy pants and side-wrapped shirt, and the look of appreciation he gives me is loaded with such desire and excitement it nearly does me in.

In seconds we're together, on my couch, pizza tossed to the table. It's a coupling that always starts with lust and attraction but quickly becomes more. It's need and comfort. It's acceptance and awe. It's the soft caresses of his hand on my hip, the kiss I deliver to the scar on his chest. It's entwining our hands as we become one, and holding on tight knowing there's nothing else that makes me this way. This safe. I clutch him knowing one day he'll be gone. There is more meaning in his touch than ever could be in his words. Maybe he knows this can't last. Perhaps we both have mastered being in the moment.

When it's over, I sit on the edge of my couch dressed in my manky pink robe and devour cold pizza. Stacy, dressed only in his jeans, does the same.

"We should meet up like this again," he says.

"I heartily agree."

"My parents are coming in two days and will stay the weekend. They'll have Cordie." He wags his brows.

"Ooh, you could sneak away during the night. Pip will be staying with Mum some until she leaves and I'll be here all alone and scared." I feign helplessness, holding my robe closed and closer to my neck.

"Yes, I can see there is a need for me," he says.

"I love a good plan."

"Not to damper the day but I've gone over more of your numbers." He pulls another slice from the box.

I groan and fall back against the couch. "Too bloody late. Just bringing the numbers up has removed all romantic and sexual ambiance."

"You don't think numbers are sexy?"

"How can they be?"

"Well, have you forgotten about sixty-nine?" He raises a brow.

"Oh puh-leez." I wave him off.

"How about seventy-one?" He nudges me with his shoulder.

"There's no such thing."

"You bent over a table, me behind you. Need I say more?" He eats his pizza like no big deal, his abs begging me to touch them, taunting me with their firmness.

"You made that up."

"Okay, how about ninety-nine? You up against the wall, me behind you—"

"All right! You win. Numbers are sexy." I fan myself with a crusty remnant of my pizza. "Now move away so I can think."

"This is way better than fighting all that attraction, right?" He bumps his knee to mine.

"For now. Ask me again when no one is talking to one another." I meet his raised brow with one of my own.

"Such a fatalist."

"Realist."

"Time will tell." He gifts me with his beautiful smile.

I dread that day. Almost as much as I dread what he's going to say about my books.

"So go on. What were you saying about the business?"

His pizza's halfway to his mouth when he stops. "It's interesting really. Your profits quadrupled when you started personal shopping. That's where the bulk of your income comes from."

"And I'll continue to do that at the new store."

"But, Jayne, you don't need a brick-and-mortar store to do it. No bank is going to give you a loan for a large square footage space to do something of that nature." He puts his hand up, telling me to wait. "I get that you need a dressing space and storage space for that. I get that combined with the store it works. But you run them under two separate business licenses. Quite frankly, my suggestion would be to keep the store here as your home base. Don't worry about another building and make yourself the traveler. Go to them if they're far away. That's where your profit and write off occurred."

"That's what I've been doing and I can't seem to spread out any more than I have. I need a location to bring fresh clients in and spread the word. Besides, with Dad out for a while and the doctor saying he should reduce his stress, I'm not sure how much longer they can keep the pub. With Pippa leaving, I'll need to be around more." I shake my head. "As it is I might have to postpone everything anyway."

"All I'm saying is that the numbers are pointing toward personal shopping. And if my initial take on the snapshots you've been doing for people is correct, that's a gold mine.

From what I can tell, when you started charging people for the outfit snapshots, which you didn't charge me by the way, those profit doubled. You could do a website, make virtual closets for people."

I put my hand up to stop him. "I only charge when I do complete wardrobes. Those are very time consuming." I twist my earring and think about what he's said, but the truth is I can't begin to piece it out. There are too many other questions I'll need to have answered first and the change with Mum and Dad's status makes everything feel more urgent. I know this is where impulse and mistakes live, so I try to steady my internal thoughts, promising to make a list of what needs to be done first chance I get.

"I'll give it some thought," I say and cross my fingers over my heart.

"That's all I can ask for." He leans over and kisses my cheek. When he pulls back, his brow is furrowed, his lips a thin line.

"What?" I ask and face him. Here it is, the metaphorical boom. "I wasn't saying the whole truth when I said that's all I can ask for."

"Go on," I say, though I really don't want him to.

"About that night at Josie's."

He's right to bring it up. But it fills me with such dread I want to run from the room.

"I'm sorry about that. I really am."

"I didn't like it. I know we agreed to keep this casual, but the moment I see you I want to walk up to you and kiss you."

I caress my hand down across his cheek. "But you understand why you can't, right?"

"I understand why you think I can't." His level stare is the one trait about him that's annoying.

"If everyone sees us kissing and holding hands, they'd think we're dating. They'd want to know where we see it going. They'd scrutinize us more."

"There's my answer." He leans away from me and rests his elbow on the far side of the couch.

"What was the question?" I take in a shallow breath.

"I wondered if you would do it again. If we were in the same situation, would you push me away?"

"Stacy—"

"Being with you is easy."

"I agree, being with you is very easy." If there were such a thing as easier than easy, it would be that. I shift toward him, which only serves to force him from the couch. He moves across the room to where his shirt landed when I tossed it after taking it off him.

"But only behind closed doors."

"You said that you and Cordie didn't need another person in your space, that you needed to be 'just us'. Has that changed?"

His sigh is heavy as he rests his hands on his hips. After a quick shake of his head he says, "Initially, that was true. When we first got here. But you're as much a fixture in Cordie's life as Josie or Pippa even. Don't you get the feeling we're missing out on an opportunity to be happier?"

I say nothing, which is enough for him.

"This pretending in front of our friends is hard for me." He pulls his sweater on and I know he's about to leave. "Can you understand that?"

I nod and just like that, the minuscule wedge I shoved between us at Josie's is now larger. Thanks to me. I want to ask him to stay, beg him to be patient with me. But this is far easier.

CHAPTER THIRTY-ONE

I drive Pippa and myself to airport. She's bound for New York City and an exciting job and I've an appointment with one of my best clients. I've had several shipments of clothes delivered to her house to fit. My biggest regret is that I can't press and hang them on padded hangers before she sees them. A practice I try to do every time. But traveling to someone makes that more difficult.

We left Mum in her glory making and baking at the pub. Dad's comfortable and happy watching telly all day. He'll be released in another day and though Pippa wanted to stay for that, I'm making her leave. It's time we all move forward.

After getting through security, we pause. Her flight leaves soon, boarding in fifteen minutes, and the time has come for us to part as our flights are in different concourses.

We face each other, no words needed.

"I love you." She throws her arms around me.

I hug her close. "I love you more, you cheeky minx."

"Ring me whenever, even if you don't need anything," she whispers in my ear.

"I'll text you all the time. I promise. I'll aim for those quiet coma pose moments, so put your phone on silent. You've been warned."

We step back from each other, both of us with misty eyes.

"I can't imagine why we're crying. For the first time in three years you're staying on the same continent." I snap my fingers as if I've made a sudden discovery. "Perhaps that's why I'm teary."

"Go on," she says then blows me a kiss.

"Don't pick up any strangers at the airport," I tell her. She'll strike some pose or another and men will flock to her like pints of beer on football night.

"Sod off." She laughs and turns, walking away.

I watch for a moment before I do the same, headed for my concourse.

"Jayne," she calls down the long hallway.

I turn and lift my chin.

"Love rewards the brave," she says, and blows me a second kiss before turning and skipping down the hall.

When I find my gate, I wait for boarding in one of those uncomfortable plastic chairs. The same ones they have at the hospital.

Over the past few weeks, I've watched Mum fight change at every step only to bow to it inevitably. How much easier would her days have been had she just admitted her fear and pushed forward?

How much easier would it be if I simply fell into this with Stacy? Rode it out? Let my naive heart get a taste of what it is that made Paisley run from her friend's wedding and the nomadic Josie change her life and plant roots? I could take the same leap. Well, perhaps not the precise same but a smaller, similar one. I could go against everything I know, everything I've told myself and believe, and let the experience, the need, and desire take me forward.

It'll hurt like nothing you've ever imagined.

Fear, a laser-hot emotion, spears my heart and spreads like a carcinogenic, feeding off old bitter feelings and memories.

No, to *Be brave* here means to cut him loose. Already, he's been hurt by my actions. I'm not the kind of girl he wants and to pretend otherwise is cruel and unfair to both of us. As soon as I get home I need to cut things off.

It's decided.

I pull my phone from my purse and pull up the messages app. We haven't seen each other since that afternoon at my place. I like to think it's because we've been busy, me getting my folks sorted and his in for a visit. Normally, I'd send a voice memo, but I fear I'll be unable to disguise the quiver in my voice, so I text.

Haven't seen you in a bit.

I can barely breathe.

Just busy.

I bite my lip. Be brave.

We should meet up. Talk.

Waiting feels like an eternity. Already my hands are sweaty and my heart races and I'm just asking him if he wants to get together. I try not to let that freak me out.

See Jayne struggle not to be a coward.

Finally a return text: *Got conned into going to Disney with folks and this weekend is Port Canaveral. Maybe when everything settles down.*

Right. No worries. Have a blast.

I'll get you freeze-dried ice cream.

Sounds delish. Can't wait.

Does he know? Could this be it?

I board, plot, and land in a haze. Thinking more about Pippa's remark about love rewarding the brave and less about all that can go wrong (read broken heart), but I'm determined to stick to my plan and Stacy was never part of that.

After a successful three hours with my client, her keeping all but one outfit, today looks very much like it's going to be a success. Maybe not measured in the way some would but that's how I'm calling it.

I've also scheduled some time with Davis, to talk about other properties. Lord knows I love the bookstore property, and Stacy's words give me pause, but I'm not yet willing to let go entirely of my dream of a second (and third) shop. I'm determined to look at all the options before I change my plan. I may not be able to afford to buy the bookstore and the owners are unwilling to let it. So back to the drawing board as they say.

Davis and I arranged to meet at a different coffee shop in an area that I'm targeting. It's not as hot as the bookstore shop but up and coming, much like me.

He's waiting for me when I arrive in what I would call a dressed-to-impress suit. Casual, dark navy trousers, and coat but no tie. Instead he opted for a checkered navy and white shirt that he's left open. The enormous amount of surprisingly dark blonde chest hair fighting to break free from beneath his shirt is startling. And repulsive. Who knew he was so hairy? There were no signs, not a single warning. No hairy hands or bushy brows. It goes to prove that first impressions can be deceiving.

Yes, I'm certain that meeting him is a lesson from the universe. Stacy, in all his threadbare clothes and well-worn trainers, is a sight to behold. Davis, though dressed impeccably, is not.

I want to laugh at myself for even considering Davis a viable option. In the past, men like him would have captured my attention, but now I see why they could never keep it. They're two-dimensional. Oh, I'm sure to someone else they aren't, but for me they now lack something. Authenticity perhaps?

I avert my gaze from him, afraid my new perception of him might show on my face.

"Whadya have?" the barista asks. "We got a fabulous blonde coffee just made fresh. It's smooth."

Instantly I think of Davis. "Earl grey latte, please."

"You want any special syrup?"

I shake my head. I no longer have a taste for fancy. "Vanilla is fine." I take the cup and make my way to Davis.

"Jayne, so wonderful to see you." He reaches across the table to hug me.

I do a quick turn and offer a one-armed side hug, patting his shoulder. "You'll forgive me but I might be coming down with something," I lie. I slide into the seat next to him.

"You sure you want to look at these others? The bookstore is still available." Davis turns toward me. He's as smooth and easy as I remember, his tone soft and lulling. I instantly relax. He'd be perfect for one of those mediation CDs. He could lull me to sleep in minutes.

"Yes, I have to exhaust all options. You understand?"

"I do. I also understand why you turned down that silent partner. I admire that you want to do this solo." His nose crinkles when he smiles.

"Thanks you." I sip my tea." If I do take on a partner—and I'm not saying I will—I want it to be the least amount of investment from their end as possible. You understand?"

He nods. "Shall we then? The three you selected are all within walking distance, if you're up for it?"

"I am," I say and show him my sensible ankle boots.

Davis pulls out my chair and walks behind me to the door.

"Ooh," I say before I step outside. "Let me just check one thing." I hand him my drink then dig through my purse to find a fortune cookie. Silly, I know. Hastily, I remove the wrapper and after slipping the thin piece of paper from the cookie, I throw everything away but the fortune.

"What does it say?" Davis asks.

I sigh heavily. "Okay to look at past and future. Just don't stare."

Davis looks bemused.

"Well, I don't like it." I withdraw another from my purse, doing the same to it as the first.

"And this one?" Do I detect laughter in his voice?

I shoot him a cross look before reading the next one. "You are cleverly disguised as responsible adult."

Davis laughs but I can tell it's an uncomfortable, forced laugh. As if he's humoring me.

"They're shit," I say, tossing the fortune in the rubbish bin before taking my drink from him then marching out the door.

Davis guides me in the direction of the first building, an above-a-shop shop, and runs through the specifics. When we arrive, the store below is a bakery. Which won't be a problem, as I like to serve food and drinks to my patrons. But it could be a problem if the bakery goes out of business and a dog groomer or butcher goes in. I like the space but give it the thumbs-down. Two blocks down and one across we start to make the U that is our path and stop at the second, narrow space, jammed between two other shops. The architectural detail is quaint and appealing but it's obvious the owner took one large space and divided it into three smaller to capitalize their investment. I shake my head and we progress to the last.

It's within a few blocks of where we started. Parking is close and convenient, as are a few trendy restaurants. This is for purchase where the others were to let and the price is higher than the number Stacy showed me that awful night but not overly so. The outside is charming red brick and it's on the end. Next to it is a plastic surgeon's office.

I cross my fingers, the most I dare to hope.

A large window is the centerpiece but it's covered with butcher paper and the door, a solid wood eyesore, will have to go. Davis goes through the specs as he swings the door open.

A moldy, sulphuric earth smell assaults us and it sounds as if a fountain resides inside. Davis steps in first. There are no lights so we leave the door open and Davis pulls a small key-sized torch from his pocket and shines it around. He makes his way to the window and pulls a corner of butcher paper back and the answer to our question is revealed.

It appears that a water pipe has burst in the apartment above. Both sit empty, Davis explains, which means that it's likely the floors are ruined upstairs as well as down here. Black mold climbs the walls.

"But the doctor's office?" I point the adjoining wall.

"I'm sure they are showing signs but may not have seen it

yet. This place and the apartment above the doctor's office taking majority of the hit."

My only response is a sad sigh, because if one were to remove the mold it would have been a charming place and, though not the bookstore, a happy runner-up that I could have made work.

"I'm going over to the doctor's office. Something to think about, Jayne, is that you could probably get this place for a steal considering the damage. Gut it and rebuild to your taste." He gives me a knowing look. Knowing because it's clear I hadn't thought of that.

"How much of a steal?" I follow him outside and breathe in the fresh air.

Davis purses his lips, his head bobbing slightly. Following a thoughtful sigh, he says, "One in your budget would be my guess. However..." He drags out the pause. "The rebuilding will be expensive and extensive." He takes my hand in his. "I know you don't want a partner. But there is a woman on the list of potential partners I gave you that is interested in your business plan. Her philosophy is to support young women business owners and wanted me to approach you."

"I could buy the building outright and she could help me do the construction?" I'm more running it through my head than asking a question.

"Precisely. Think it over on the plane. I'll talk to these owners and see what I can work out." Assumingely, he nods.

"Right. I can do that." I squeeze his hand before letting go.

"Good. Good. Are you all right if I don't put you in a cab? I'd like to get on this right away." He waves to the room.

"I'm good," I say, feeling lighter in my step than before, if that were possible.

I easily catch a cab, hit no traffic, and am back at the airport, where this morning I landed with sadness and hope and the day is ending with opportunity and a potentially golden future. Who wouldn't feel that way when their dreams might be realized?

CHAPTER THIRTY-TWO

Today is bang on the worst day I have had in recent memory and I don't see how it can get any better. A shipment of Italian shoes lost somewhere between Italy and the United States, invoices that simply aren't adding up, no matter how many times I put the numbers in the calculator, and my daft employee, who I should have sacked ages ago, used a box cutter to open a package from France with a special order dress. Consequently cutting the dress right down the center. The long overdue sacking happened, which then put Heather and I in such a tight bind with the timetable that I changed my store hours. Reduced them. Which means a loss in revenue. I've an advert placed and hope to find someone soon. Hopefully before Heather and I get desperate. Unfortunately, I've been talking to Mum about a similar option as they are struggling as well.

It's been a week since Stacy and I texted. His parents extended their stay and with Pip gone and Dad out, I pulled more shifts at the pub. Even Josie's worked a few. Time has been in short supply.

My highlight? Davis said the owners came in less than he expected, which means I wouldn't be in for as much as I thought with the partner. The downsides are her list of co-owning necessities. Items such as sending monthly budgets for approval and a higher, faster payoff should the business show a profit less than twenty percent. Which, if you ask me, is worrisome. If profits decrease and more goes to her, how do I adjust so that I can try to raise profits as well as feed myself? Pippa says that's when eating junk food will come in handy, as that's all I'll be able to afford. Instant noodles for me, she teased.

When I think back to Stacy's comment about my twenty percent coming from the shop, that it rarely made much more than that, a slight tremor of fear courses through me. That and knowing I have forty-eight hours to decide about Atlanta.

And if that isn't enough to keep me moving forward, I only have to look at the fortune cookie from lunch today which read: *Every exit is an entrance to new experiences.*

I pull into my driveway, give Stacy's flat a quick glance and find the lights are all out. His presence has become as familiar to me as everything else in my life. Just like my daily texts with Pippa, I look forward to my interactions with Stacy. How many times today did I want to text him about the chaos at the shop? But like an awful sugar addiction, I'll have to suffer through the withdrawals.

Watch Jayne be in complete denial.

A movement in the park catches my eye and I squint against the evening sun. It's Cordie. Sitting on the park's swing and kicking up sand with her toe. Her head is resting against the chain, her gaze cast downward, away.

I hesitate the briefest of moments. I'm probably the last

person she wants interrupting her playtime. Yet, there's something so forlorn in her demeanor it makes my day seem inconsequential. This is not a child playing.

Leaving my handbag in the car, I make my way to her. She doesn't notice me until say I her name. When she looks up at me her face is streaked from recently shed tears.

I scan the park. "Where's your dad, love?" I ask. I see a teen a few picnic tables away. Her back is turned to us and she's on the phone.

"He's on a date." Her voice is barely a whisper and she gives the sand another kick.

Air crystallizes and freezes in my lungs, making breathing impossible. A date?

"A date?" I don't realize I've said it until I hear the words.

"With Jill."

And just like that, in the second it takes to say the words I've been replaced, am no longer chosen, my heart and soul shatter into large deceiving chunks. Pieces big enough I think I might be able to paste them back together but they no longer fit together as one because who they used to fit is suddenly gone. Replaced.

Cordie sniffs and I'm brought away from my pain and back to hers. There will be plenty of time to wallow in a tub with cupcakes and tears but right now focusing on her provides me with a purpose and distraction I desperately need.

"Well, who are you here with?" I squat down so I can look at her. I try not to think of Stacy being on a date. When I see the sadness pulling her face downward, I'm able to put it aside.

Cordie looks toward the teen sitting on the top of a

picnic table. "That's my babysitter. She was supposed to order pizza but she pocketed the cash and made me a hot dog instead."

I sit back on the grass and process this. Regardless of whatever it is going on between her father and me, I don't want to leave her alone with this babysitter. Digging in my skirt pocket, I pull out a fortune cookie still in the wrapper.

"Want to know your fortune?" I hold the cookie out on my palm. She stops kicking long enough to take it.

She removes the cellophane, hands it back to me, and I tuck it into my pocket. The state of mother's purse is now clearly understood. Cordie cracks it into two pieces and offers me one. Of course I take it. After sliding the fortune from her half, she plops the cookie in her mouth and holds the tiny strip out for me to read. Her lips lift into a grin.

Don't panic, it reads.

"That's a good one. It's a keeper. Post it someplace where you can see it often."

"Like you do?"

I nod. "Gets me through some bloody awful days. Got me these shoes, too," I say and stretch out my leg to show her my ankle boots.

"I don't have a mom and my Mimi's gone again," she says from seemingly nowhere.

I fall back onto my bum and let it hang between us, giving her words the proper weight they deserve. A declaration like that does not require an immediate response.

"Well, we have something in common then. I bet you would never guess I didn't have a dad."

"But I met your dad. At the restaurant."

The ground is cool and a wee bit damp but I pay it no

never mind. I want Cordie to know that what she has to say is the most important words heard today.

"Yes, you did. But that's not my biological dad. My biological dad left when I was eight. Mum met and married the dad I have now when I was ten. He's been my dad since then."

"What happened to your other dad? "

"He moved on and had a different life." I shrug and look right at her so she can see I'm not upset by that fact.

"Did you ever want to find him?" She starts swinging, a little bit at a time, kicking off with the tips of her toes.

"Sure. When I was sixteen I became fairly obsessed with the idea of finding him and I did."

She catches herself, balancing her swing on the tips of her toes. "You did?"

I nod. "I've never told anyone this. Not Pippa. Not my Mum. You're the first."

"Why not?" She's watching me closely.

"I thought it would upset Mum mostly. When I found him he was living about a hundred kilometers from us, just over an hour away. He was married with a family." I leave out specifics.

Her eyes widen as she lets her toe grip on the earth go and swings forward. "He has kids?" She doesn't look at me.

"Yes, two girls."

"Did that make you mad?"

I watch her face, her emotions so easily seen as she bites her lip and narrows her brow.

"At first I was very angry. I came home and acted quite the terror actually. Mum tried to talk to me but I wouldn't have it. Later that night Dad came to my room and asked if I wanted to talk. I said some awful things to him, Cordie. Just awful." I put my hands to my face, hiding my embarrassment. "I told him he wasn't my father so why should I talk to him. You know what he said?"

She shakes her head.

"He told me that the day my biological dad left Mum and I was his luckiest day ever. You want to know why?"

She's stopped swinging and is staring at me open mouthed. "Why?"

"Because the day he met Mum he was given the gift of me too. He's the only dad I've known and the only dad I would ever have."

"But I don't have a second mom."

"You might one day, and what woman wouldn't love having you? When they get you, they'll be getting an amazing gift, a blessing. You're a smart, funny, fashion forward girl," I say and wink. "Anyone should be so lucky. Like Jill. I bet she adores you."

See Jayne be a wanker for probing a poor distraught child.

"She's okay, I suppose." She toes the dirt. "She cooks better than Pippa; she's a chef. That's cool."

"Indeed it is. You know how important good food is. Lest I remind you of nutritional yeast and black bean brownies." I put on a brave face.

Cordie laughs. "Don't tell but I kinda liked those brownies."

I gasp and quickly place a hand over my heart. "I'll pretend I never heard it. Besides, who would I tell that would believe such a thing?"

And speaking of food, Cordie's stomach gives a low rumble. I raise a brow in question.

"I may not be a chef or, well, even a decent cook, but I

can ring up a mean order of Thai, Chinese, or pizza. What do you say?"

"Pizza please." She kicks off the ground, lifting her swing into the air.

"Right, I'll call your dad first and then we'll get the pizza." I pull my phone from my pocket. The sitter is still sitting away and has yet to check on Cordie. I call Stacy but it goes straight to voice mail so I click on the message icon. I smile at Cordie.

Call me. It's about Cordie and this bloody shite of a sitter you've hired.

In seconds my phone rings.

"Stacy." It comes out hard, bitter.

"Is Cordie okay?" He sounds as if he's trying not to panic and keep his voice low at the same time.

"She's fine, but your sitter has pocketed the pizza money and took Cordie to the park where she spent the last twenty minutes on her phone completely ignoring her."

"I'm coming home right now," he says.

I turn to Cordie and give her a smile; the sitter has yet to disconnect her call but is standing closer to us.

"Don't come home. Let me take Cordie. You should stay and enjoy your date." It pains me to say it. Deep guttural pain, and I hope it causes him indigestion at the very least.

The pause is long. Through the phone, I can hear the murmur of other diners in the background. Though I can't see him, my mind's eye knows he's struggling to find the words and I can see his mouth working with nothing coming out.

"Ah, Jayne about—"

"Stacy, I'm going to pay your sitter. Then I'm going to take your daughter to my house and we're going to eat cupcakes whilst we wait for pizza to be delivered. Enjoy your night and pick her up at my place when it's over." If he was my friend, one that I wanted to find endless happiness, I would offer to keep Cordie so he can stay out for the night. I have no intention to offer that to him.

"Are you sure?" he asks.

"I'll see you when your date's over." I disconnect the call and walk over to Cordie.

"How much did your dad leave for the pizza?" I whisper.

"Thirty dollars."

"What time did she come over?"

"About five. Am I coming with you?" She stands and starts to follow me as I walk toward the sitter.

"Yes, love. You are most definitely coming with me." I march over to the sitter, who has the audacity to still be on the phone. I swipe it from her hand.

"When you are being paid to care for someone else, whether it be a child, a dog, or someone else's elderly granny, your job is to pay attention to that charge." I don't bother waiting for a response; instead I disconnect her call then swipe through her contacts list until I find the word mom. "You drive here?" I ask her.

"Yes, ma'am." She's gone pale but I don't feel sorry for her. Not in the least bit. I'm about to make her a more aware teen. "You live at home with your—"

"Mom and Dad. Listen, I was only—"

I press the call button and put her phone to my ear. When a woman, this teen's mother, answers, I tell her the story. She thanks me and after I disconnect, I give the teen her phone back. "Your mother wants you to come straight home."

The girl retrieves her handbag from Stacy's and is

pulling out of the car park before we've made it to my front door.

"You're badass," Cordie says.

"Thanks, but I'm not sure if you should be using that word." I call my local pizzeria, where I place my standard order for a mushroom and pea pizza for me and cheese for Cordie.

CHAPTER THIRTY-THREE

We've eaten an obscene amount, including two cupcakes and more fortune cookies. And there is no plan to cease anytime soon.

Mine reads: *You have many talents left to explore.*

Cordie's: *You will find a thing. It may be important.*

"That's a stupid one," she says.

"I agree. Open another." We're lying on opposite ends of my couch watching some show about a high school spy. "I'm not sure I like this show. It sets unrealistic standards for girls. Not everyone can be a spy, good student, master in black belt, wear cute clothes, and have great hair like that," I say.

"It's fiction." She rolls her eyes. "My teacher says with fiction you suspend your reality."

Like I had with Stacy, pretending this moment *might* not happen.

There's an ache in my chest so painful I consider seeing Dad's cardiologist. But I know this is not from any medical condition. Unless one counts stupidity. Isn't this what I was trying to avoid all along? This pain makes even my bones hurt. I suppose the one silver lining is that we didn't take it further.

Just thinking about coming out to our friends, letting them see us together, only to have him go on a date with this Jill is what I focus on. It fuels my anger and tamps back the weak and weepy Jayne.

"Does that gifted program not teach you important things like history and social studies? Seems like you've learned to be a smart arse."

She laughs and sticks her hand in the fortune cookie box but a quick, loud rapping on my front door has us both sitting up, Cordie clutching the box to her chest. "That scared me."

I give the obligatory glance through the peephole but I already know who it is. I swing open the door to Stacy and my heart weeps. Yet, my brain tells me to kick him in the shin. How dare he go on a date? Also, for the love of the Queen, in an outfit that I picked out for him. It's a double betrayal.

"Enjoy your date?" I ask, not allowing him passage.

"I was in Orlando when you called. I left as soon as we hung up."

"Mm. And where did you pick up that nightmare of a sitter? Off the road? At a store? Did you even know her?" For more proof that he is not welcome, I extend my arm across the doorway and block the gap.

"Online." He ducks his head briefly.

"On-bloody-line you say? All these people you know and no one can watch Cordie? I don't recall you asking me. Instead you go online." Ha, do the math on that one, genius.

He presses his lips together before saying, "And how would that have gone over, Jayne? Me asking you to watch my daughter while I meet up with an old friend?"

He's got me there. "We'll never know, will we? Because not only did you not ask but you didn't have the balls to tell me you were going on a date."

In one swift motion he pulls me out the door, says, "We'll be out here, Cords," and closes the door behind me "First, I was not on a date. I was seeing an old friend—"

"Yes, Jill of the let's-get-married group of old friends you keep." I cross my arms over my chest and notice a pizza sauce stain over my right boob.

"Yes, Jill. I don't know what you think you know or what Cordie told you but it wasn't a date. She happens to be in Orlando—"

"And you happen to be out with her."

"It's not like you and I have gone on a date. We just meet up for sex and occasional takeout." He crosses his arms over his chest and I try desperately not to stare at the bulging biceps. Even angry he makes me hot.

"In what world does a man not like those arrangements? I thought I was giving you every man's dream."

"In this world, mine." He circles with one hand the space around us. "I was hoping you'd see that we were pretty good together and—miraculously—Cordie wasn't suffering for it. But you're so stubborn and shortsighted you can't see what's in front of you." He turns away, his arms going from his chest to his hips.

I look at this moment with two opportunities before me. I could confess that I fantasize about ending my days with him. That I find comfort in his arms; in a bottle of wine, takeaway, and occasionally an entire giant-size Toblerone. In that order. And when I picture myself there with him, I also picture Cordie.

Or I could preserve what's left of my wounded heart.

This will take time to get over but it won't destroy me. I'll still be able to function and breathe.

I envision what both those lives might look like.

Fear wins every time. There's no chance in hell I'm going to give more than I have.

"So this date was to prove something to me?" I force my fear to convert to anger.

"I don't get why you're so mad."

Because it's a way to disguise my heartbreak, you dolt. Only I don't say anything. I cross my arms and wait him out.

"Jill came to town for an interview. She called and asked if we could meet and—"

"Off you went. In such a hurry you look online for a sitter. Not your finest moment." I like to make my wounds deep. It's petty, I know. I hate myself for it, but it's what needs to happen between us to make this a clean break.

"In my defense, it's a vetted and well-established child-care site. These people come with references."

I scratch my nose. "And they pocket your pizza money and ignore your child. What were you thinking? It's not like you."

He tucks his hands in his pockets. "I wasn't. Jill suggested it."

"Oh, she sounds lovely." This time my anger isn't forced.

"It's not my finest moment. But jeez, Jayne. I don't know if I'm coming or going anymore. With you I'm walking a thin line. I can't push you too far, too fast, or you'll run off like that weird cat you feed." For the first time he looks me in the eyes and I look away.

Did he just call me weird? This night just keeps getting better.

"Jill and I broke up because I caught her sleeping with her sous chef."

I gasp.

"So when she called and asked to meet, I decided I wanted to put some things away permanently. It's not the cheating that really pissed me off, it was how easily she walked away from Cordie."

A high-end SUV pulls into the car park closer to Stacy's house.

"Shit," he mumbles and shifts on his feet. "I didn't ask her to follow me. I thought she was staying behind."

A petite woman gets out. She's Pippa's size. Precisely. Height and build. I could break her over my knee she's that tiny.

And she's perfect. She's wearing a high-end brand I use as a go to for several of my clients because of how well made it is. She has long, dark hair that curls and bounces with perfection.

"Jill? I assume."

The chestnut beauty spots Stacy and gives a hesitant wave.

He moves to my front door. "It comes down to this. I want to be with you. I want to see where it goes. You don't want that. You want a quick fix. Something that doesn't require a lot of energy. But I like energy, Jayne. I like putting work into something and seeing how great it turns out. Funny, you being a business owner and all, I thought you might like the same thing. I was wrong about a lot of things." He pushes open my door and tells his daughter to head home. She comes out carrying my box of fortune cookies.

"Can I keep these, Jayne?" She looks at me hopefully.

"I don't see why not. Save some for tomorrow though." I

fight back the rising panic, the knowing that everything has suddenly changed. The tight grip of grief wraps around my throat, making any further words impossible.

Cordie stops midstride and reverses her steps. "Yay, there's Jill. Can't I stay the night with Jayne?"

"She's not staying." He pushes her forward.

She clutches the box to her chest. "I'm not sharing any of my fortunes."

"Night, Jayne. Thanks for keeping Cordie." He steps past me but stops and turns half way. "It was good while it lasted. Thanks."

If love rewards the brave, what does it do to the cowards?

CHAPTER THIRTY-FOUR

When one is about to actualize their dream, one should be crying tears of joy. Not sadness. Yet I can't stem the flow and I've overstayed my welcome at this bank's ladies loo. The same woman has come in twice under the ruse of refreshing her makeup and asked me both times if I am okay.

Sure. I'm fabulous. Isn't that obvious? Can't she tell by my tears? Thankfully, I wear mascara that flakes off in giant tarry black blobs; at least I have that going for me.

No raccoon eyes for this savvy fashionista.

I pull in a heavy shaky breath and try to let it out smoothly.

I got this. Right? I do.

I'm about to sign the docs to take on a partner and with the same pen, in a moment later, sign the docs to buy the busted pipe building. The fast turnaround inspector I hired supplied a report that was encouraging with a reconstruction estimate slightly over what I had hoped. But in less than one hour I can have exactly what I've been working toward these last eight years. Well, almost exactly. I never imagined a partner. I never imagined it would be a project as large as this at a time when being away from home may not be the wisest of decisions.

"Jayne?" Davis raps on the door. He pushes it so a slender crack is present. "Are you okay?"

I stare at my owl-eyed expression. "I am. Just nervous."

"We need to wrap this up. The loan manager has an appointment following ours."

"Right. Give me three," I say and push the length of my index fingers against the underbelly of my eyes. Moisture gathers and spills over.

"Sod it." I pull more than a handful of tissues from the dispenser. So what if I cry my way through this experience? I won't be seeing this loan officer again. If I don't pull it together then they'll invite me to leave and both opportunities will be lost.

I fling the door open and startle when I see Davis leaning against the wall.

"Let's do this," I say and nod toward the main lobby where my dreams await.

"Are you sure?" he says.

I nod, dab at my eyes then indicate for him to lead the way. Once we're back up front I take a seat facing the loan officer. Davis' investor has already been in to do her share of the paperwork; I just need to sign my life away.

I fold the tissue over my index finger and tab again at the endless stream.

Tears of joy, right? Perhaps some of fear.

"Are you ready, Ms. Grandberry?" the loan officer asks. She's a nice looking lady. One who would likely shop at my store. Not overdone like the loan offficer in Miami, this one is softer, more pastels and kindness.

Maybe it's because she's giving me what I want and not lowering the boom of bad news.

I nod, unable to force words past the constriction of my throat. Clutched in my other fist is the stupid fortune cookie that started this entire display.

You will soon have an out of money experience, it reads, and I can't help but feel that it's likely the most accurate fortune I've had. Ever.

"We'll begin by signing the agreement between you and your partner so that you can then purchase the building."

I nod. A mute to the end.

My phone buzzes in my jacket pocket. I tucked it there when I made the dash to the loo to bawl my eyes out.

I try to ignore it.

It buzzes again and lacking any and all willpower, I try to covertly pull it from my pocket while listening intently as the lady goes over all the papers and the terms. Davis hovers to my right.

A text from Paisley: *UR a lifesaver. Those snapshot pics of dresses you made me saved my ass. I love u.*

I texted back a question mark because I honestly can't remember if she had an event that required a gown this weekend.

Paisley answers: *Semi-formal event with his boss, an Admiral. Last minute. I was trying to call you when I saw the text pictures and knew what to do. U da best! ;-)*

Lady Loan Officer continues to review the terms, this time about my budget and quarterlies.

"I offer a service that provides customers with a snapshot of outfit ideas. Combinations they can use when they find themselves in a pinch," I say this more for myself than for them.

"I beg your pardon?" She's so nice to stop and though she's casting fleeting glances at Davis, she's not looking at me like I'm barmy.

"Do you think that's something people would like? Snapshots on hand to help them decide what to wear each day or for those occasions like first dates or formal events?"

Paisley texts me a picture of her and Hank leaning against the wood railing of a pier, her navy blue bridesmaid dress looking less like what it was intentionally purchased for and more like a cocktail gown with the thin silver metal scarf I'd convinced her to buy as an accessory. Her arm decorated with several bangle bracelets. She pulled it off precisely as I told her to and she looks stunning.

"Ah, actually." Loan Lady looks again from Davis to me before she continues in a lowered voice. "I know I would *love* something like that. Some days I can't bother to think about what to wear, much less be creative. Kinda like planning dinner for a family. Sometimes the guesswork needs to be taken out."

"Like takeaway. Each Thursday is shrimp korma but sometimes you need someone to tell you to try the daily special." I dab at my eye but there's nothing but dryness there.

"Yes." She nods for further emphasis.

"I could do that." I run it through my mind, the ways I could make it work. According to Stacy, my recent boost of income has come from this entirely. Imagine if I put my wits to it and came up with something brilliant, which could be tricky.

"You could offer a website that shows combinations. A virtual closet if you will where people can go to search out options based on what they have in their closet. That would be something. A dream, really." She sighs wistfully.

As do I.

Hang on. Why can't I do that? Surely, Josie, if not Brinn, has to know an IT person who could help me make this happen.

"Let's keep moving forward, shall we?" Davis says over my shoulder.

Loan Lady and I make eye contact and I know she knows I need a moment.

"Let me get a glass of water and then we'll continue," she says before rising and quietly leaving the room.

I text Paisley: *Would you pay for this service? To have the photos?*

I'd pay 1 million dollars.

Seriously?

Sure, especially if it were a subscription service. That I could add to and change. You bet.

I swallow. I need a moment to clear my head. I need to talk it out and see if it's more than a pipe dream. If it has the potential I think it does. I stare at my screen, knowing the one person I want to be my sounding board is Stacy. The one person not taking my calls.

"All right. Are we continuing?" Loan Lady, her tag says Clara, comes back into the room and resumes her place before me. She gives me an inquiring look.

"Er—"

My phone chimes and I'm caught off guard when I see Stacy's name come across the screen. I jump from my seat.

"I have to take this. Excuse me." I rush from the room, catching the last bit of Davis' exasperated sigh. I find a quiet space back toward the loo, answering the phone as I make my way there.

"Hallo?" I hate that I sound breathless.

"Jayne." It's Cordie.

My hope and heart deflate like a punctured balloon. Then I move into worry.

"Cordie, love. Is something the matter?" It could be a number of things and I can't seem to grab onto one that I could live with.

"Your cat, what's her name?" She sounds a wee bit panicky.

"I don't have a cat." I softly kick my toe into the wood paneling of the bank wall.

"Yes you do. The one you feed by your shrub. What do you call her?" There's a faint mewing in the background.

"Well, mostly arsehole. Wait! Don't tell your dad I said that. I've tried several names but he doesn't answer to any." There's a small nick in the panel and I pick it with my finger, running my nail into the groove, making it deeper.

"That's because he's a she and she's at your door with her mouth full of kitten trying to get you to open the door. Dad and I have been trying to get her to come to our place but she gets real hissy when we get close."

"A kitten, you say?" I try to recall how the cat looked last time I saw him—er, her.

"Who wants in your house," Cordie repeats.

"Right. Well, there is a key in the light. If you unscrew the bottom, it should fall out. That is if Pippa ever put it back." I wait while Cordie relays the info. "So, your dad's there helping?" I ask without an ounce of self-respect.

"We found the key, hold on. Dad's opening the door."

"Tell your dad to put a bowl of milk and water down

and that there is cat food in my garage." I've made the groove an inch longer. I know it would be going too far for me to ask her how her dad's been. But darn if I don't want to.

There's some exchange of words between them and Stacy's voice fades away. He must be walking to the garage. I try to picture the state of my apartment. The impression that it's giving him. Yes, I've been moony for him. Lonely. Likely I left several empty cupcake wrappers on my table. At least there are no penned and abandoned love letters scattered across the floor.

"The cat's put her baby on your robe."

"My robe?" Ah, yes. I'd spent a fair amount of time slouching around in my robe, staring out the window across the lot. I shed it there, by my couch and window at the last minute where I also dressed for this trip. Because heaven forbid I go to my room and be out of sightline of Stacy's house.

Bloody hell, I've become a stalker.

"Yeah, she's tucked her kitten into it and then went back to the door so I let her out."

"She just left her baby on my robe?" Cat really is an arsehole.

"This kitten is too little to be alone. What should I do?" I can hear Cordie worry her hands through the phone.

"I dunno, love. If she's abandoned her then you can take her home. Talk to your dad. Is the kitten cute?"

"So cute, Jayne. So cute. Hold on, I'll take a pic." There's some quick fumbling and seconds later a photo comes across my screen of the cutest brown tabby kitten I've laid eyes on.

"Oh, she's coming back," Cordie says. There's a vibration of excitement in her voice.

"What. What's happening?" I stop working the groove and begin turning my earring.

"She's bringing another kitty. Oh, so cute. Like the other." Cordie sighs with delight. "She's dropped this one and left again. I wonder how many there are?"

Turns out the answer is four. Three brown tabbies and an orange one. A saucy ginger, I'm thinking.

"Dad says that because she chose you and won't let us near them we're going to leave them here. We'll go get a litter box." I hear Stacy tell her that they'll also get some piddle pads, as that's likely where they'll go. "We'll stop by and check them every few hours. Until you get home."

I glance at my watch. "I'm on the first flight back," I tell her. "Listen, Cordie. These kitties will need a home when the time comes. So don't get too attached."

"Too late." She sighs with adoration. "We'll see you later."

"Okay." We disconnect and it doesn't escape my attention that Stacy and I did not talk once, that his daughter was our intermediary.

But I'm not devastated, wasted on the floor like I was a few hours earlier. Something wonderful has shifted inside me.

I text Pippa a picture of the kittens with the added text: *Look at who's come to live with me!*

She responds with: *Love rewards the brave. She couldn't have picked a better place to find shelter. Buy her good food. Not junk!*

I toss back my head and laugh. Of course Pippa would be worried about a cat's diet. Bless my cousin, who always sought shelter at my place at the times I needed her the most.

I kick the paneling one more time, this time more in

thought than uncertainty. Holding my phone close to my chest, I decide what needs to be done and there's no second guessing my decision. It's right. Feels right.

With a sure foot, I return to Davis and Loan La—Clara. "Er, I'm so sorry. But I must leave."

Clara stands. "Is everything okay?"

I rush to the chair where I was sitting and weeping only moments before. "Yes, it's fabulous." I turn to Davis. "I'm so sorry, Davis. This isn't going to happen. This is not right. What I mean is that it's not right for me."

"You'll lose your escrow monies." He crosses his arms over his chest and I see it all. See how foolish I've been, how this man would have made the cut per my list only to find he's more a Wickham at heart. Yet Stacy wouldn't have even had a chance because he has a child. I'm a mad bitch. At least I can try to right my wrongs.

"I'm aware of that, but I'd rather lose that than everything else that's at stake. I really am truly sorry." I grip his forearm but he doesn't move. He's an alabaster statue of disappointment. I'm about to apologize again but I stop myself. There's nothing more to be said.

"I'm sorry for all your wasted work, Clara." I pick up her business card. "But I think I'm going to go in a different direction." I slightly wave her card before I tuck it in my handbag. "I'll let you know how it goes."

"Please do." She extends her hand. "Good luck." We shake hands, not the typical brief clasp but an excited pumping of energy before I dash out the door. Moments later I'm in my rental car driving toward the airport and opportunity.

CHAPTER THIRTY-FIVE

I lucked out and caught an earlier flight home. On the short trip I made copious notes plotting my new business idea including a list of questions that needed to be answered before I could move forward.

The first stop, however, will not be at Josie's with hopes of her calling in her IT connections, but to Mum's pub. If I'm going to be all in on this venture then I'd better make sure my family is all in with me, or at the very least, know where I stand with them.

I don't go through the back, as is my normal custom, instead entering through the front and assessing the vibe. Mum, understandably stressed, might have brought her troubles to work. I want to know what I might be up against. For the most part, the restaurant is quiet. No slamming doors or crashing dishes. Not that I really expected that, mind you. But these are new and difficult times; one can never assume.

A waitress is leaning against the bar and waves as I pass. No one scrambles or stumbles when they see me. This is definitely a good sign.

With trepidation I step into the kitchen, letting the swinging door block most of my body. No one is there. This, perhaps, might not be a good sign.

"Mum?" I suck up courage and step fully into the room.

"In the office," she calls from down the hallway.

With my shoulders straight I make my way there. She and Jeff are sitting around the desk looking at a large disheveled stack of papers.

"How'd it go, darling? I'm surprised you're home so early. I thought you'd still be up there taking pictures of your new building. My daughter, the real estate mogul and shop owner." She claps her hands together with delight.

I try to smile, only it's an act of forcing my muscles to comply.

"Funny thing that, Mum. When it came to sign the papers I couldn't do it." I lean against the doorjamb to steady my nerves and ready myself.

"What do you mean you couldn't do it? They weren't ready or they were wrong? I hope someone reimburses you for going all the way up there and them not being prepared." She slaps her hand on a stack of papers.

I glance at Jeff. "Actually, the papers were fine. The problem was me. Opening another shop is not what I want—"

"Course it is. It's what you've wanted forever." She looks at Jeff. "How many nights she'd call from university and talk about her grand plan. She had it worked out long before she graduated, my girl."

I duck my head and twist the earring in my left ear. "You're right, Mum. It has been something I've focused on for years and because of that I nearly missed out on the opportunity that was right before me. A better opportunity.

So I walked away from the deal." I look at her through my hair, my head ducked not in shame but in apology.

"What about all that money? The escrow—"

"I lost it." I hurriedly hold up my hand. "I know what you're going to say and yes, I hate losing that much, but better that small amount than so much more over the next few years. Because in my gut I know that would happen."

Mum shakes her head. "What will you do now? Did you even think of a next step?"

Following a disbelieving snort, I say, "Of course, Mum. But you're a fine one to talk. Do you have a plan?" I knew this conversation was inevitable. Much like I knew I was moving forward with my dreams for the wrong reason. But denial is a powerful emotion that can trick the mightiest of minds and I've never professed to be one of those, that's for sure.

"I'm just trying to get through today." She looks at her pencil and the paper before her.

"My answer was right in front of my eyes." I say, shoving off from the jam and stepping further into the office. "I just had to acknowledge that change was inevitable and that I was going to be better for it. Like you and Dad. Change has come and we need to embrace it." I kneel before her. "Mum, I love you."

"I love you, Jaynie-girl." She drops her pencil and takes my face between her hands.

"I'd do anything to make that stupid thermometer all red. Even take on a building and a loan that would have put me in way over my head," I say, cutting off her protest. "I know you only wanted me to be successful and self-sufficient. But I'm already those things, Mum."

"And I'm proud."

"I met a man, one I want to keep. More than anything."

Startled, Mum sits back, then suddenly is squealing and clapping her hands. "That's wonderful. Wonderful. I'm so happy to hear it. Relieved too."

I look between her and Jeff. He's been around since my folks opened their doors and has witnessed many a set down from Mum about men.

"What is happening here? When does the idea of me getting domesticated make you happy?"

"I've always wanted you to find someone, luv, but only after you knew you could take care of yourself. And you know that now."

"What about my thermometer? About having an article written about my success?"

"All worthy accomplishments but you'll want someone to share that with and if you've found that person, then hold on to them." She clasps my hands between her rough ones. "Who is it? Is it that lovely Stacy? He was at the hospital an awful lot."

I ask my question to Jeff, who's been sitting quietly. "Did I get shoved in a Tardis? Is this real?"

Mum caresses my cheek, pushes back my bangs, then tucks her hands in her lap. "Now we need a plan to get this place sorted. Your Dad can't come back to this, at least not in the way he was before."

I gently scoop her hands in mine and turn them so the bulbous knuckles and scars prominently show. "You can't keep this pace up either, never mind your hands."

"Jeff and I have been in here talking about alternatives." She pulls her hands from mine and crosses her arms, tucking her hands out of sight.

Jeff clears his throat. "I offered to buy the pub. It sits on prime land. Doesn't flood like the beachside and is central to everything." He rubs the bristle on his chin, before pushing his floppy curls out of his face. Deep, sun-darkened skin, with light blond-streaked curly hair, and a propensity for a quick easy smile, Jeff looks more like he belongs on a surf board and cooking out over an open fire than he does talking to Mum about food deliveries. He can't be but five years older than me. He looks from between Mum and me.

I sit back on my haunches, "Bloody hell."

"Jayne!"

"I mean that in a good way. It's perfect really." I look to Jeff. "Assuming you don't tell us your plans, because it will destroy them if you turn this into a surf shop."

"I want to keep the pub going. I have some ideas to increase business." He shifts his attention to Mum. "Ideas that might not suit you all, but I'd like to keep the general theme and menu." He nods to emphasize his point. "I love this place."

"And you make the food just like Mum." Mentioning this makes Mum sit up taller.

"You are rather good at dredging the fish—"

"And the stout is the secret ingredient." He winks.

Mum smiles brightly at him. "You are a fine young man, Jeff."

"Not to be nosy but you think you can get a loan for this place?" I ask.

Jeff smiles. "I already own the lot next door. This hasn't been my only job. I run an online business. I kept this job because it got me out of the house and off the computer. It would be a cash offer."

I fall back onto my bum. It's like the universe is sending me a message.

"Do you want to own this place forever, Mum? Or do you want to travel and do other things?"

Mum takes his hand in hers. "There is no finer person to sell my business to than you."

They both break out in large smiles. It's a real love fest in here.

"Right," I say. "Isn't this grand? You two should start talking over the details so that when you go see Dad tonight you can, you know, lay the groundwork, as they say." I squeeze her knee before rising.

"Oh, dear. What will Thomas say?" Her smile turns downward with worry.

"Just tell him you'll have more time for Grace_and and other holidays. I think Dad will like the sound of that. There's lots that has to be worked out first. But let's start the conversation."

"This is the finest day ever, man," Jeff says, coming to a sudden stand. "I'm gonna go call my folks and tell them. Excuse me." He's gone in a flash.

"He would be a good fit," muses Mum.

"He'd be an excellent fit. He's very loyal." I lean against the desk. "How do you feel about selling?"

"Scared yet excited." She looks up at me and there's a twinkle in her eye that's been long missing. "You know, I never said this to your Dad, but I'd like to go home and spend some time. No more than three months, mind you, because my sisters and I would murder each other, but I'd like to have longer visits. I'd like to travel across America in an RV. Doesn't that sound lovely?"

"Mm," is all I can say, because time in an RV for one day sounds bloody awful. The fridges are tiny. "You want me to help you talk to Dad, let me know."

Mum stands and folds me in her arms. "I'm a lucky woman to have you for a daughter. You and Pippa."

"You should tell her that. She'd love to hear it. I think she sometimes still feels like a burden." I hug her back and breathe in the scent of fish, clotted cream, and the lavender water splash Mum uses to freshen up with.

"I'll call her and tell her right now."

After a final squeeze I leave Mum to call Pip and make my way back to my car.

Now, it's time to face what's waiting for me at home.

I've cracked one nut. Time to take on the tough one.

CHAPTER THIRTY-SIX

A text from Josie tells me that everyone has gathered at her house for the evening. Another impromptu get-together really designed to provide everyone with a chance to relax. Paisley and Hank are preparing for their first long-term separation as his deployment date is creeping closer. Heather's divorce is starting to wind down, and Kenley and Doug have yet to conceive. Brinn and Stacy have come across some unexpected issue that has once again slowed their plans. Who wouldn't need some good food and maybe a refreshing drink?

Josie texts me to stop by if I get home in time. She thinks I'll be in Atlanta until late tonight. That was the plan, after all.

After leaving Mum's, I swing by my flat and drop off my bag and change out of my tailored suit and into my yoga pants and jersey T. I don't refresh my makeup, but I do brush my teeth, because there are messages one might want to send and then there are messages one *doesn't* want to send.

Before I leave, I take a few moments to fawn over the

kitties. Surprisingly, Arsehole Cat allows me to scratch her between the ears. I let them be and leave for what will probably be the biggest night of my life. I don't need a fortune cookie to tell me that.

Following the quick drive over, I let myself in the front door and can hear everyone out back. I text Pippa and tell her to answer my call but to listen and not say anything. Then I quickly make a FaceTime call so she can be present too.

I come around the corner and run smack into Josie.

"Jayne, I thought you were in Atlanta. How'd it go? Why are you home? What's happened to you?" She scans me up and down.

I turn her around and push her toward the others. "You'll know soon enough.

Here. Hold this." I hand her my phone. "It's Pippa. She needs to see this too." Once outside I step up on the bench so I am over everyone.

"Excuse me," I say and wave my hands in the air. "Excuse me. Will everyone look at me please? I have something to say." And just like that my courage flies away. Stacy turns his blue eyes toward me and just as quickly averts them. He starts to move toward the house and I call him out.

"Stacy, please. I would like you to hear this."

He goes to stand by Cordie, his hand resting on her shoulder, and continues to not look at me.

Fine. Right. It's do or die.

I take in a shaky breath, glance at Josie then look back toward him.

"My name is Jayne." I cross my hands over my chest. A few people laugh. "Many of you have known me for a while."

"More like your whole life," Pippa says.

"Yes, Pip. But I'm introducing you to the new me." I can't help it but a tear escapes.

"You are now the business owner of two stores!" calls out Heather.

I hold up a finger. "When you think of me, do you think of me as someone who has it together?"

"For the most part," Josie says in all her honesty. Bless her.

"Right. For the most part. As you all know, today I was supposed to sign papers and buy a building. I was supposed to make a dream of more than eight years come true. But then I got a text." I look at Paisley. "Thank you for that text, by the way; it's changed my life. I didn't sign the papers. In one moment I was staring at what I had long thought was my dream but in the next moment I was thinking that nothing was right but how *that* made complete sense." I wipe away a few more tears on my shoulder.

"A few days ago I stood before someone I care deeply about and lied. I lied to hurt them and make them go away." I stare directly at him and when his gaze flicks up to mine, I know it's time to let it go. "By nature I'm a fearful person. I never really thought that to be true until I was asked to push past my fear. I was presented with two paths and I chose the one of least resistance. The one that let me be a coward. But that's who I am. I like yoga pants and trans-unsaturated fats. Sorry, Pip. I like to watch the er—" I glance at Cordie and Tyler. "Late night adult channel while I eat those fats. I have a cat who just now decided to be mine and I have a dream-man wish list. Well, you know. About that." I stare at Stacy.

"I eat Indian food every Thursday and Chinese on Mondays. I wear flats because I'm afraid I'll be too tall and for some asinine reason that will make people not like me. I'm not very good at minding children but I'm a loyal friend."

"You're a great friend," Paisley says.

"And I am in love with you, Stacy."

"About time," Heather mumbles.

I ignore her and continue, "But because I'm too scared to take personal risk I was too scared to say it. I thought that you should know how I feel. That you should know that I don't care if all our friends know about how I feel." I do another shoulder wipe. "I'm terribly scared. Not of loving you. Of losing you. So I felt it best to let you go now before it got really awful. Before I fell so terribly hard there would be no coming back from it, only I'm too late. It's already happened. I thought you should know."

He cuts through the crowd, coming toward me. Not a single muscle on his face has moved and I can't tell which way this is going. But I prepare myself for the worst. The part where he walks out. Or actually, the part where he shakes my hand, says it's all good and all that but he's changed his mind about me. About us. That would be the worst.

Unequivocally.

He stands before me, looking up, searching my face with his gaze. "I love transunsaturated fats, too. I like Indian food on Thursdays and I'm open to Chinese on Mondays. I like when you wear heels and I think you're the most beautiful, sexy woman I have ever laid eyes on."

"Gross," says Cordie from the back.

"Honestly?" I sniff in the most unbecoming way. Loud and certainly not girly.

"Yeah. I like watching you crack open a fortune cookie

and how hopeful you get before you read it. You look at me like that, you know."

I shake my head.

"Right before I do this." He steps up to the bench, wraps his arms around the tops of my thighs, and lifts me up and off, pulling me against him.

Slowly, I slide down his length until we're lined up perfectly.

"See," he whispers as he lowers his lips to mine. A breath before they touch, he says, "There it is."

EPILOGUE
ONE YEAR LATER

WE SLIDE INTO THE BOOTH AT AMIT'S. AS PER OUR custom, Cordie and I take the same side and I weave my legs between Stacy's. There's no use for menus as we get the same thing every time we come. Amit doesn't even bother trying to convince me to try the specials.

"So California was a success?" Over the table, we hold hands.

I landed from my trip only a bit ago, and we went straight from the airport to dinner, filling the ride over with Cordie's stories of her sleepover, which thankfully was a smashing success. She's still adjusting but it's slowly getting better.

I squeeze his hand. "It was insane. You'll have to go to the next meeting with me because I can't even begin to relay everything they said. I have the proposal in the car and of course, it looks like a cracking good offer." Who knew a year ago when I started *The Daily Closet* I'd have offers from tech companies to buy it? Who knew that I'd do so well in this time frame that I'm mere inches, Stacy projects two more months, from making Mum's goal thermometer fully red?

She'll be excited to hear and when they come back from RVing in Parts Unknown, Canada, she'll probably laminate the silly thing.

"What will you do with your time if you sell?" He's asked this a million times since the offers started coming in.

"That's the question, right?" I wag my brows.

"You could ask a fortune cookie," offers Cordie.

I gesture around us. "Much to my displeasure, Amit doesn't stock those here.

We'd have to go to his cousin's to get one and I'm all out."

"I have one." Stacy takes one from his pocket and puts it on the table.

"Why ever do you have a fortune cookie? Though I'm happy you do." I take the cookie and find it surprisingly heavy. "Gads, where did you get this?"

"From the box. Open it." He sits back in the booth.

I lean toward Cordie. "It doesn't look too promising. The paper is missing. One of those, you know." She's shared enough with me that she now has her own fortune board going.

I crack it open but instead of a slip of paper a ring tumbles onto the table.

A simple, one-stone ring. A large sapphire.

Stacy takes my hand. "I love you, Jayne. We love you and want to know if you'd like to marry me, marry us."

"We want to be your family," Cordie says and leans against me.

I look into his blue eyes. He's my home. They're my everything. "You already are my family." I hold my hand out for him to slide the ring on my finger.

"Is that a yes?"

"Of course it's a yes!" I lean across the table and kiss him soundly. When I sit back, Cordie is bouncing in the seat.

"Do you like it? I went with Dad to pick it out. I told him we should get one that looks like a cupcake. Don't you think it kinda looks like a cupcake?" Cordie grabs my hand and pulls it close.

I look down at the round stone and chuckle. "It absolutely looks like a cupcake and I can't imagine a better ring. Thank you." I wrap her in a hug and squeeze tight. "I love you, kid, you know that right?" She nods against my shoulder. "The only reason I'm hooking up with your dad is so I can have you."

Stacy comes from his side of the booth and slides in with us, squishing Cordie between us, and then he folds us in his arms.

Our gazes meet over her head. This is what Josie was talking about on her wedding. When I look at him I see a lifetime of worn math t-shirts, takeaway food, and naughty TV. There's also laughter, fighting, and a bliss from being a part of something greater than myself. Something I never knew existed.

I see love.

LOVE HANGING OUT WITH JAYNE? Next up is Heather. If the boy that got away broke your heart, would you give him a second chance?

Go here—> THE GIRL HE LOVES

who's hid behind photography, on her adventures in her new life
as a Private Investigator. A job she inherited when her new
husband died unexpectedly and left behind a mess and another
wife.

One Hit Wonder

All Bets Are Off

Best Laid Plans

Caught Off Guard

Two Time Loser

Dodged A Bullet

The Meryton Brides

(Sweet romance) The Meryton Brides is a complete series (for
now) that is a light, pleasant modernization of Jane Austen's Pride
and Prejudice with a twist on the characters. These sweet
contemporary romance books are full of love, friendship, trust, and
family. Darcy and Elizabeth's story spans the series and ends in
book 5, but each book provides the happily ever after we seek.

To Have and To Hold (Book 1)

With This Ring (Book 2)

I Do (Book 3)

Promise Me This (Book 4)

Marry Me, Matchmaker (Book 5)

Honeymoon Postponed (Book 6)

Matchmaker's Guidebook - FREE

Hey! I'm Kristi. I write romances that will tug your heartstrings and laugh out loud mysteries. In all my stories you'll fall in love with the cast of characters, they'll become old, fun friends. **My one hope** is that I create stories that *satisfy any of your book cravings* and offer a get-away from everyday life. When I'm not writing I'm repurposing Happy Planners or drinking a London Fog (hot tea with frothy milk).

I'm the mom of 2 and a milspouse (retired). We live in the Pacific Northwest.

Here are 3 things about me:

- I lived on the outskirts of an active volcano (Mt.Etna)
- A spider bit me and it laid eggs in my arm (my kids don't know that story yet)
- I grew up in Central Florida and have skied in lakes with gators.

I'd love to get to know you better. Join my Read & Relax community and then fire off an email and tell me 3 things about you!

Not ready to join? Email me below or follow me at one of the links below. Thanks for popping by!

You can connect with Kristi at any of the following:
www.kristirose.net
kristi@kristirose.net